The
Reckoning

To Lynda,
Your Reckoning Awaits!

Dale Cut
10/24/2009

The Reckoning

a novel by

Dale Crotts

THE RECKONING

Cover Design by CH Creations
Interior Layout and Design by CH Creations

Published April 2009

HEARTLAND

HeartLand is an imprint of RoseHeart Publishing
www.roseheartbooks.com

ISBN 10: 0-9822337-6-0
ISBN 13: 978-0-9822337-6-4

Printed in the United States of America

Dedication

I would like to dedicate this book to my dear wife Becky, whose inspiration and encouragement made this, and all of my dreams, possible.

Chapter One

Lorraine gripped the railing as she held on desperately. It was a long fall to the first floor below causing the fear to well within her. She pleaded for him to take hold of her arms and rescue her from impending death, but he ignored her. Instead, Joey grabbed the stone bust from the pedestal in the corner and lifted it high above his shoulders, bringing it down swiftly, striking her full against the side of her head. Blood splattered against the railing as her hands let go and she fell backward to the floor below.

Joey rushed down the stairs to check for signs of breathing. Finding a faint pulse, he struck her again, listening intently to the last gasp of air seeping from her lungs. He stood over her limp body, peering into her cold, lifeless eyes as the film of death turned the once beautiful blue color to a cold, pale grey. Joey spat on her face, turned and walked back up the stairs carrying the stone bust with him.

He removed a leather bag from the closet and placed the bust inside, then placed a call to his father and within just a few minutes, several men in dark suits were swarming all around the estate. As his father barked directions, the men went to work on the sanitizing of the crime scene. Mr. Van-

Warner climbed the steps and headed to the master bedroom. As he entered the room, the face he saw was not Joey's, but that of Spencer Rawlings.

***

Spence sat straight up in bed, beads of sweat trailing down his forehead as the phone blared its familiar ring. That same dream had haunted him for the past fifteen years, one from which he couldn't seem to escape. He reached for the phone as he tried to control his shaking.

"Hello."

"Spence, its Agnes. I have some bad news," she relayed on a tentative note. "Your father passed away sometime this evening. He requested I call you when this time came."

"I'll be there as soon as I can," said Spence, placing the receiver back in its cradle.

The sun began to rise as Spencer Rawlings crossed the Michigan border from Indiana. It had been a long drive from his home in Versailles, Kentucky and the trip started to take its toll as he began to nod his head, finding it difficult to keep his eyes open. He slapped his face a couple of times, even stuck his head out the window hoping the cold air would jolt him back to his senses, but he still had two hundred more miles to go and wondered if he'd be able to make it there in one piece. He'd received the news of his father two nights ago before beginning his journey back home, a place he'd avoided for the past fifteen years. He'd refused to show up for the ceremony to swear his father in as District Judge. Yet now he felt an obligation to return, not just because he was the executor of his father's estate, but because he needed closure to end the heartache and guilt he'd held in for so many years.

The drive through Indiana had been quiet enough, especially at night, since there was nothing but flat farmland as far as the eye can see once you pass Indianapolis. The solitude gave Spence time to reflect on the past and come to grips with the fact that his father was now gone. Even in death, it seemed his father still exerted power over his life, because he was heading home, was he not?

It had been so many years since he'd last seen his father. The thought of seeing him again stirred up old memories, somehow making Spence fearful and yet sad at the same time.

He'd left Michigan at the age of thirty, having spent three years working in his father's law firm. He had received his bachelor's degree in political science, and law degree, from the University of Michigan in Ann Arbor, and had been eager to work alongside his father. That eagerness lasted until his third year with the firm, and the VanWarner case. Then everything changed.

Joseph VanWarner III, or Joey, was the son of Joseph VanWarner Jr., one of the wealthiest men in Michigan. They lived in an estate in Grosse Pointe Woods, east of Detroit overlooking Lake St. Clair. The elder VanWarner inherited his fortune from his father, who owned several automobile parts factories all across Michigan. The senior VanWarner also owned an investment banking company, a publishing company, and a chain of bars in the Detroit area as well as Toledo and Chicago. He was also a major shareholder in one of many riverboat casino operations with ships along the Ohio River from Rising Sun to Evansville, Indiana. He also had a stake in one of the casinos in Biloxi, Mississippi. Although involved in these well-known business ventures, rumor made him a major player in organized crime in Michigan.

When Spence began working at his father's law firm, he learned the firm did a lot of contract work for the Van-Warners, especially dealings with the casino operations. He believed the VanWarners were legitimate business people with a need for legal expertise, and besides, the fees were terrific. The VanWarners were less concerned with how much it cost, than with the results being well in their favor. He even prepared a few of the contracts himself, catching the attention of Mr. VanWarner with some very lucrative results.

Spence heard the rumors of illegal activity, but since he worked so closely with their contractual affairs, he thought they must be legit. Besides, if there were any illegal operations, he would have discovered them by now.

Then the big case broke. His father, saying to meet him at the office in ten minutes, startled Spence awake at three a.m. one morning. His voice was very serious and to the point, hanging up before Spence finished mumbling he'd be right there. He wondered what was so important his father would call a meeting at three in the morning, but being still too fuzzy from just waking, he wasn't able to give it much thought. He threw on his clothes, and in eight minutes pulled up in front of the building. His father and Mr. VanWarner were already there. As he walked inside, his father called for him to come to the conference room. Upon entering the room, he saw his father seated at the head of the table, and Mr. VanWarner at his immediate right. Joey sat next to Mr. VanWarner, very distraught, shaking and sweating as he mumbled incoherently.

"Spence," his father began, "There was a terrible accident at the VanWarners tonight. It appears Joey's wife, Lorraine, came home rather intoxicated. Apparently, she lost her balance, and fell over the banister railing from the second floor, her head striking one of the marble sculptures on one of the tables in the foyer. Mr. VanWarner and Joey have come to ask for our assistance because the District Attorney has issued a warrant for Joey's arrest charging him with murder. I have already contacted the D.A. and told him Joey will surrender to him this morning at 8:00 a.m., which gives us a little time for damage control."

What did he mean by 'damage control'? Spence wondered.

"Mr. VanWarner got the situation under control after Joey called him, and now believes the police will not have enough evidence to convict Joey since it was an accident," his father continued, "But never the less, we must begin preparing a defense, so I asked them both to come here before Joey turns himself in."

The four of them sat together going over every detail, and making sure everyone was on the same page. Spence had never prepared a murder defense case before, although he'd argued one in moot court when in law school. He believed in his father, and the innocence of his client, but something about the whole situation continued to disturb him. Joey admitted that Lorraine was having an affair, and he'd recently found out about it, but was not mad enough to kill her. He felt certain the prosecutor would use the affair as the motive for the murder. Joey and Lorraine were alone in the house after the maid left for the night off, so there were no witnesses. Lorraine was supposed to have been at an art auction for the hospital, but witnesses confirmed she was not in attendance. According to Joey, she came home drunk, but managed to crawl up the stairs. As she stood up at the top of the stairs, she lost her balance, grabbed for the banister railing, but flipped over it, unable to hold her grip. The prosecutor would argue that either she came home intoxicated after spending the evening at her lover's, or she was home all night. Either way, they would argue that Joey became so enraged over the affair, he pushed her over the balcony.

Joey, accompanied by Spence's father, turned himself in at eight o'clock sharp. After they processed him, they scheduled his bail hearing for eleven a.m. The prosecutor argued for no bail given the seriousness of the crime, but since he had no prior record, the judge set bail at one million dollars. They had Joey out in thirty minutes. The trial began three weeks later, and Spence's father saw no need to try any delay tactics. He'd tried many such cases, and felt confident in his approach. He also knew the Judge presiding over the trial, and believed they were in good shape. Spence noticed an unfamiliar name on the prosecution's list of witnesses, which would turn out to be the alleged lover with whom Lorraine was having an affair. He'd testify to the affair, and she wasn't drunk when she left his place. Spence also noticed the piece of sculpture they said Lorraine fell on did not appear on the list of evidence obtained at the scene. Even though his father felt the prosecutor would argue Joey used the sculpture to bash her head in, with no murder weapon, it would be hard to prove.

   The trial began with the typical opening arguments from both sides. The prosecutor painted Joey to be a monster, subject to fits of rage, while making Lorraine out to be the victim of a jealous husband. Spence's father, on the other hand, described Joey as a model citizen, citing his philanthropic works for the community, while Lorraine, an alcoholic, had injured herself many times while in a drunken state. The prosecution began with testimony from the police describing the scene that night, and the missing sculpture. When the medical examiner testified Lorraine died from blunt force trauma from a blow to the head, the defense asked if the blow could've resulted from her fall from the second floor, striking her head on something. The medical examiner agreed, as long as the size and shape were consistent with the wound, it was a possibility. With that, the defense recalled the detective who processed the scene and asked if the police had recovered any such sculpture. The detective said they had not. Next the defense asked if the police examined any of the marble stands on display as various art objects in the foyer. Again, the detective admitted they had not, and the defense proceeded to add as an exhibit, pictures showing what appeared to be blood on the corner of one of the stands. His father pointed out that one of their investigators obtained this evidence, but one of the maids had since cleaned the stand after they had taken the picture. Although the prosecution objected to the authenticity of the photograph, reasonable doubt had already begun growing.

   The last witness for the prosecution was Henri DuBois, a young unknown artist who had recently come to America from France. When asked about his relationship with Lorraine, he said she'd helped him exhibit some of his artwork at local showings and studios, but denied they were having an affair. This caught the prosecutor off guard, so he asked for a recess to confer with Henri. After the recess, it was apparent Henri would not recant the testimony he'd just given. He said the police threatened to revoke his green card if he didn't say he and Lorraine were lovers. The crowd began to hum, growing from a faint murmur to a loud roar, as the Judge pounded his gavel to restore order. Spence's father immediately moved for a dismissal, given this enlightening testimony, and the Judge agreed. He found insufficient evidence to prove the state's case, and ordered an investigation into the allegations of witness tampering within the police department. With Joey a free man, Spence and his father celebrated the victory.

Not until the following weekend would Spence learn the truth. This revelation would cause the rift between him and his father that lasted until his father's death. That night after the trial, as Spence left the office, he noticed Mr. VanWarner and his father talking in the conference room. He saw his father open a briefcase full of money Mr. VanWarner had placed in front of him. Then Mr. VanWarner handed his father a brown duffel bag. Spence decided not to let them know he'd seen them, and slipped out of the building. The following Saturday, they were back at the estate in Traverse City for the weekend when Judge Rawlings decided to go sailing. Spence insisted he go along, much to the discomfort of his father.

His father sailed to the center of the bay, then asked Spence to go below and bring up his fishing gear. He thought it odd to fish in the middle of the bay, but shrugged his shoulders and walked below deck. He returned to the deck just in time to see his father toss the brown duffel bag Mr. VanWarner had given him over the side. When he questioned his father about it, the Judge said, "Where do you think the sculpture was? Are you that naive? Besides, it was still an accident, and we will speak no more about it!"

At that moment, Spence began to believe the rumors about the VanWarners, and decided he could no longer work for criminals or his father. That was why he had to leave Michigan, and why he kept having the same recurring dream of Lorraine's death, as if he were guilty of the crime himself. He didn't intend to set foot in Michigan ever again, much less work alongside his father. Yet, as he headed north through Michigan on his way back home, he felt a strange sensation that his intentions would fail. He slammed his fist against the steering wheel and muttered, "Why didn't you at least give him a chance to explain?" Then he cursed himself under his breath for not working harder to repair the damaged relationship with his father before now. Now that his father died, it was too late. His eyes began to moisten with emotion as all of the past came flooding back in one second, so he pulled his Mercedes into a rest stop and wept for what seemed an hour.

As he neared Holland, Spence decided to stop for breakfast. The wind coming off Lake Michigan still felt biting cold, even in March. He devoured his food, eager to get back on the road. He decided to take Highway 31 North toward Traverse City. It ran a little longer than taking Highway 131 out of Grand Rapids, but he remembered this way as more scenic. As he drove, a deer darted out alongside the highway, but thought better of entering the lanes and instead paralleled Spence's car until it ran back into the woods just off the road. As he passed Muskegon, the sky darkened as thick gray clouds banked together, blotting out the sun in a fluffy blanket of impending snow. This area could receive a lot of snow in a short period due to the lake effect, snows as fronts moved across Lake Michigan, even in March.

Spence turned the heater off when the sun warmed the interior of the car, but now that the sky had turned darker, he began to shiver from the cold. He could even see his breath in front of him. His fingers were stiff and hurting from lack of warmth, so he turned the heater on, being careful not to make it too cozy for fear of falling asleep at the wheel. By the time Spence reached Ludington, the snow cascaded, covering the pavement in front of him. A heavy wet snow blanketed the highway, making it difficult to see where the lanes were, but Spence was no novice at driving in bad weather. He had spent his young adult life driving in conditions such as this, and felt confident he would have no trouble.

His father's estate lay just outside of Traverse City overlooking Grand Traverse Bay, one of the more picturesque settings in the area. Some liked to winter here, watching as the snow fell on the water and accumulated around the shore, while others preferred the warmth of summer where they could watch the ducks and geese swim on the cool blue water as they sat on the lush green grass surrounding the bay. Numerous boats were harbored along the shore for the sailing enthusiasts.

As he neared the turn off toward his father's estate, his stomach knotted as a wave of nausea swept over him and he broke out in a cold sweat. He felt a multitude of emotions swell within him as he remembered some good times and bad, feeling the joy, pain and guilt he'd felt throughout the years, and now with his father gone, how he missed him so.

Nearing his destination, Spence couldn't hold back the tears that crept down his cheeks as he wished he could turn back the clock and make things right with his dad. However, he realized he must find some inner strength in order to get through the next few days of settling his father's affairs. Then, he told himself, there would be time for healing and self-forgiveness.

Chapter Two

S pence eased his Mercedes into the drive of his father's estate, following a long and winding paved path lined with spruce trees. He remembered his father wanting evergreens so the driveway wouldn't look so bare in the winter, and the fullness of the branches obstructed the view of the estate from the rest of the world. As the snow settled on the branches, it looked like a scene from a Currier & Ives Christmas card, red birds perching among the limbs, trying to find shelter from the falling snow. Spence couldn't help but think it looked just as he remembered, but somehow more vivid. As he continued up the winding drive, he peered through the trees hoping to see it still there. Then, just through the snow, his eyes caught a glimpse of it. His old tree house he used to play in as a little boy. He remembered playing hide-and-seek with his father on the rare occasions he stayed home. His father used to say, "You always were the best," meaning Spence could find him no matter where he hid, but now Spence wondered how many times his father let himself be found. Spence smiled as he felt a warm glow of comfort flow over his body as if to say how good it felt to be home again.

The driveway stopped in front of the garage, and that's where Spence left the car. He didn't see the maid's car in the driveway or the garage of the guesthouse. He scurried through the snow, as it continued to come down hard and had already laid three inches on the ground. In front of the house were two large planters on each side of the small front porch. Each one had a small, sculpted evergreen tree that spiraled to within three feet of the porch roof. Spence felt alongside the rough edge of the inner rim of the left planter and pulled out a key, still there where his father kept it twenty years ago. He remembered his father told him where to find it should he ever decide to come home. Spence stuck the key into the lock, gave it a turn, then slowly opened the door. He stomped his feet to remove the snow, and stepped inside.

The heavy scent of pine and disinfectant flooded his nostrils as he stepped into the foyer, revealing no doubt Agnes had been there. Agnes Morehead had been cleaning and cooking for the Rawlings ever since Spence reached the age of six. Judge Rawlings had hired her two months after Spence's mother died. She lived in the guesthouse, but never married. The Judge had always said he couldn't perform domestic work as it should be, and truthfully didn't have the time. Once Agnes began her duties, Spence's father found more reasons to stay at his apartment in Royal Oak, even on weekends.

Spence adored his mother, and felt a tremendous sense of loss without her. She had given him her maiden name, Spencer. His middle name was Thurman, the same as his father's, but he seldom told anyone what the "T" stood for. His mother had always spent hours with him, playing and teaching him the alphabet. She worked with him on his writing before the age of four because she wanted him to be ahead of the other children his age. Perhaps the most memorable thing about his mother, though, was the way she smelled. As far back as he could remember, his mother wore Windsong perfume. It was her favorite, and had a distinctive fragrance that Spence could still smell to this day. He was heartbroken at the news of his mother's death.

Spence remembered his father kneeling in front of him as tears streamed down his cheeks. He told Spence his mother had gone to heaven and would always be watching over him. It was not until he was twelve that his father told him a drunken driver killed her in a car accident. She was on her way home from playing bridge with her friends when the other car crossed the centerline and hit her head on.

Agnes found Judge Rawlings' body and called Spence Monday night. Agnes was like one of the family, and told Spence she'd have the house clean for him when he arrived Thursday, and so it was. In fact, Spence thought it seemed super clean under the circumstances, almost as if no one had lived in the house for a while. Yet how hard would it be to clean up after one old man, Spence thought.

According to Agnes, the Judge was in his bed when he died sometime during the night on Sunday. She'd been cleaning the rest of the house, not wanting to disturb the Judge, until she realized he hadn't been down all day. When she knocked on his door late Monday evening and heard no answer, she entered his room and found him dead. Judge Rawlings was seventy-five years old; an age Spence thought was too young to die. However, when is it ever a good age to die?

Spence laid the house key on the long table in the foyer and proceeded to carry his overnight bag to his old bedroom upstairs. He crept up the steps at first, as if he were afraid he'd wake someone. He almost felt like an intruder since it had been so long since he was here, but soon realized he was alone in the house. He walked past his father's room, but did not go in, deciding there'd be plenty of time for that later. As he reached the door to his old room, he hesitated for an instant, almost unsure of what to do next. Then, taking a deep breath, he turned the knob and opened the door. He hadn't been in this room since his college days, but it looked just as he'd left it. He picked up the album that held his collection of old baseball cards and casually flipped through the pages. His father had told him he could leave his things here as long as he wanted. That was fifteen years ago.

On one wall was the infamous Farrah Fawcett poster that adorned almost every teenage boy's room when Spence was in school. The other held a framed copy of The Constitution of the United States of America. He felt it gave the room a balance between stud and nerd, a twilight zone of teenage angst. Spence could not believe his father had left the room the way it was, and was almost embarrassed as his eyes met Farrah's smiling back at him.

Next, he retrieved his old record collection from the cardboard storage box with which he had used years ago to keep them in. Spence waxed nostalgic as he flipped through albums of the Stones, Aerosmith, Led Zeppelin, and Boston. It was a wide variety of rock and pop, from Bee Gees to Foghat and ZZ Top. Spence drew the line at country, though. Even after the emergence of modern day pop artists like Shania Twain and Faith Hill, he never once had an interest in country music, not that his assistant didn't try to convert him on a daily basis. Being from Kentucky, she was well versed in country and western artists and songs, and even had the office radio on a country station at first. After several bouts, they agreed to a pop station that played some of both, and Spence found he liked some of the songs, but assured himself in his mind that they were not country.

Spence began removing the contents of his travel bag. He hung his trousers in his old closet, and placed his underwear in the dresser, along with his socks and T-shirts. He had traditionally been a "briefs" man in his younger years, but lately wore the boxer briefs, the ones with legs that fit more snug than traditional boxers did. Spence smiled as he remembered how his ex-wife used to buy silk boxers for him, telling him how sexy he looked. However, that was a different life, thought Spence, and the ones he had now were just fine. Besides, for whom did he have to look sexy?

When he finished unpacking, Spence decided to look around some. Although he was tired from the trip, his emotions would not let him sleep. He wandered downstairs to the den where he stopped to look at the various photos on the mahogany sofa table. As he scanned over the same photos, he remembered from fifteen years ago, he couldn't help but feel sentimental. His favorite was the one of himself with his mother and father taken at the lake one summer. He'd caught his first fish, and was holding it up with a big smile on his face. That picture reminded Spence of the happy times when all of them were together. He wiped away a tear as he re-played the death of his mother in his mind. Now with the death of his father, he wished she was there to comfort him. A chill ran over him, suddenly feeling all alone in the world.

Spence placed the picture back on the table and walked to the sunroom. He could see the whitecaps through the glass windows as they roiled across the gray water in the bay from the wind of the storm. He shivered as he thought about the cold wind slicing across the water like a knife cutting to the bone. He'd always preferred the summer with its beautiful sunshine reflecting off the blue water where he watched the geese swim and dive for food. As a child, he'd lie on the lawn and watch the white fluffy clouds as they made their way across the blue sky. His mother would often lie with him and they would compare what they saw in the clouds. Of course, her descriptions of majestic swans, hurtling acrobats, and fire-breathing dragons were much more vivid than his simple dog, horse, or car, but he loved the way she described them. Now, as he looked out over the gray foaming water, it re-minded him of how his life had become. Cold, dark and lonely.

Feeling that was a long enough trip down memory lane for now, he decided to lie down for a while and rest, even if he could not sleep.

Chapter Three

Spence jumped up in bed trying to shake the cobwebs from his head as his cell phone rang incessantly. He recognized the number flashing on the display. It was his office number, and he knew Sherrie would be on the other end. Sherrie had been his assistant since he began his practice in Lexington. He'd located a prime office space at 103 West Vine Street, and although the rent was more than he originally wanted to pay, it had turned out to be worth every penny. Vine Street was the center of the financial district with banks and investment houses, and of course, attorneys.

The office Spence rented once belonged to one of the most prominent attorneys in Kentucky, Sam Ballard. Spence found himself receiving calls simply because of his location. They remembered Sam, and believed anyone who was in the same place must be a relative or associate of Sam's. Even with the sudden onslaught of customers, Spence kept the practice relatively small, handling mostly contract law along with some trial work. He loved working a jury, a trait he must have inherited from his father, so he occasionally wound up the defense attorney arguing his client's innocence to the dismay of the District Attorney, Tom Fiedler. Yet he and

Sherrie were the only two employees of the firm. Sherrie insisted it was not too much work for her, but Spence had already decided to hire a paralegal when he returned from Michigan.

Sherrie was a local girl complete with an adorable Kentucky accent. Spence recalled how she was twenty-five when he hired her, and now at the age of forty still looked the same as the day they met. His mind began to wander as he replayed fond memories of watching Sherrie move around the office. Her five-foot four body was slender yet muscular in all the right places. She exercised every day after work at the gym down the street. He smiled as he thought about her short red hair that rested just below her ears, never out of place, and how her cute little bangs would rise and fall every time she'd blow upward when she was frustrated.

Spence felt a connection with Sherrie, as he did with most red heads, but reassured himself that his and Sherrie's relationship would remain strictly professional. Moreover, it had for the past fifteen years, although Sherrie had thrown many hints his way that she was open to exploring a more intimate relationship. Nevertheless, after ten years she gave up on Spence and settled for a local banker who was eleven years older than she was. They met at the gym. After six months of dating, they were married. Neither wanted children so they adopted two Golden Retrievers from the local animal shelter. Now she considered it a personal goal to find a good Kentucky woman for Spence, yet she still liked flirting with him.

"Hello Sherrie," Spence muttered rather sleepily into the phone.

"How's my man?" Sherrie replied as she pictured him blushing.

"I'm okay I guess, just trying to get a little rest."

"Well wake up! You're supposed to be at the funeral home by four o'clock."

Spence looked at his watch. It was 3:30. He'd been asleep for only a couple of hours. "Thanks for the wake up call."

"No problem, honey," Sherrie drawled. "And don't worry about the office. I have everything under control. You take all the time you need, but make sure you bring your cute butt back to Kentucky, ya hear?"

Spence said with a laugh, "All right Sherrie. I'll call you tomorrow."

"Not if I call you first," she giggled, and with that, the call ended. Sherrie was a tease, but Spence knew he could count on her to run the office while he was gone. Now, time for a quick shower and change before heading to the funeral home.

Cowell Funeral Home had been a mainstay in Traverse City for over one hundred years. James Cowell was the third generation currently in charge of the company. He inherited the reins after his mother, Emma, had died last spring. Of course, Cowell Funeral Home handled all of her funeral arrangements, the largest funeral Traverse City had seen in years. Only the funeral of Mr. Cowell, James' father, attracted more people, but then many of their friends had passed on before Emma's death. After her death, James had an extra wing added to the funeral home in memory of his mother. Now they were able to accommodate both small and large funeral services.

Spence pulled into the Cowell Funeral Home parking lot at exactly five minutes before four. He had always been a stickler for details, and punctuality was a necessity. He often berated clients who came to an appointment late so they learned quickly never to be late unless there was a very good reason.

Spence was not sure what instructions his father left regarding his funeral. All he knew was they were not included in his father's will. Spence read where to find the tape in a letter of instruction his father mailed to him a few years ago when the Judge made the last version of his will. He'd never opened the letter. He knew he had plenty of time to attend to it after the funeral, so it was still in the dresser underneath the clothes he placed there earlier.

Spence opened the beautiful wooden door that led to the

foyer of the funeral home and stepped inside. Just past the viewing rooms on the right was James' office. Across the hall was an office for his son, Josh, who no doubt would follow in his father's footsteps and one day take over the family business. Spence knocked lightly on the door and the hinges creaked a little as the door, which was already slightly open, opened a little farther.

"Come in," James called out, and as Spence stepped into the room, he saw James sitting behind his desk looking up over what appeared to be some important paperwork. James began working at the funeral home right after college, and now at the age of fifty, he had almost thirty years' experience in handling the final wishes of the recently departed and comforting the loved ones they left behind. He was very soft spoken with kind brown eyes, traits you would expect from someone in his profession. His hair was receding, but he insisted on sporting a dreadful comb over to try to hide his baldness. Most people said he reminded them of an old southern minister. James was a gaunt six-foot five without an ounce of fat on him. Even as a child, he was tall for his age. That, coupled with the family business, earned him the nickname "Lurch" among the neighborhood children. However, the nickname really didn't suit him, considering he'd grow up to be one of the best citizens Traverse City ever had. James was a very kind and generous man.

"Well, Spence, it sure is good to see you again after all these years, only I wish it were under better circumstances. Come in and tell me what you've been up to for the last several years."

"It's good to see you too," Spence replied. "It has been a long time."

After several minutes of catching up and idle talk, Spence got right down to business.

"James, I understand my father left specific instructions for his funeral with you. I just need to know the details so I can take care of the arrangements."

"Well actually," James replied, "Everything is already taken care of. Your father was very precise in his directions, right down to the cremation."

"Cremation?" Spence almost shouted.

"Yes," continued James, "Your father requested his body be cremated upon his death and the ashes placed in an urn. Once that was complete, he asked to have a ceremony here in the new chapel, announce it in all the papers, and then have his ashes placed in one of the mausoleums at Cedar Ridge Cemetery. He even requested a large article in the Detroit paper, I assume since he had many business associates in the area, but he was very insistent on no visitation. The service will be Saturday at two," James finished.

"Can I at least see him before you cremate him?" Spence asked.

"Certainly. Of course, due to the nature of his death, we were unable to make him presentable since it was a while before his body was found," continued James, leading Spence to the basement. James led him to a coffin on a gurney beside the wall.

"Here he is," he said. "Take all the time you need." Then he stepped back a few feet from the casket.

Spence stared into the coffin unable to recognize his father. Of course, it had been fifteen years since he'd last seen him, but still Spence thought he'd look more familiar. Apparently, James sensed his confusion so he stepped closer and in a half-whisper said, "Unfortunately, the stroke left him rather distorted. I'm sorry, Spence, but we did the best we could."

Spence recognized the lapel pin his father was wearing as the one Spence's mother had given him for their tenth anniversary. Recovering somewhat from the initial shock, Spence thanked James for his assistance and assured him there were no hard feelings, that he wanted his father's true wishes carried out. James invited him to play golf the next day since his schedule was free, and seeing he had no arrangements to make, Spence accepted.

He was still somewhat in a state of shock as he left the funeral home and walked back to his car. He settled in the seat and remained there for what seemed an eternity before he started the engine and drove out of the parking lot.

Chapter Four

A s he headed back to the estate, Spence suddenly felt hungry again. Not knowing if there was any food in the house, he decided to stop at Antoni's for some Italian. Antoni's had opened when Spence was still a junior in high school, and was a favorite for prom night. It was an upscale Italian restaurant, but not too stuffy, and moderately priced, famous for lasagna. Spence almost drooled as he thought about how long it had been since he'd eaten good lasagna. The place was just north of town up Highway 31 in a small brick building with a nicely carved wooden sign hanging on an old-fashioned lamppost.

The sun had just disappeared over the horizon as Spence pulled into the parking lot at Antoni's. It was still too early for the main crowd, and he was hoping to grab a quick bite and leave before anyone who might recognize him came in. He knew he'd see them at the funeral, and for now wanted some time to digest not only his meal, but also the conversation earlier with James.

As he entered Antoni's, Spence noticed the sign that read 'please wait to be seated,' but saw no hostess at the front. After a minute, a woman yelled "be right there!" in

Spence's direction. He saw her turn the corner heading toward him, a woman probably in her early fifties, plain yet attractive, with short blond hair that reminded him of his Aunt Margaret. She was average height, and her weight was proportionate to her frame, filling her black pants and white shirt nicely. A red bow tie completed the ensemble, and Spence couldn't help but think she should have a more feminine uniform.

"Sorry about that," she said, "we don't usually get many customers this early. Did you want smoking or non-smoking?"

"Non-smoking, please," Spence replied. She quickly turned, grabbed a menu, and led him to the first booth on the right. "If it's not too much trouble, can I have a booth in the back?"

"Sure, you almost have the place to yourself anyway," she said, and led Spence to the farthest booth on the right hand side where he slid into the booth as the woman disappeared into the kitchen.

Soon Sharon appeared and asked for his drink order. She seemed to be in her early twenties with brown hair neatly tied in a ponytail, deep brown eyes, and very thick pouting lips. She was almost Spence's height, slender yet not too thin. Her black dress revealed a nice pair of legs with smooth thighs and very toned calves, with black stockings to match her outfit. He noticed her ample size thirty-eight breasts spilling from her low-cut blouse. The back was very low cut, revealing much of her creamy white skin, with a few freckled moles here and there.

"I'll have a Jack and Coke," he ordered, his usual drink of the evening. Jack Daniels and a splash of Coke had been Spence's favorite drink, and closest friend, since shortly before the dissolution of his first marriage. He'd tried rum and coke in college until one party where they ran out of Coke and he began drinking rum straight. He'd never been so sick in his life, as he spent most of the night paying homage to the porcelain god. He occasionally drank wine, but had never acquired a taste for beer. However, he could always count on his friend Jack to clear his head and make him feel better.

As the waitress retreated to the bar to place his order, he couldn't help but watch the sway of her hips as she walked away. At least the senses still work, he told himself as he felt that familiar tingle inside. Sharon quickly returned with his drink and began to list the specials of the evening. Spence could've stopped her at any time, knowing he wanted the lasagna, but was enjoying watching her lips move too much to interrupt her. When she finished, he ordered the lasagna, and again watched her walk to the kitchen. He had an urge to ask her for a date, but feared she'd laugh in his face because of their obvious age difference, so he decided to simply finish his Jack and Coke and enjoy the view.

The lasagna was piping hot, and Sharon warned Spence to be careful not to burn himself. He was so looking forward to it, that he almost dove right in, but decided to heed her warning and sip his drink while his meal cooled. After a few minutes, he could no longer wait, and proceeded to place a large helping in his mouth. It was just as he remembered, with the right blend of spices in the sauce, and enough cheese to feed a small nation. Antoni always said it was the cheese which made his the best, and the man wasn't lying.

Spence dipped some of the warm garlic bread in the sauce, and took alternate bites of bread and lasagna until it was all gone. Satisfied, and very full, he asked Sharon for the check. She was back in less than a minute, and he handed her his credit card. She turned and left again, only to return with the card receipt for him to sign. Spence mused it would be worth paying a dozen different checks just to be able to watch her walk back and forth. She thanked him for dining with them, and Spence returned a kind 'Thank You' for the service. He was so enamored with her that he left a very large tip. When he was through signing his name, he placed the receipt in his pocket, drained the last of his drink, and as he was rising to his feet, he heard a familiar voice call his name.

"Spence, is that you? I can't believe it after all these years!"

As he looked up, he saw a rather tall woman approaching. She had short, brown hair just past her ears in a Dorothy Hamill style, which revealed her beautiful milky neck. She was wearing a red dress, high enough at the bottom to reveal her shapely legs, yet low cut enough at the top to enhance her breasts. Spence was racking his brain, trying to come up with her name, when he realized it was Arlene Hurst, or at least that had been her name in high school.

"Good to see you, Ally," Spence quickly replied. That was what everyone in school called her, and he felt proud that he remembered it.

"Why, you remembered," she cooed. "I heard you moved out of state. What brings you to town?"

"My father passed away this week, so I had to come home for the funeral and to settle his estate."

"I'm so sorry to hear that," Arlene said as she patted his arm. "Tell me what you've been up to all these years."

Spence called Sharon back to the table, ordered another drink, and Arlene ordered a salad and a carafe of Rosemount Cabernet. Apparently, he noted, she was in no hurry to leave. He began his story, sticking mainly to the mundane facts and leaving out the intimate details of his life's history to date. After he arrived at the present in his story, Arlene said, "I guess you'll be one of the richest eligible bachelors now."

"Why do you say that?" Spence questioned, rather shocked at what she'd alluded to.

"Well," she continued, "I heard your father was very wealthy, but I didn't mean to pry."

"Don't worry about it, I'm not really sure how much he was worth, but probably not very much. So, tell me about yourself, Arlene."

Arlene recalled her life story of how she married the star quarterback of the high school football team; only to wind up divorced after five years of living with an alcoholic. He began drinking when he blew his knee out in his second year of college and realized his football career was over. After graduation, he ended up selling used cars and spending what little money he earned on booze. She'd graduated from Michigan State with honors, and after earning her CPA, landed a good job with a government agency. She realized she was wasting her time in the marriage, and decided she was better off alone. They had no children, and she hadn't remarried, yet. She enjoyed the single life, and became accustomed to the independence of living alone. At this point, she wasn't sure if she'd ever be able to, or want, to be married again. At least, that's what she told herself on those nights when she had trouble falling asleep. Spence wondered why she was telling him all of this, but he had asked, and at one point found himself actually pondering what it would be like to be married to Arlene. She was definitely more interesting than his first wife had been.

Spence met his first wife, Greta, at a college party. She could trace her family roots back to some of the original Dutch settlers in Western Michigan. She was a natural red head with a fiery temper to match. They'd been married for two years when the VanWarner case broke. Because Greta was a very passionate lover who became bored easily, when Spence was distracted over the crisis with his father, she'd found excitement in the arms—and bed—of Harry Wolciez, one of Spence's college buddies. When Spence announced he was leaving Michigan, Greta told him she didn't intend to leave her exciting life for a mundane existence in rural America. She adored men, but she adored money more, and considering Harry came from a very wealthy family, she would be able to party with him from now until eternity. As he became lost in the past, Spence realized Arlene had stopped talking and he was staring at her as if his eyes were boring through her skull.

"Penny for your thoughts," she said.

"Just thinking about Dad," he lied, knowing he could get away with that response for now. The truth was, he was remembering how his mother used to say the same thing to him when he would stare off into space. Although there were very few days that passed without him thinking of her, the trip back to Michigan made the memories more frequent and depressing.

After another hour of small talk, Arlene invited Spence

to her place to continue the conversation, but he declined the invitation saying he still needed to go over his father's will and take care of some last minute preparations. In addition, he was meeting with James tomorrow at the funeral home. Of course, he conveniently left out the part about playing golf. She said she understood, kissed him on the cheek, and told him they should definitely get together before he left town. Spence agreed, after all, it was always a good idea to keep your options open. As Arlene walked out, he remained at the table for a minute, just long enough to watch her walk away. 'Yes, you're a dog,' he told himself, but how many days was he able to enjoy so many good views in such short time. With that, he sighed, got up from the table, and walked to his car for the return trip to his father's estate.

As he made his way up the winding drive, Spence noticed that although it was dark, the moon reflected off the snowy trees, making a magical lighted path that sprang up on either side of him. He stopped the car in front of the garage, glancing in the direction of the guesthouse. There was still no sign of Agnes, and with the funeral still to take place, he thought surely, she was not out of town on a trip. She must be out for a late dinner, he told himself.

He walked to the house, retrieved the key that he found earlier from his pocket, and entered the dark house, cursing under his breath for not leaving a light on. He felt along the wall just inside the door until he found the switch, and soon the foyer was fully illuminated.

As he blinked to adjust to the sudden burst of light, he noticed what appeared to be wet footprints down the hallway and leading to the door of his father's office. He followed the path they made, slowly trying not to announce his presence in case someone was still in the house. Then he realized he had no protection should he encounter an intruder, so he slipped his shoes off, climbed the stairs and entered his bedroom, retrieved his old baseball bat, and crept slowly back to the office door. He held the bat drawn back with his right hand as he reached with his left for the door. Slowly turning the knob, Spence inched the door open and quickly turned on the light.

There was no one in the room, but the footprints continued across the floor, disappearing into the den. He followed the trail and again turned on the light in the den, only to find no one there and wet footprints that ended in front of the entertainment center.

He examined the contents of the entertainment center and quickly noticed someone had rifled through the videotapes. There was a case marked 'NFL Super Bowl Highlights' left open, but no tape was inside. The remaining cassettes appeared to be undisturbed. Spence looked at the VCR and noticed the power was still on. There was also a tape inside, and he realized someone had been watching it while he was gone. He turned on the television, rewound the tape, and pressed the 'play' button. After a minute of snow, his father appeared on the screen announcing that he was of sound mind and body and this was his last will and testament.

Spence was very surprised by this, since he hadn't yet opened the envelope containing the location of his father's taped will. The question at hand now was who had already watched the tape, and why? More importantly, how did they know exactly where it was?

Since the tape was already playing and it was apparent no one else was in the house, Spence decided to go ahead and watch the video. It seemed weird at first, watching his father after all those years, but uneasiness gave way to serious attention, especially since Spence was to administer his father's estate.

It began with the usual legalese followed by some general comments about family and friends. Then the Judge, looking directly into the camera, declared his love for Spence, described how he missed having a normal relationship with him, and finally asked for his forgiveness, stating that he, not Spence, was to blame for the strain on their relationship. The years had been kind to Judge Rawlings, giving him the appearance of someone ten years younger. He always kept in top shape, jogging through the woods on the estate every morning, and working out in the gym at least three days a week. Spence could still see the kindness in his eyes as he watched his father speaking to him.

"And now to the disposition of the assets of my estate," the Judge began. "The law firm has a buyout agreement whereby the surviving partners will buy out my interest with the proceeds of a key person insurance policy in the amount of one million dollars. You will need to contact Ed Harris, one of our senior partners. He should take care of the details and wire the funds to the estate account once you give him that information. Agnes has moved to Key Largo to live with relatives. I bequeath to her the sum of one hundred thousand dollars, which you need to deliver in person. I'm not sure of the address, but you should be able to find her. There's a checking account, a money market account, and various CD's at Comerica, which are to be yours. You also inherit this estate, the only real estate holding I own. That is the sum of my affairs. If you have been in town long enough, I'm sure someone told you I had a lot of money hidden somewhere, but I'm sorry, this is all I have to give you. I love you very much, son. Just remember, 'You always were the best.'" With that, Judge Rawlings disappeared from the screen and the tape ended.

Spence stared at the blank screen for a minute to collect his thoughts. He played the tape again just to make sure he understood, but it was actually a very simple will for someone of Judge Rawlings stature. He remembered Arlene's words as his father mentioned rumors of money. Why did she believe he would inherit a lot of money, and why did his father specifically mention it? It was very puzzling indeed, but Spence was tired and decided he should sleep on this. Maybe James could shed some light on this tomorrow during their golf game.

He grabbed a mop out of the pantry and erased the drying footprints as best he could. There was no point in calling the police, considering there were no signs of forced entry, nothing taken, and nothing was disturbed except the tape, which Spence felt would be of little benefit to anyone but himself. He locked the front door and climbed the wooden staircase once again to his room. He set his cell phone to alarm at six o'clock in the morning, which should give him plenty of time to shower, dress and grab some breakfast before meeting James at ten. Spence pulled back the sheets, undressed, and slipped into his old bed. It felt good to be home again, but he missed his father, and seeing him on the tape made the feelings stronger. With all that was spinning through Spence's head, he was sure there would be no sleep for him tonight. However, the cocktails and the long drive won the battle, and Spence was sound asleep within fifteen minutes.

Chapter Five

The cell phone began to chime, waking Spence from a hard sleep. It was six, and he eagerly climbed out of bed, anxious to start the day and perhaps find some answers to the questions last night's events had posed. He showered quickly and dressed for a cool day on the golf course. The temperature should reach fifty-nine degrees today, but the morning would be quite chilly, so Spence donned slacks, a long-sleeved shirt, and his favorite Polo vest. He would also wear a windbreaker, which he'd probably remove if the temperature became warm enough. It, too, had the Polo emblem embroidered on the front. Spence couldn't help but think about the events of last night and began to formulate a plan of discussion with James that would provide some answers.

He stopped at Nick's, one of the small local restaurants open until two and serving breakfast and lunch. He sat at the counter between two truck drivers who were just finishing their plate of ham and eggs. The waitress removed an order from the shelf, then turned and took it to the right end of the counter, calling "Be right with you" in Spence's direction. She quickly returned with a pot of coffee and a cup, and he noticed her nametag read 'Shirley.'

"Coffee?" she asked as she placed the cup in front of Spence. He nodded his approval and she began to pour as she handed him a menu. "Specials are on the board," she said, which were listed on a dry erase board hanging on the wall behind her.

He ordered the ham and eggs with toast and hash browns. She quickly turned and placed the order on the wheel above the shelf to the kitchen, and was off in the direction of a young couple who had just sat down at the booth along the left wall of the diner.

Spence was glad she was busy, or perhaps she would have recognized him. Shirley Jessup, the girl voted most likely to succeed in his senior class, was apparently not living up to that distinction. Shirley had been a beautiful girl in high school, but the burden of life as a waitress had taken its toll. She looked ten years older than she actually was, and Spence found himself wondering what cards life had dealt her. He decided it was best to leave well enough alone. After all, he had his own mystery to solve. Besides, she was much too busy with her work to waste time talking to him.

She rushed another order to the kitchen, grabbed the coffee pot from the warmer, and topped off Spence's cup. She paused long enough for a smile, making sure there was nothing else he needed, rushing off to the next customer, never giving Spence a second glance. He finished his meal and left the restaurant.

The snow which arrived during Spence's trip had melted, so it would not interrupt the golf game. James had mentioned the possibility of heading a little south in order to find a course not covered in white, but Mother Nature had cooperated with a slight warming trend, removing the remnants of the last storm. As Spence turned into the funeral home parking lot, he noticed James was already there. It was five minutes before ten, and again Spence was a little early. Before he could climb out of his car, James was walking out of the building toward him.

"We'll take my car," James said. "It's already warmed up."

"Sounds good to me," Spence replied as he lifted his golf clubs from the trunk of his car. He always carried his clubs with him, just in case there was an opportunity to play. He placed the clubs in James' trunk, closed the lid, and proceeded to the passenger side of the car. James' Cadillac was black, matching the other funeral home vehicles, causing Spence to hesitate for a moment before opening the door.

"It's okay," James said with a chuckle. "A lot of people think of it as a funeral car. The truth is I rarely carry clients in it, especially not the dead ones." They both laughed at that, as they pulled out of the parking lot and headed in the direction of the country club.

"You look like someone with a lot on his mind," James began. "Of course I understand the process, having seen the effects of the passing of a loved one many times. Is there anything I can do to help?"

Spence shifted in his seat. "Let me ask you something, James. I know you and my father were very close. Did he tell you what was in his will?"

"No," James replied. "We never discussed that, only his funeral arrangements. Why?"

Spence hesitated. "I ran into an old friend last night, and she had the impression my father was a very wealthy man. Don't get me wrong. He has substantial assets. However, not what I would consider wealthy, especially after reviewing his will. Have you heard any rumors to the contrary?"

James replied, "Well, there was this rumor that started a few years back about the Judge coming into some money. Some said the VanWarners were involved, others said he just rather found some money. Either way, no real evidence of a sudden windfall ever appeared, so I assumed it was just idle gossip." The name VanWarner sent a chill up Spence's spine, but he listened intently to see if he could discern whether James was lying to him. "Besides, I'm sure if he had this money, he would have mentioned it in the will."

"I guess you're right," Spence agreed, but he had this feeling James wasn't telling him everything. Maybe he would open up more during their round of golf.

It turned out to be a beautiful day, and Spence was thoroughly enjoying himself, at least his golf game. Every time he tried to uncover more information about his father's finances, James deflected his questions and avoided making any response that Spence could interpret as him knowing more than he let on. James insisted the money rumor was just that, a rumor, and offered no other information except that he remembered the Judge making an occasional trip to the casino in Mount Pleasant. His reaction made Spence even more curious, frustrating him in the process. However, he decided not to let James see how it affected him, and instead changed the subject, asking about his family. The small talk continued throughout the rest of the afternoon until they were finished and it was time to head back to the funeral home.

"I don't know what you plan to do, Spence," James said. "But if you were to move back to the estate, we could pick up where your father and I left off with our Thursday golf outings."

"I don't know, I still have my practice in Kentucky. But we'll see," Spence replied, knowing he had no intention of ever moving back to Michigan.

"Think about it. It would be good to have you home again."

"Thanks," Spence said, as they pulled into the funeral home parking lot. He placed his clubs back into his car, shook James' hand, and drove off in the direction of Traverse Bay and his father's estate.

As he pulled his car in front of the garage, Spence automatically looked in the direction of the guesthouse for Agnes' car. Then he remembered what his father said about her moving to Key Largo. He didn't remember Agnes ever mentioning relatives, but that was a long time ago. He hesitated as he opened the door, just in case last night's visitor had returned. There was no sign that anyone else had been there, so he strode into the foyer, tossed his keys on the table, and closed the door. He walked to the wet bar in the den, fixed himself a Jack and Coke, and collapsed in the chair in front of the entertainment center. The tape was still in the machine from last night, so Spence decided to watch it again, just in case he'd missed something. The Judge repeated the same words, and about half way through the performance, Spence drifted off for an afternoon nap.

The cell phone was ringing again as Spence awoke from his rest. It was Sherrie checking up on him.

"Hello, Sherrie."

"Hey, babe," she teased. "How was your day?" Spence recounted the day's events, even telling her about his score of seventy-five at the country club. He also told her about last night, the mysterious intruder, the rumor of money, and the will that made it all seem like a dream.

When he finished, Sherrie asked, "What's your next move?"

"Well, the funeral is tomorrow. I think I'll wait and see who shows up and what rumors they bring."

"Sounds like a plan, hon, but do be careful. You don't know who that was in the house last night," Sherrie reminded him.

"Don't worry about me," he told her. "How're things at the office?"

"I told you I have it all under control," she said in a huff. "You just take care of yourself." After a few more words and some extra flirting from Sherrie, Spence ended the call.

He decided to stay in for the night. He found some frozen microwave dinners in the freezer Agnes had obviously placed there for him before she left. He decided on a pizza sub as he opened the box, removed the sandwich, and placed it in the microwave. As it was defrosting, he fixed another Jack and Coke. The funeral was to be at two in the afternoon, so he could sleep in. He watched the tape again, remembering he still needed to contact Agnes about her inheritance, but how would he track her down?

He rewound the tape and turned off the VCR, deciding to flip through the channels to see what was on. Suddenly his cell phone began ringing again, but the caller ID stated the number was private. Spence hesitantly answered, "Hello?"

The voice on the other end asked, "Are you alone?" She

sounded sultry and sweet at the same time, and he recognized it was Arlene.

"As a matter of fact, I am."

"I realize the funeral is tomorrow," she continued, "But I wanted to check on you, to make sure you're okay."

"I'm fine."

"I don't mean to pry. But, did you play the will?"

Spence was surprised at the question. "Why do you ask?"

"I'm sorry," she said. "Forget I mentioned it. Would you like some company?"

"Not tonight," Spence replied, "Maybe after the funeral."

"I understand. Let me give you my number in case you need me."

Spence wrote the number on a pad on his father's desk. He assured her again he was fine and had no need for company. Reluctantly, she agreed to let him go, telling him she'd see him at the funeral tomorrow. She reminded him one last time to call her if he needed anything, then told him goodbye. Spence really was not in the mood for company, but was glad she'd called. Still, he wondered why she had mentioned the will, and how did she know it was a tape? Of course, taped wills had become very popular, so maybe she just assumed that it was. Either way, he'd get no answers to his questions tonight, so he fixed another Jack and Coke and sat back down to watch some television.

Spence awoke to the sound of sirens, which caused his heart to race. He squinted, trying to focus his eyes, and soon realized it was just the television. He fell asleep after his fifth Jack and Coke, and awoke to an old rerun of Hawaii Five-O. 'Book 'em, Danno,' he said toward the TV as he reached for the remote. He glanced at his watch. It was three-thirty. He turned the TV off, and made his way to the bedroom to finish the terrific dream he was having, when McGarrett abruptly interrupted it with his pals chasing the suspect. He was dreaming about Arlene, actually he and Arlene together, and couldn't wait to pick up where he left off.

Spence slid beneath the covers, but found it difficult to return to sleep. Why was he dreaming of Arlene? Surely, she was not the girl for him after all these years. Whoa, slow down, he told himself, who said anything about a long-term commitment? After all, they hadn't even dated yet, and something about the whole situation didn't feel right. Sure, he could stand some female company, but that didn't mean he was ready to settle down with anyone. Besides, there were too many unanswered questions about Arlene, her actions in the past few days, and the probing questions, which all led to one thing—money.

Spence decided he would play this thing out with Arlene and see where it led. Who knew, maybe she had more knowledge of his father's money than he did. Since she would be at the funeral it would be the perfect time to schedule a date for later in the evening. He would try to catch her early and get it settled so he could concentrate on the other guests, who they were, what they said, how they acted. Spence wondered if his uninvited visitor from last night would be there, but how would he know? He had no clue as to who it was. He felt good about his plan, and after he had everything laid out neatly in his mind, he drifted off to sleep.

Chapter Six

The parking lot at Cowell Funeral Home was almost full when Spence arrived at one-thirty. James promised to block off a space for him near the front of the chapel since he declined the use of a family car. The idea of riding in one of those large black funeral home limousines made Spence's skin crawl, and besides, since he was the only family member, the limo wasn't necessary.

One of James' employees stood ready to remove the orange parking cone as Spence drove toward the designated space. Once he pulled in, the man and the orange cone disappeared somewhere inside the building and James was standing just outside the car waiting for Spence to exit the vehicle and walk with him into the chapel. After shaking hands and a cursory exchange of words, James led Spence inside where he had reserved a spot in the front right pew.

People packed into the chapel waiting for the service to begin so they could pay their final respects to the dear departed. Spence's eyes darted back and forth, as he proceeded down the aisle, trying not to appear too obvious as he checked out the attendees. He recognized the partners in his father's law firm and a few of his friends. Some of the Van-

Warner clan were assembled in the back left pews, trying to blend into the crowd, but the silk suits and slick hair made them stand out like a bridegroom at a toga party.

As he neared the front, Spence noticed Arlene was sitting just behind the first pew on the right. Very convenient, he thought, was it just coincidence or by design? No matter, it made it easier for him to locate her in the crowd. After he sat down, he turned around in Arlene's direction and leaned back in the pew. Arlene leaned forward and touched him gently on the arm.

"Will you please come by the estate this evening around six?" he whispered.

"I thought you would never ask," she replied. "I'll be there with bells on."

The urn that contained the ashes of Judge Warren Thurman Rawlings sat on a marble stand in the front of the church directly in front of the pulpit. A picture of the Judge rested on another stand beside the urn. The picture was from a few years before, but Spence thought it looked very much as he remembered. The Judge had requested Pastor John Mitchell preside over the service, considering he had been the Pastor at Grace Reformed Church for twenty-five years, and a good friend of his.

Pastor Mitchell was sixty-five years old, with snow-white hair that had been that way since he was forty. His five-foot eight-inch frame hunched over from years of poor nutrition. At first glance, one would believe him to be a feeble man. However, when he spoke, his voice resonated with the strength of a man in his twenties. He had a soothing tone that demonstrated his kindness and compassion. Truly, he lived a life that proved his faith in the way he dealt with his congregation and the community with his many charitable works. Spence was glad Pastor Mitchell was performing the service.

Although he grew up in the Reformed Church, Spence was not devout in his faith. It had been three year since he'd seen the inside of a church, and that was for an old college friend's wedding. During college, he'd read about the many different religions, and found himself questioning some of the church teachings he'd learned as a youth. However, he never converted to any other faith, instead opting to remain a non-practicing Christian. He believed in a higher deity, but wrestled with the ever-present questions of why certain things happened if there was indeed a God. These were thoughts he chose not share with others, but kept them buried in the hopes that one day he'd find an answer and meaning to life. Sherrie had tried for years to get Spence into church, inviting him to come with her and her husband, but so far, he'd managed to find enough excuses not to go. Maybe one day, he thought, he just might take her up on the offer and possibly find the peace he so often heard about.

The service was a wonderful combination of music and message, with one of the church's choir members singing beautiful renditions of *Amazing Grace* and *The Lord's Prayer*. Having known him for many years, Pastor Mitchell accurately described the life and faith of Judge Rawlings. He revealed some things about his father that Spence never knew, like his financial support of needy families in the community; details that displayed a more human side of his father that Spence had forgotten all these years. Sure, he remembered many good times, but Pastor Mitchell's words bore straight to Spence's heart, making him yearn for all the lost years he'd so stubbornly refused. These feelings swelled up inside Spence until he could no longer hold back the floodgates, and wept openly for his father, and the lost wasted years.

The service concluded with a hymn Spence had never heard before, but found to be beautiful and comforting at a time of loss. Spence found it a very different service than some funerals he'd attended in the past, refreshing and more personal. He decided not to speak himself, although Pastor Mitchell asked if he wanted to eulogize his father. Because of their relationship, Spence felt it would sound better coming from someone who actually knew his father, especially in the more recent years. He was proud of his decision to allow only Pastor Mitchell to speak, believing no one else could have done a better job. After the service ended, the urn was removed to the cemetery by the hearse as per the Judge's instructions. There was a short graveside eulogy, the reading of *Psalm 23*, and then the remains placed in the vault. Spence removed the rose he'd placed in his lapel, and laid it in front of the mausoleum that now held the remains of his father. He gently touched his hand to the cold marble, wiped away one stray tear, and turned in the direction of his car.

Many of the guests had already returned to their automobiles, but several stayed behind to speak to Spence. As he made his way through the throng of people, he politely shook their hands and thanked them for coming. Most of them expressed their sympathy, and a few recounted a specific memory they had about Judge Rawlings. Spence suddenly felt a large hand grab his and another firmly patting his back. He looked up to find Joseph VanWarner or Joey as to most, staring down at him.

"Really sorry about your old man," Joey began. "He was a dear friend of the family and will surely be missed by us all."

Spence managed to choke out a 'Thank you,' having been caught off guard by the encounter.

"If there is anything we can do, or if you happen to run across anything in the Judge's personal effects you don't know how to dispose of, don't hesitate to call me. I know a lot about the Judge's business dealings since we were friends for so long."

"I'll keep that in mind," Spence replied almost questioning, wondering what Joey was referring to and how he had the nerve to be so bold at a funeral. Of course, grace was not one of Joey's strong suits.

After thirty minutes of meeting guests, discussing the old days and recollections of Judge Rawlings, and a few token 'Don't be such a stranger, come visit for dinner' invitations, Spence was finally able to leave the cemetery. It was now four o'clock, two hours before Arlene was due to arrive at the estate. This gave Spence time to pick up a nice bottle of wine and all the necessary ingredients to make his famous spaghetti; at least his friends from college called it that. He remembered seeing a grocers on Highway 31 as he came into town, thinking how neat that it was still in business after all these years. He'd shopped there many times when he was home from college and wanted to cook for his father and Agnes. Cooking was his way of saying thanks to Agnes for all the meals she'd made for him and his father over the years.

Only a few cars were in the parking lot of Nell's Grocery when he pulled in. Nell had passed away several years earlier, but her daughter Muriel kept the business going, in spite of the large chain grocery stores that had been trying to squeeze the little people out of business for years. The people of Traverse City bought their groceries from Muriel because she offered one thing the larger stores did not, the personal touch. Muriel made it her business to know her customers and their families, right down to their pets. She had a knack for remembering each name, never confusing one for another. Sure, the patrons could probably purchase some items cheaper at the larger stores, but it was worth more to trade with family, and that was how the customers felt about Muriel.

It had been years since Spence last saw Muriel, but upon seeing her again, it was as if time had stood still. She hadn't changed, looking much the same as the last time he saw her, with the exception of a few additional gray hairs. Muriel was a petite woman, standing just under five feet, plump but not obese. She wore her hair in an old-maid style bun, a few stray hairs hanging around her face. A face still smooth, with few wrinkles, and a warm inviting smile that made you feel right at home.

Before he could speak, Muriel almost shouted, "Why, Spence! It's about time you came to see me. Are you making some of that spaghetti of yours again?"

Spence smiled and replied, "Yes ma'am, as a matter of fact I am."

"I'm sorry about your father," she continued on a somber note. "I would've come to the funeral, but I had to stay open. Too much competition these days."

Spence nodded in agreement. "I understand and I'm sure he would too."

They spent the next ten minutes catching up, as Spence told her all about his life since leaving Michigan. Muriel updated him on her sons and their families, asking Spence why he wasn't married, considering it had been so long since the divorce. He just had not met the right woman, he assured her, but there was always hope. Muriel walked with him as he collected the meat, bread, produce, and spices he'd need. As he paused in front of the wine aisle, one of her clerks summoned Muriel. She patted Spence on the arm and asked him to stop in before he left town, and then hurried away in the direction of the employee needing her assistance.

Spence mulled over the selection of wines before settling on a nice Cabernet. He also grabbed two bottles of Merlot, hoping they would need more wine after the meal. The cashier was a cute blonde who couldn't be much older than twenty-one, probably a college student working part-time when she came home on weekends. He paid her for the groceries, waved in the direction of Muriel, who was in the middle of disciplining a clerk, and headed out the door to his car. He placed the bags carefully in the trunk, and sped off toward what was now his house.

Chapter Seven

It was five o'clock when Spence walked back into the house. He placed the groceries in the kitchen and went straight to work on the meal. With a little luck, he would be finished just as Arlene arrived, but thought it would be nice for her to see him in action, so he purposely waited until just before six, the time she was to stop by, to begin preparing the garlic bread.

The doorbell rang just as Spence was placing the bread in the oven. He opened the door to see Arlene smiling back at him, wearing a tight leather skirt that stopped several inches above her knee, and an equally tight red sweater that revealed her shapely body. She wore black silk stockings with seams down the back and black stiletto heels, definitely an outfit for style or play, Spence mused.

Arlene was definitely different from his first wife, Greta. He'd been married two years to Greta, a Dutch girl whose family had settled in western Michigan. They met at one of the many parties he attended while in school, and shortly after he graduated, they were married. Greta was a natural redhead with the noted fiery temper to match. She was also a very passionate lover who became bored easily, and when the crisis for Spence with his father began, Greta found excitement in the arms of Harry Wolciez, one of Spence's college friends.

The passage of time hadn't made it easier for Spence to discuss Greta's affair, having internalized the pain and feeling of inferiority to the point of embarrassment at the thought of someone so close to him betraying his trust and crushing his spirit. He preferred to avoid any discussions of the affair for fear of showing how emotionally devastated it had left him. When Spence announced he was leaving Michigan, Greta informed him she did not intend to leave her exciting life for a mundane existence in rural America. She adored men, but she adored money more, and Harry came from a very wealthy family, enough to keep her partying from now until eternity. She quickly divorced Spence with no claim to any of his assets, so he left and settled in Versailles, Kentucky, establishing a law practice in Lexington.

"Thanks for coming, I hope you like spaghetti."

"What, lasagna last night and spaghetti tonight? If I didn't know better, I'd swear you were Italian," Arlene said with a giggle. "At least, all I had last night was a salad." With that, she leaned over and kissed Spence softly on the cheek. He held the door as she walked in, making sure he lingered behind for a view from the back.

"I brought some wine," she whispered as if it were something naughty.

"Great!" he replied, "We can have a glass while we wait for the bread to finish toasting." With that, he retreated to the kitchen with the wine and soon returned with a glass for each. Arlene was already sitting on the sofa in the den.

"What's this tape?" she asked, holding the tape of his father's will. "I didn't know your father was into football."

"I'm not sure," he lied, "maybe someone gave it to him."

"But it looks like you've been watching it," she continued.

"Guilty," Spence said, raising his hands. "I found it the other night when I couldn't sleep and decided to watch some of it, your honor," he said, hinting that she was asking too many questions.

"Oh, I'm sorry if it sounded like I was prying. I just

thought at first that it might be your father's will," she replied.

Spence seized the moment. "Why would you think the will was on video tape?"

Arlene froze for an instant, a bead of sweat glistening on her brow, then, nervously answered, "Well, I just assumed it would be since most people were doing it that way."

Spence just smiled and retreated to the kitchen to take the bread out of the oven, and give Arlene time to consider her blunder.

The dining room was just off the kitchen through an open arched doorway. There was the usual dining furniture, a table, six chairs, a china cabinet, and a server, all made of solid cherry. The crystal chandelier hung beautifully from the fifteen-foot ceiling, resting above the table just high enough so no one could accidentally bump their head into it. Spence had already set two places at the near end of the table to shorten the trip from the kitchen, and ensure Arlene sat next to him. Once he placed the dinner on the table, he poked his head in the den and told Arlene it was time to eat. As she sat down, he refilled their glasses, taking his seat next to her.

"I'm really sorry I asked about the will earlier," she began. "It wasn't very thoughtful of me."

"It's okay. Don't worry about it."

"Everything smells delicious," she said, changing the subject.

He thanked her, as he served up a nice helping of sauce over her spaghetti. He had thought of everything, salad, spaghetti, sauce, garlic bread, and wine. He even had cheesecake for dessert. Of course, he bought it from Muriel's refrigerated case.

The remainder of the dinner conversation was limited to old stories each remembered from school. It was interesting how people remember events differently from others, as they found to be true when it came to recalling certain events. Each memory produced a laugh or an embarrassed sigh, but they both were enjoying the evening. Spence especially liked hearing Arlene laugh. He found it very attractive.

After they finished eating, Arlene helped Spence clear the table. He placed the dishes in the dishwasher and the leftovers in the fridge. There was barely enough twilight left to make out the bay, but Spence insisted they take their wine to the sunroom. Arlene eased into the overstuffed sofa as Spence handed her a full glass of Merlot. Then he settled next to her, taking another glass for himself. The shadows of twilight shining across the bay made for the romantic setting that he wanted. He thanked Arlene again for the company as they sipped their wine.

"I was wondering," Spence began. "Where do you live around here exactly?"

Arlene took his hand. "Come here." She stood and led him over to a telescope the Judge had used for bird and people watching. She looked into the viewer, adjusted it somewhat, then pushed Spence's head down toward the eye-piece. "There," she said. "That's my sunroom."

Spence stared through the telescope at a room that appeared to be right in front of him. Her house was actually around the left of the bay in the direction of Grellickville. He was awestruck at how close their houses seemed to be so far apart. The view was so good, he could make out every piece of furniture, including the art on the walls. She has good taste, he told himself, as he admired the way she'd decorated. The remainder of the house was dark, but he could tell by the shape and dimensions that it was above average in size. Then his eye caught something in the back right corner. A telescope. Had she been watching his house?

"What do you think?" she asked.

"Nice," was all Spence could get out. He wanted to ask if she'd been indeed watching the house, but he needed to play it cool for now.

"You said you work for a government agency," Spence said, switching gears. "Which one?"

"FBI," she said quickly, without hesitation. Then she broke out in laughter. "Relax, I'm just a staff accountant. Besides, you don't have anything to hide, do you?"

"Maybe," he said smiling. "Why don't you tie me up and

beat me with a rubber hose to see what I know?" With that, they both burst into laughter. The wine was definitely beginning to have an effect on them both.

As they returned to the sofa, Spence topped off their glasses. After a few minutes, Arlene informed Spence she needed to visit the powder room. He led her to the downstairs guest bath, and returned to the sofa, his mind racing with all sorts of questions and scenarios, each one more perplexing than the last. He felt like there was more she was not telling him, but how would he get her to open up? Moreover, in the process, would he blow his chance with her? Then he thought, maybe he really had no chance. Maybe she was just here trying to get information from him.

Suddenly, he felt used and alone. 'Snap out of it,' he told himself. After all, he was with a beautiful woman. He might as well make the most of it, with no expectations about what the future would hold. Just then, he realized several minutes had passed since he left Arlene at the powder room. He decided he should check on her and make sure she was okay.

As he neared the bathroom door, he noticed the light was off. He quickly began looking around to see where she could've gone. Walking through the den, he noticed a light on in his father's office. He eased the door open just enough to peek inside. Arlene was standing over the desk, frantically reading the papers that lay on top. Spence decided not to let her know he was on to her, so he eased the door shut and quietly slipped back to the sunroom. Turning around, he called out to Arlene, asking if she was okay. As he stepped into the den, Spence almost ran into Arlene coming from his father's office. She was flustered; sweat popping out on her brow.

"Where were you?" Spence queried. "I thought for a minute something was wrong."

"No," Arlene reassured him. "I just got lost on my way back. This certainly is a big house."

"I'm sorry," Spence said. "I should've waited for you outside the powder room. I guess I'm not a good host."

"Nonsense," she quickly replied. "I'm having a wonderful time, but I would like a tour, just so I don't get lost again."

Arlene took his arm and he led her through the house. He described every room in detail, recalling childhood memories along the way. As they made their way back through the kitchen, Spence grabbed another bottle of wine, then proceeded back to the sunroom where it was now dark.

As they settled back down on the sofa, Arlene commented on how nice the house was, pointing out that his father must have really done well to afford such an estate. Another hint about his father's money, but Spence decided to let it go. As he leaned over to pour Arlene more wine, he could feel her hot breath on his cheek and smelled the sweet aroma emanating from her mouth. Unable to control himself, he kissed her gently on the lips. She ran her fingers through the grey temples of his otherwise brown hair, then placed her hand behind his head and pulled him toward her for another kiss, lingering for what seemed an eternity. Obviously she did not mind, Spence thought as he silently congratulated himself for finally doing what he wanted to do that night in Antoni's.

Just as they were finishing their third and longest kiss of the evening, Arlene's cell phone began ringing.

"Don't answer it," Spence pleaded.

"I'm sorry, but I have to," Arlene said as she spoke into the phone. Spence could only hear her side of the conversation.

"Now? Are you sure? Can't it wait until tomorrow? Oh, all right. I'll be right there." With that, Arlene ended the call, looking up at Spence as if she were a little girl who had just broken something very valuable and was awaiting her punishment.

"Everything okay?" Spence asked, trying to ease her guilt.

"I've got to go," Arlene explained. "There are some important reports that my boss needs first thing in the morning and it seems I'm the only one who can retrieve them since they're stored under my password protected files."

"Sounds pretty important for a staff accountant," Spence said. "When can I see you again?"

"I'll call you tomorrow," Arlene promised as she

grabbed her purse and headed for the door. She paused long enough for one more kiss, not as long as the last, Spence noticed, but just as sweet. Then she climbed in her car and headed back toward town.

Spence couldn't help but be curious, especially since he was not aware of any FBI offices anywhere near Traverse City. Of course, they could have offices any number of places disguised as something else, and no one outside the family would know. Even Cowell's Funeral Home could be a front for an FBI field office, Spence chuckled to himself, imagining James as an agent.

He frowned as a thought suddenly occurred to him. Since when is a staff accountant important enough to have secret files hidden under password protected codes? Spence found himself imagining all sorts of possibilities, from Arlene being an FBI agent to some hired gun for the mafia, but finally decided he was definitely making too much of the circumstances. Besides, she was too good of a kisser to be that bad. In time, Spence reasoned, he would find out more information about Arlene, but for now would remain satisfied with the moment.

Chapter Eight

Spence awoke at ten, after sleeping off the effects of the wine from the night before. It was Sunday, and he had no specific plans for the day. With most businesses closed on Sunday, he wouldn't be able to take care of any of his father's estate business. He wondered what he should do with an entire free day, considering he hadn't enjoyed a leisurely day in three years. He spent most weekends working on legal issues or cases involving work, anything to fill the time since he had no one with whom to share his life. This morning felt a little different though, as he thought about calling Arlene to see if she finished replicating the reports her boss needed and was free for the day. Just then, his cell phone rang.

"Hello," he responded rather cheerfully.

"Well, it sounds like someone is feeling good today," Arlene teased. Spence could hear her smiling through the receiver, remembering her beautiful lips pressing against his last evening.

"An evening spent in the company of a special lady can do wonders for a man's psyche," Spence returned. "I was just getting ready to call you myself."

"Oh, really! Why I was afraid after leaving so abruptly last night that I wouldn't hear from you, at least not until you felt you had punished me enough for running out on you like I did."

"Arlene, you definitely do not know me at all. I'm not that petty. Besides, I had a wonderful evening the short time we did spend together."

"Well, if that's the case, then why were you going to call me?" Arlene flirted.

"I was wondering if you had any plans for the day. I was thinking of taking my father's boat out on the bay, and wanted some company. Kind of like a picnic, only on the water instead of a blanket on the grass."

"Well, let me check my schedule and get back to you."

"Wait a minute," Spence objected. "You called me!"

"I'm just teasing, dear," she said. "I would love to spend the day with you."

"Great! How about meeting me here in a couple of hours? That should give me enough time to get the boat ready and whip up some lunch."

"Sounds great. I'll see you then, but don't go to a lot of trouble just for me."

They said their goodbyes for the time being, and Spence raced to the shower to begin getting ready. There was a lot to do in a couple of hours, and he wanted the day to be perfect. As he was showering, he caught himself whistling, which made him burst out laughing. He couldn't remember the last time he felt this way, but he told himself to settle down. There was no need to fall too hard too fast, only to end up with a broken heart if things went awry. Besides, this was only their second date. Then he began whistling again.

Spence dressed in blue jeans and a teal pullover sweater, which should be warm enough, he figured, but would take a jacket just in case the wind picked up. It was a good thing he bought some chicken salad and ham at Muriel's, because he only had enough time to whip up some sandwiches. He placed them in a picnic basket he found in the top cabinet over the fridge, and added two slices of cheesecake. He also included a bottle of wine, and lunch was complete. Good enough for a bachelor, he thought to himself.

The boat was actually a Hatteras yacht that his father had purchased after a visit to North Carolina. The Judge had an old school chum who owned a chain of furniture stores, and had invited the Judge to join him for a week of fine dining and high-class parties at the spring furniture market in High Point. During one of the parties, they overheard one of the sales representatives bragging about his Hatteras yacht he'd purchased, and since they had a plant right there in High Point, the Judge visited the Hatteras plant for a tour the next day, and was so impressed he ordered one as soon as he returned to Michigan. He was proud of "The Scarlett," which he named after Spence's mom. He used to tell Spence that every time he took the boat out, he felt her presence, and that kept him going through the years.

The Judge had a boathouse built just in front of the dock, which made it easy to take the boat in and out of the water. He had the contractor install a special winch and tracks along the ramp and into the boathouse, so all he had to do was push a button and the trailer would descend down the ramp and into the water. When he wanted to store the boat, he simply lowered the trailer, guided the boat onto it, and pushed the button to pull it into the boathouse. The Judge liked things to work simply, and was quite pleased with the contractor's work.

The dock had two walking piers on either side with a ramp in the middle. It had an overhead cover with padding so the boat could remain docked between the piers. Usually his father removed it from the boathouse in April and returned it in October, but Spence felt it was warm enough to make an exception. Besides, there was no ice with which to contend.

He pushed the button and watched the boat descend into the water, then backed it off the trailer and secured it to the dock. He then made his way back up to the house to wait for Arlene.

As Spence was walking into the house, the doorbell rang. Perfect timing, he thought, as he walked through the foyer to open the front door. He could barely contain his pleasure as he grinned like a Cheshire cat when he saw what waited for him on the other side. Arlene was dressed in jeans that couldn't have been any tighter. They revealed every curve of her body, which Spence definitely found to his liking. She wore a pink angora turtleneck sweater, with a pink beret to match. Completing her ensemble was a pair of black high-heeled boots, which Spence thought to be somewhat odd for boating, but he wasn't complaining.

"It's great to see you again," she said as she smiled and gave him a quick kiss.

"I'm glad you could make it," Spence told her. "I hope sandwiches are okay. They're all I could put together that quickly, unless you wanted some of last night's spaghetti."

"No, I think you've had enough Italian food lately. Sandwiches are fine. I'm not hard to please."

Spence led her through the house and out the back down to the boat dock. The wind was calm, perfect weather for sailing. He stepped onto the boat first, then, held her hand as she joined him. There was a small table and two chairs situated on the deck. Spence had already placed the picnic basket on the table, the bottle of wine and two glasses beside it. He eased the boat away from the dock and proceeded slowly across the open water. The crisp air reddened Arlene's cheeks, her hair gently blowing as the boat eased along the water. Her beauty mesmerized Spence, as he steered toward a small inlet. This was a favorite spot that he knew well from many trips with his father.

He slowed the boat and dropped anchor just inside the inlet. Hardwoods grew tall and strong on either side of the bank, with a few evergreens mixed in. This time of year you could see further into the woods between the branches, but during the summer the leaves filled the limbs like a thick carpet. A few Canadian geese were swimming in the shallow water toward shore. There was a pair of squirrels on the right bank chasing and playing with each other, not seeming to care that a boat with spectators had arrived in their neighborhood.

Spence opened the wine and poured a glass for each of them, then carefully removed the sandwiches from the basket.

"Which do you prefer, chicken salad or ham?" he asked.

"Chicken salad," Arlene replied, as Spence placed the sandwich in front of her. She began removing the plastic wrap when he asked, "Were you able to get those reports last night for your boss?"

"Finally," she said. "It took me six hours to locate and retrieve the files, and then another hour to print them out. I don't understand what happened. Of course our system is old, so maybe there was a glitch somewhere."

Spence found it odd that she had so much trouble finding her own files, so he decided to press the matter a bit.

"I thought they were your files to begin with. Did you forget where you stored them, or does anyone else have access to your computer?"

Arlene appeared taken off guard by the question, and hesitated as if she were collecting her thoughts before she spoke.

"No, I'm the only one who has access to them. That's why I had to go myself. I don't know what happened unless the system somehow stored the files in the wrong folder, or maybe I accidentally saved the files in the wrong location. At least I was able to retrieve the data, or I probably would still be there today."

"Thank goodness for that," Spence said. "I would've hated to spend today all by myself. Especially as nice as the weather is."

He decided not to press the issue any further, as he could see the topic was making Arlene uncomfortable. He found himself wondering why though, and decided to pay close attention whenever she mentioned her work again.

They continued with their meal with very little conversation, just some small talk to fill the time. They marveled as the geese retrieved their lunch from the shallow water, and laughed at the squirrels as they chased each other from tree to tree. Spence kept Arlene's wine glass full, hoping the alcohol would ease her anxiety over their earlier conversation. She ate only half of her sandwich, and tossed the other half in the direction of the geese. Afterward, Spence brought out the cheesecake, and with some protest, Arlene finally gave in and agreed to share a piece with him. She was probably afraid of gaining an ounce considering how tight her jeans were, Spence was thinking.

When they finished eating, Spence took the food downstairs, and returned with two fishing rods and a Styrofoam bucket. He'd collected some earthworms earlier after taking the boat out, and stored them in the container along with some dirt.

"I thought we could do some fishing," Spence said.

"I haven't fished since I was a little girl," she exclaimed as she let out a shriek of joy. "My Dad used to take me to the lake on his boat and we would fish all day."

"Well, I'm not sure if we'll catch anything, but I find it relaxing. Plus, it's been a long time since I fished too."

He placed a worm on each hook, and cast the lines into the water. He'd placed corks on the lines at the depth he remembered from the last time he fished in this area. Then he handed Arlene a rod, and she sat down on one of the deck chairs facing the water. Most people used artificial lures, especially when fishing in such a large body of water, but Spence had always liked the fight of the little fish you typically caught with live bait. He topped off her wine glass, and settled in a chair next to her on the deck. They watched the corks float along the surface, comfortable in the silence of the moment. After about five minutes, Arlene's cork began to bob a little.

"I think I've got something," she shouted, and stood up from her chair.

Spence stood up too, and looked over the edge of the boat as the cork disappeared under the water. The rod bowed greatly as Arlene struggled to reel in her catch.

"Boy, it must be a big one," she exclaimed as she struggled with the rod.

"Careful," Spence cautioned, "Don't try to reel it in too fast or he'll break the line."

He placed his hand on top of hers and helped her guide the rod as she played the fish for a few minutes in order to wear it down. Then once it appeared to have given up the fight, she began reeling again. He grabbed the net and lowered it beside the boat; ready to retrieve the whale she'd hooked. As it surfaced, he recognized the victim as a catfish. He scooped it up into the net and brought it over the side of the boat. Arlene was breathing heavily from her battle with the fish, which appeared to weigh all of six pounds, although she swore it was larger.

Spence proceeded to remove the hook from the fish, being careful not to let it sting him with its fins. Then he released it back into the water, and it swam away under the surface. Arlene plopped down in the deck chair and took a big gulp of her wine as she brushed her forearm across her brow.

"That takes a lot out of you," she claimed, taking a deep breath as Spence placed her rod against the side of the boat, leaving her line dangling out of the water. He reeled in his line only to find the worm had died without a single nibble. They decided to sit for a minute and relax before trying their luck with the fish again.

Spence tried his luck a couple more times, but was unable to get even a nibble. As the evening approached, he decided to pull anchor and head for shore. As he started the motor, Arlene howled at her triumph of out-fishing a man. He declared he wanted a rematch another day, to which Arlene gladly agreed.

The breeze had picked up somewhat and the air grew cooler, but the wine had managed to keep them warm. Spence made sure Arlene drank the majority of the bottle, which was apparent when she tried to walk from the chair to where he was piloting the boat. After stumbling, she quickly sat down and decided to stay put until they reached the dock.

After he secured the boat, Spence lifted Arlene over the rail and onto the pier, making sure he held onto her as he exited the boat himself. As they walked toward the house, Arlene stumbled in her boots, and twisted her left ankle. Thank goodness for the wine, Spence thought, as it seemed to lessen her pain.

He picked her up in his arms and carried her into the house. He laid her on the sofa in the sunroom, and proceeded to the kitchen for a towel and some ice. He returned with the ice, and removed her left boot, placing the ice-laden towel gently on her swollen ankle. Leaning over, he kissed her, tasting the wine on her luscious lips. She pulled him over onto her as she kissed him back. Then he rose up from the couch and scooped her up in his arms, carried her upstairs to his bedroom, pulled back the sheets, and laid her on the bed. He lay down beside her again, and they started kissing and removing each other's clothes. Arlene ran her hands down Spence's muscular chest, and pulled his five foot ten inch frame closer to her, digging her nails into the soft flesh of his back. After a long session of lovemaking, they fell asleep in each other's arms.

Arlene awoke to Spence stroking her hair.

"What time is it?" she asked.

"Nine o'clock. You've been asleep for some time."

"I'm sorry. It must have been the wine, or the exercise," she said, laughing.

"Or both," Spence finished.

"I've got to go. I've got a big day tomorrow."

"You can stay here tonight," suggested Spence. "I'll wake you in time."

"That's sweet. But I can't. I had a wonderful day, though."

As she got out of bed, she suddenly felt the pain in her left ankle. Nevertheless, she acted as if it didn't hurt, as she got dressed.

Spence pulled his robe around him and followed her downstairs to see her out. They kissed again at the front door, before Arlene walked to her car, got in, and drove off toward her house. Spence returned to the bed and basked in the warmth and smell of where she'd been. Remembering how she felt in his arms, he fell asleep holding the pillow still carrying the scent of her perfume.

Chapter Nine

At eight the next morning, Spence awoke to the sound of his cell phone. It was Monday, time enough for Sherrie to have her computer up and ready and be on her second cup of coffee. Spence spoke sleepily into the phone, "Hi Sherrie."

"Hey babe, is everything okay?"

"Fine. Have I missed anything at the office?"

"No, it's been kind of quiet. Everything's hunky dory."

"I need a favor," Spence disclosed. "I need you to find someone for me."

"Ooh, sounds mysterious. Who is this mystery person?"

"Agnes Morehead, my father's maid. She's supposed to be in Key Largo living with relatives. I need to find out exactly where she's staying."

"Where should I start?" she asked.

"Try searching for her in Key Largo. If you don't have any luck, check the Michigan records for info."

"I'm on it," she told him. "I'll buzz you when I get something."

"Thanks Sherrie. I have other estate matters to attend to, so this will really save me some time. Besides, I don't want you to get too bored while I'm gone."

"Don't worry, hon, this should get me to lunch. Bye-bye, sweetie."

"Bye," Spence said, shaking his head. He snapped the phone closed and headed for the shower. He had a list of errands a mile long, and hoped to be able to finish them all today. First, he'd clean up and head to Nick's for breakfast.

As Spence pulled into the parking lot at Nick's, he wondered if Shirley would be working again today. Should he remind her of who he was, or just let it go? He decided it was probably best not to say anything. After all, he didn't want her to feel ashamed that someone from her past knew how her life had turned out. Then again, what is the true definition of success in life? Maybe for Shirley, she was already there.

Since there were more people at the diner than his previous visit, Spence had to settle for a small booth in the left corner. Shirley was on duty again today, moving more quickly as she sped from station to station. There was another waitress helping her, who happened to be covering the side of the diner where Spence sat.

"Know what you want?" she asked in a manner revealing she really didn't care.

"I'll have two eggs over easy with sausage and toast," Spence answered.

She quickly turned and sped off toward the kitchen without another word. Spence didn't even notice her nametag. He was too busy trying to think over the noise of her chewing gum popping in her teeth. When she returned, she hastily thrust the food in front of him and topped off his coffee. Then she asked if he needed anything else while already turning to leave. Spence managed an audible no, wondering if it registered with her, considering she was already half way back to the kitchen. She would no longer bother Spence again, since she never came back to the table. However, she had conveniently left the check under his basket of toast.

After he finished eating, Spence tossed a dollar on the table, just in case the waitress was having an unusually bad day and didn't intend to provide such lousy service. He decided not to complain, not that he saw anyone working who resembled a manager. Instead, he took the check to the counter and paid Shirley for the meal. She still didn't let on as if she knew him, but she was too busy for small talk if she had. He managed to get a smile and a 'Thank You' from her though, before she closed the register and was off again to other customers.

Once back inside his car, Spence opened his day planner he'd left on the front passenger seat to look at his 'to do' list for today. He'd worked on it while he was talking to Sherrie, trying not to forget anything. His first stop would be the courthouse, where he would present the necessary documents and legally become executor of his father's estate. The will pretty much sealed it, but he'd need some official documentation from the clerk in order to open an estate account at the bank and transfer the money from his father's accounts.

He arrived at the courthouse at exactly nine, and headed straight to the probate clerk. After presenting the will, the death certificate, and the necessary identification, the clerk asked him to wait while she processed the paperwork. After about thirty minutes, the clerk called his name and handed him a manila envelope with all of the documents he would need. Now that he'd completed the first item on his list, it was off to the bank.

Spence entered the local Comerica branch where a woman, who was standing behind a tall circular stand in the center of the lobby, greeted him. She was dressed in a professional two-piece, gray pin-stripe business suit, with her name-tag that read 'Angela' on the right lapel He told her he needed to speak to someone about opening an estate account. She directed him to a sofa in the waiting area just behind the round counter where she was positioned, and assured him someone would be with him in a moment.

As he sat waiting, he glanced around the lobby. The teller line was just inside the front doorway on the right facing him, with six stations, but he could only see three tellers. Two offices were on his left, and two on the right past the teller stations. In addition, several doors were along the back wall behind the waiting area. Spence assumed they were either private offices or storage. He also noticed the video cameras mounted behind each teller window, one over the entrance, and one in each corner of the back wall.

Spence had been waiting less than a minute when he noticed a young woman in a purple business suit walking toward him from across the lobby. When she reached him, she thrust out her right hand and gave him a firm handshake.

"Hello. My name is Heather Pierce," she greeted. "How may I help you?"

"I'm Spencer Rawlings," he replied with a smile. "I'm here to open an account to administer my late father's estate."

"If you'll follow me to my office. I'll be glad to assist you."

She turned and began walking back across the lobby with Spence following close behind her. She led him into the middle office and gestured toward the two chairs facing her desk. "Please have a seat," she said, maintaining her smile.

He sat down and began pulling the documents he'd need from his leather portfolio. Heather reached into her left middle desk drawer and retrieved a folder, which she opened and placed in front of her. She explained to Spence how the estate account worked and asked if he brought a check to deposit or if the funds were already held in accounts at Comerica.

Handing her his father's account information, he made small talk while she punched some buttons on her keyboard. As she continued, the printer beside her computer suddenly sprang to life. When it finished, she handed the paper to Spence and asked him to verify the accounts and amounts with his records. The accounts totaled just over a half million dollars, and Spence nodded in agreement as he handed the paper back to her.

She punched more buttons on the keyboard and the printer sprang into action again. Once she gathered all the papers together, she had Spence sign as executor in the necessary places, attached the necessary probate documents to her copies, and handed Spence a folder with his copies and a few starter checks. She asked if he'd need more checks, but he assured her the ones provided would be more than enough. Very few bills were left to pay since his father had already taken care of most of them, including pre-paying James for the funeral expenses.

As Spence rose to his feet to leave, Heather also stood up and extended her hand, her lips breaking open into that crooked smile again. He thanked her for her help as he shook her hand, then turned and headed out of her office, across the lobby, and out the front entrance. Another item on his 'to do' list complete.

The next stop was American Mutual Insurance Company, just three blocks from the bank. It was such a beautiful sunny day, Spence decided to walk. As he stepped into the building, he noticed a receptionist behind a counter just inside the front door. She was on the phone, so he waited patiently for her to finish. She quickly transferred someone on the other end to a back office somewhere, and glanced up with a smile, asking if she could help him. Spence pulled out a piece of paper with the name Jack Thomas scribbled on it, and asked the receptionist if he could see Mr. Thomas. She asked his name, then pushed a button on her phone. After speaking with someone whom Spence believed must've been Mr. Thomas, she informed him that someone would be with him in just a moment, gesturing toward some chairs along the sidewall. Spence took a seat and picked up a Field & Stream magazine to leaf through while he waited.

He had no more than turned a couple of pages when a man walked out from behind the counter and called his name. Spence looked up to see a man who appeared to be in his mid-fifties with dark brown hair slightly graying at the temples. He wore navy slacks and a gray herringbone jacket. He extended his hand toward Spence as he approached.

"Jack Thomas," he said, smiling at Spence. "It's good to meet you. Your father talked about you so much I feel I've known you for years."

"Well don't believe everything you hear," Spence chuckled as they shook hands.

Jack led Spence around behind the counter and to a back

office, all the while assuring him that his father had only good things to say about his son. Jack's office had an old wooden desk and a leather covered chair that squeaked as he sat down. Spence sat in one of the two chairs facing the desk that had a flame patterned orange fabric. His hands curled over the cotton stuffing protruding from both arms, well worn from years of use. Glancing at the insurance company calendar on the desk, he thought to himself 'typical insurance agent office.'

Spence explained he was here to make sure the necessary paperwork was in order for Ed Harris from his father's law firm to be able to collect on his father's insurance policy in accordance with the buyout clause. Jack informed Spence the insurance company had already been taken care of everything, and in fact, they mailed a check to the firm that very morning. Feeling relieved that one more item on his list was complete, he thanked Jack for his assistance and stood up to leave. Jack rose as well and took hold of Spence's arm.

"Aren't you here to take care of his other policy, too?" he asked.

"What other policy?" Spence said, sounding surprised.

"Your father took out a second million dollar policy a few years ago. He named you as the beneficiary."

Spence nearly fell back down, feeling as if someone had knocked the wind out of him. He hadn't seen his father in fifteen years, and now he learns his father loved him enough to leave him a million bucks? It took a few minutes to sink in, so Jack sat in silence as Spence collected his thoughts.

Having been an agent for thirty years, Jack had seen many reactions similar to the one Spence had. When he was able to speak again, Spence asked Jack what he would need to do to settle this second policy. Jack opened a folder already sitting on his desk, and retrieved a check, which he handed to Spence. Spence took the check and looked at it for what seemed like thirty minutes. Jack assured him the insurance company had already received copies of the death certificate and had processed both claims. Spence was suddenly a millionaire. He took another couple of minutes before he stood up, just in case he was dreaming. Then he thanked Jack for his help and headed out the door.

As he walked back to the bank parking lot, Spence held on tightly to the check. His head was still spinning from the news that he was now a millionaire. Since he wasn't sure how long he'd be in town, and didn't want to carry a million dollar check around, he decided to open an account in his name and deposit the check.

Walking back into the bank, he asked for Heather. After waiting a few minutes, she stepped out of her office and walk toward him.

"Is everything okay?" she asked as she shook his hand again.

"Everything is fine," he said. "I just received a check I feel should be deposited rather than me carrying it around."

"I can deposit that into the estate account if you would like," she said.

"Well, actually the check is made out to me, so I need to open an account for myself," Spence replied, handing her the check.

Heather glanced down at the check, looked back at Spence with wide eyes, and breathlessly said, "Follow me." With that, they headed back to her office.

Heather began with a litany of financial services, offering to schedule an appointment with the bank's financial planner. Spence thanked her, but explained he was from out of town and just needed to park the money in an account that was liquid and easy to retrieve when he left town. She explained a money market would be best. Although he'd earn very little interest, the money would be readily available. She asked again if he would at least consider a CD, but he shook his head. She went straight to work punching buttons again until the printer began spitting out papers. She placed them in front of Spence for his signature, then handed him another folder complete with starter checks for his new account. As she disclosed the limit on the number of checks allowed each month, Spence could tell she had rehearsed her delivery well and had given it many times over the course of her career. He smiled as she continued her account speech, knowing he would only write one check for the balance when he decided to head back to Kentucky.

As Spence walked out of the bank, he was still trying to grasp the fact that he was now a millionaire. Feeling good about his accomplishing most of his 'to do' list, he decided to grab some lunch and contemplate his newfound fortune. He decided to have lunch at The Fatted Calf, a local restaurant known for having the best steaks around. He drove the two miles from the bank to the restaurant, and realized that since it was eleven-thirty, he'd arrived ahead of the usual lunch crowd.

The hostess greeted him as he entered, quickly leading him to a booth near the bar. The waitress appeared just as quickly, and took his drink order, the usual Jack and Coke. He decided it was late enough for a drink, and besides, he was celebrating his recent windfall. The waitress soon returned with his drink and some peanuts to munch on while he waited for his filet mignon. The restaurant was famous for allowing patrons to snack on peanuts and throw the hulls onto the floor. Spence noticed the floors were clean, and it would be later when the lunch crowd arrived before there would be very many hulls thrown down. Spence decided he'd do his part, though, as he grabbed a handful of peanuts and began cracking the shells.

He was on his second Jack and Coke when his steak arrived, medium rare, perfectly cooked. As he bit into the filet, it seemed to melt in his mouth. Spence savored every morsel until he had eaten it all. He even polished off the loaded baked potato that came with it. The waitress had just picked up his empty plate and returned to the kitchen, when his cell phone rang. He recognized the office number and answered. "Hi Sherrie. Find out anything on Agnes' whereabouts?"

"As a matter of fact I did," she answered. "But I'm afraid you're not going to like what I have to tell you."

Her statement caught Spence by surprise as he asked, "What do you mean?"

"Well," she continued, "it appears Ms. Agnes Morehead

died in an automobile accident three years ago. The obituary even listed your father as her employer."

Spence sat silent for a few minutes feeling as if someone had punched him in the gut and knocked out all his wind.

"Are you okay, hon?" Sherrie asked after a while.

He mumbled a yes, and then blurted out, "But she called me the night my father died. How could she do that if she'd been dead for three years?"

"I don't know, but something doesn't smell right."

"Were you able to locate an Agnes Morehead in Key Largo?"

"Actually, I did find an address for an Agnes Morehead in Key Largo," Sherrie told him. "But I'm telling you, this dead woman sounds like the one you are looking for. There was very little info on the other one."

"Do me a favor and send me a fax with the information on both women," Spence said. "I want to do a little digging of my own."

"Please be careful, Spence," she pleaded, knowing this was a dangerous game he was playing. "After what you've told me so far, there's no telling where this will lead."

"Don't worry about me," he assured her. "I'll be fine." With that, he closed the phone and sat back in the booth.

He motioned for the waitress and ordered another Jack and Coke. He needed to think for a few minutes and decide what his next move should be. As he sat there, the same question kept eating at him. If Agnes was dead, who called him the night of his father's death? Spence decided he'd get no more answers from his drink, so he headed back to the estate to wait for Sherrie's fax.

Chapter Ten

By the time Spence arrived back at the estate, Sherrie's fax was waiting in the incoming tray of the fax machine. He picked up the papers and walked into the sunroom to study them closer, noticing how beautiful the view was as he watched the geese wading near the shore of the bay. Gradually, his mind wandered to Arlene and yesterday's adventure. He hadn't heard from her today, and wondered what she was doing. Maybe they could get together for dinner, he mused, as he sat down on the sofa where they first kissed.

Spence first read the article regarding the death of Agnes Morehead. According to the police report, she was traveling south on Highway 31 from Elk Rapids to Traverse City at approximately eight o'clock in the evening, when her car suddenly left the road and hit a tree head on. Police believed she swerved to avoid a drunk driver, since several reports of someone driving erratically came in from that area about the same time as her accident. She died instantly. The county medical examiner pronounced her dead at the scene. The next paragraph gave a brief overview of her life, ending with her current employment listed as a maid and housekeeper for

Judge Rawlings. According to the article, the reporter spoke with Judge Rawlings by phone, where the Judge expressed his deep sorrow at the loss, and described Agnes as a 'member of the family.' This is why Sherrie was so sure she was the Agnes he was looking for, Spence thought, but was a little upset that she'd failed to mention this part of the article.

The next page was a copy of a white pages search from the Internet showing an Agnes Morehead at 1116 Cabana Way, Key Largo, Florida. No phone number was listed for the address. There was also a page showing Sherrie had attempted a public records search to obtain more information about the Key Largo Agnes, only to come up empty.

Spence ran his left hand through his hair as he stared at the papers. Why had his father mentioned Agnes in the will if she was already dead? Maybe he recorded it before she died, and never took the time to change it. No, that didn't sound like the Judge Rawlings he knew. There was something missing, he thought. However, what it was he was not sure.

Spence decided to watch the tape of his father's will again, hoping to find some clue that would answer these questions. When he reached the part just before his father mentioned Agnes, he paused the tape and studied it carefully. Then he pushed play again and watched closely as the Judge delivered his instructions regarding Agnes. There was something different, Spence thought, but what? He reversed the tape, studying every gesture, movement, and background image. Then he played it again, closely studying everything as before.

After about ten times viewing back and forth, something suddenly stood out at Spence he'd missed all the other times he'd watched it. The calendar on the desk had a black border, but the border appeared smaller just as the Judge began his bequeath to Agnes. Spence thought at first that it just appeared smaller because of a shift in camera distance, until he realized the camera was in a stationary position. The year on the calendar wasn't visible, but he could make out where it was at the top. He wanted to be sure before he jumped to conclusions, so he immediately grabbed his cell phone and punched in a number.

"Sherrie, I'm leaving for Grand Rapids and I'll catch the first flight to Lexington. I have a brief for you to finish for me, and then everything should be up to date. I'm going to take a trip to Miami and maybe hop on a cruise or go snorkeling or something. I just need to get away for a while, what with the funeral and all. Can you handle things for me while I'm gone?"

"Sure, hon," Sherrie answered. "Don't you worry about a thing. I'll see you when you get here."

Spence hung up and quickly packed his bag. He called Sherrie back from his car on the way to Grand Rapids, and asked her to book a flight for him from there to Lexington. Then he asked her to book a flight to Miami for the following day. He'd check in and pick up his tickets at the airport counter. She agreed and again told him to be careful. Spence took Highway 131 South toward Grand Rapids, since he knew it would be four lanes just past Cadillac and he could make better time. He drove as fast as he felt he could get away with and not attract the attention of a patrol officer trying to fill a monthly ticket quota. He arrived in Grand Rapids about one hour and forty minutes later.

Sherrie had booked Spence on a Delta flight connecting in Cincinnati before continuing on to Lexington. He never liked to fly propeller-powered planes, so Sherrie made sure both flights were jet service. He checked in at the counter, and heard what gate his flight departed from. He had no bags to check, so he proceeded directly to the security checkpoint leading to the concourse. As he started to place his bag on the conveyor, he quickly asked the security guard if the X-ray machine would damage film or videotape. When the guard told him they would be fine, he placed the bag on the belt and walked through the metal detector. Once through, he grabbed his bag and headed to the gate. His flight left in twenty minutes, and had already begun pre-boarding.

Once the plane was in the air and had reached cruising altitude, Spence reached in his pocket and pulled out a credit card. He swiped it in the slot beside the phone on the back of the seat in front of him, and removed the receiver. He quickly punched in the office number and waited for Sherrie to answer.

"Rawlings Law Office," Sherrie politely answered.

"Sherrie, it's me, Spence."

"Oh no, did you miss your flight?" she asked, sounding alarmed.

"No," he replied. "I'm calling from one of those on-board phones. I need you to contact George Merit. His number is on my Rolodex. Tell him I need to meet with him tonight at the lab. It's extremely important, and he still owes me a favor."

"Ooh, this sounds spooky, what with all the cloak and dagger," Sherrie said with a giggle. "But why didn't you tell me this stuff when we talked before?"

"Because," Spence answered, "I wanted to make sure no one knew exactly where I'm going, and I figured these plane phones are probably not bugged."

"Okay, hon," Sherrie said. "I just hope you know what you're doing."

Spence said goodbye and placed the phone back into its cradle. The flight attendant had just arrived at his seat, so he ordered a soda and took the pretzels she handed him. He pulled down the tray in front of him, and placed the plastic cup full of cola on it, then opened the pretzels and munched on them as he reflected on the news about Agnes and his planned meeting with George.

George Merit worked in the crime lab for the State Bureau of Investigation. Although Kentucky's state capital is in Frankfort, the lab he worked at was located in Lexington. Spence first met George three years ago during a trial. He was the expert witness for the prosecution in a case against a man accused of murdering his wife, and of course, Spence was the attorney for the defendant. The accused claimed his wife fell down the basement steps one morning while doing laundry, and he found her when he came home from work that evening. George testified the injuries to the body were not consistent with a fall, but instead the position of the body indicated a heavy object struck the woman while standing at the foot of the stairs. His findings had led police to search the basement, where they found an old bowling trophy belonging to the accused, containing blood and hair on one corner of the base. George further testified that the defendant's fingerprints were on the trophy, and the blood and hair were from the victim.

After the trial, Spence scheduled a lunch meeting with George to get his opinion on another case he was working on. George actually helped Spence with some of the medical jargon, since it was a malpractice case. They quickly became friends, and met once a week to play racquetball. Spence would bounce theories off George, and George would lead Spence in the right direction. Occasionally they were on opposing sides, and had to limit their conversations to non-case related topics. However, once the trial was finished, they went back to comparing notes. Less than a year ago, Spence helped a client with her deceased husband's estate. Afterward, she took Spence to dinner as a 'Thank You' for his help. As they were eating, George sat down at the booth beside them, so Spence introduced them. Three months later, George and his client were married, and Spence was the best man. After that, George told Spence he owed him for introducing him to the most beautiful woman in the world. Now, Spence thought, it was time to call in the favor.

The plane touched down on the runway with a jolt that startled Spence. He'd fallen asleep for a short nap, exhausted from his thoughts of his father, the funeral, questions about money, and now Agnes. Once off the plane, he walked quickly to the rental car counter, where Sherrie had already reserved a mid-sized vehicle in his name. He left the counter, and walked out of the airport to the parking area. He carefully placed his bag in the back seat, and drove out of the lot toward downtown. Spence arrived at the office, tired but restless. He wanted desperately to find the answers to his questions, but knew they would not come easily. Sherrie had fresh coffee waiting for him when he came through the door. When she hugged him tight, Spence wondered if she was still just flirting, or did he detect more from her embrace. He decided to act as if it was innocent, considering he had no time for such distractions. Besides, she was married, and even though Spence found her very attractive, he'd never get involved with a married woman. He'd seen too many of those situations go badly in court.

"Okay," Sherrie began as she slowly released her grip on Spence. "Tell me everything and don't leave one detail out."

Spence recalled the trip back to Michigan and the meeting with James. Then he told her about the funeral and Joey VanWarner's comments. He briefly touched on his chance encounter with Arlene and her mention of his father's money, but conveniently left out the intimate details. The rest she already knew from their phone conversations. She asked why he was meeting with George, but he decided not to tell her at this point. There was no need to divulge too much information until he knew for sure his instincts were correct. He simply told Sherrie he wanted to confer with George before he left on vacation.

Sherrie brought Spence up to date on the office, and made it clear she'd taken care of everything so there was no need to worry. He'd be able to leave and enjoy his time in Florida. Spence smiled as she debriefed him on the past week's events. He knew she loved running the show while he was away, and was always careful to let her enjoy the moment and assure her of how much he needed her. The truth was, she was very good, and Spence wanted to make sure she was content and never wanted to leave. After all, Sherrie would be hard to replace.

After an hour of office talk, Spence stood up and informed Sherrie he had to leave now if he was going to make it to the lab before George left. Of course, he knew George would wait for him, but it was a good enough excuse to escape Sherrie's litany of office details. He usually enjoyed listening to her talk on and on, but today he had business more pressing if he was going to find any answers to the questions that kept haunting him. Sherrie hugged him again as he was leaving, this time not lasting nearly as long as before. She was ready to leave the office herself, and return home to her husband. They drove away in opposite directions, already missing each other after being apart for two minutes.

Spence arrived at the lab after most of the employees had already gone home. He parked beside George's Jeep, and walked quickly to the side door carrying his bag. He knocked three times, then two, and then once, a signal George had given him to use in case Spence ever needed to meet him at the lab after hours. Technically, no one except lab personnel could enter the building after five o'clock in the evening. The side door was rarely used, and the only entrance without camera surveillance.

George opened the door carefully and peeked out into the darkness. The light inside the lab was extremely bright causing George to hesitate while his eyes adjusted enough to recognize Spence. He motioned for him to enter, and quickly closed the door behind him. It was now Spence's turn to adjust to the contrast of entering the brightly lit lab from the outer darkness, as he blinked a few times until he could see.

"Sorry about your dad," George began. "Did everything go okay up there?"

"Thanks, George," Spence replied. "I'm not sure yet how everything went. I'll know more after you take a look at this for me," he continued, handing George the videotape.

"What's this?" he asked.

"It's the video tape of my father's will. I can't put my finger on it, but something's not right here. I was hoping you could analyze it and tell me if he taped the entire will at one time, or if he added more to it later. Specifically, there's a desk calendar in the picture I'd like you to see if you can read the date on. If my hunch is right, he recorded the second part of the will at a different time than the first part. Retrieving the date will tell us which came first."

"How soon do you need it?" George asked.

"As soon as you can get it," Spence replied. "I'm heading down to Florida in the morning to check out something, and I may be back the day after. It depends on what I find there. In any case, do you think you can check it out tomorrow in case I come back early?"

"Sure," George answered. "It shouldn't take too long to

examine. Are you concerned about the authenticity of it?"

"No," Spence replied. "I'm sure it's my father, and for the most part these are his wishes. I just need to know if it's one continuous recording, or two separate dates put together to look like one."

"Why do you think he'd do something like that?"

"I don't know, George, but if he did, I'm determined to find out."

Spence left the tape with George and returned to the dark night waiting beyond the lab door. He drove to a nearby hotel and checked in for the night. There was no need to drive all the way to his house, considering his flight left early the next morning. Sherrie had taken the liberty of packing some additional clothes in a larger travel bag he'd retrieved back at the office. She knew he kept a spare key inside one of those fake rocks in the front landscaping behind the azaleas, just for times like this. He was thankful for the additional clothes, especially considering it would be much warmer in Florida and he'd taken only winter clothes to Michigan.

Spence ordered a cheeseburger, fries and a cola from room service. After it arrived, he settled into a hotel chair and started surfing the cable channels as he ate. Then he placed an order for a wake up call for five o'clock the next morning, turned off the television, and climbed into bed.

Chapter Eleven

Spence awoke to the sound of the phone ringing to announce his wake up call. He'd slept through the night, but still felt tired as he headed to the bathroom. Maybe a shower would wake him up, he thought, as he turned on the water. After showering, he dressed quickly, and gathered up his things so he wouldn't have to make a trip back to the room after breakfast. He took his bag to the car, returning inside for juice and a bagel at the continental breakfast buffet. After he finished eating, he took a large coffee for the road and headed west on Versailles Road toward the airport.

Sherrie had booked a flight from Lexington, connecting in Cincinnati, and continuing nonstop to Miami. If both flights were on time, Spence would arrive in Miami around eleven. That would give him time to pick up his rental car, check in at the hotel, and grab some lunch before he began his 'vacation.' The bag Sherrie had packed for him was too big to carry on the plane, so he had to check it with baggage claim. He carried his smaller case on board just in case his luggage was lost. He had heard too many horror stories of people arriving at their destination only to find they'd have no change of clothes for a couple of days until their lost luggage was located and returned to them.

The flight to Cincinnati was more crowded this morning than yesterday evening's flight. Spence noticed many of the passengers were dressed in business attire, and assumed they were traveling to Cincinnati for the day, and would return to Lexington later in the evening. Once the plane reached cruising altitude, the flight attendants began serving beverages. Still feeling a little sleepy, Spence decided he'd have another cup of coffee, hoping both this cup and the one earlier would soon kick in and revive him. The man in the seat next to him was afraid to order anything. He was on his way to Cincinnati for an interview with one of the major banks, and didn't want to risk spilling anything on his new navy pinstripe suit. Spence noticed that the man seemed nervous, so he decided to begin a casual conversation in hopes it would settle the man's nerves. His name was Dennis Burke, and he lived with his parents just outside of Lexington. Spence learned Dennis had recently graduated from the University of Kentucky in December with a degree in Business Administration, but had been unable to find a job. His interview was with Bill Wilson at Fifth Third in downtown Cincinnati. Spence remembered Bill from his college fraternity, and decided that after talking with Dennis, he'd put in a good word for him with Bill. After all, Spence was impressed with Dennis' ability to converse on an intellectual level, and believed he'd fit well into the banking world based on his observations of other bankers.

When the flight landed in Cincinnati, Spence and Dennis shook hands as they walked from the plane into the terminal. Dennis headed toward the rental car counters, while Spence remained in the gate area. His connecting flight departed from the next gate over in about thirty minutes. Just enough time to check in with Sherrie, Spence thought as he dialed the number on his cell phone. It rang several times before Sherrie answered, half out of breath.

"What took you so long?" Spence asked, almost laughing.

"Do you realize how early it is?" Sherrie replied. "I just now came in and had to run to catch the phone. Why are you calling so early?"

"Relax," Spence said. "I need you to look up a phone number for me."

Spence waited while Sherrie looked up the number for Bill Wilson at the Fifth Third Bank. Thanking her for her assistance, he chuckled as he told her she could now take a nap. She started to snap a quick retort, but he snapped the phone shut, ending the call before she could. Spence figured it was too early for Bill to be in his office yet, but dialed the number anyway. When Bill's voice mail began, Spence waited for the message and the tone so he could leave a message. Spence knew by yesterday's date on the recording that Bill wasn't in yet. After the tone, Spence said the usual niceties of it being so long since they last saw each other, and suggested they should get together. Explaining the reason for the call, he stated how Dennis Burke impressed him during their conversation during their flight. Spence went on to say he believed Dennis would be a good asset to the bank, stating that even though he just met Dennis this morning, it was obvious Dennis was outgoing and a people person based on their conversation. Spence concluded with some more niceties of wanting to get together, etc., and ended the call. He smiled after having done his good deed for the day. The flight to Miami had begun boarding.

Vacationers packed the flight to Miami to board cruise ships for the Bahamas. Spence sat next to a single mom and daughter who were taking a cruise on Disney's Big Red Boat. The little girl appeared to be about six years old, and based on her energy level, must have been full of chocolate or sugar-filled goodies. She never sat still for one minute, fidgeting in her seat when the FASTEN SEAT BELT sign was on. The rest of the time, she was jumping in and out of her seat. The mother kept apologizing to Spence for her daughter's behavior, but only mildly scolded the little girl, which made matters worse. The little girl had obviously learned the word 'No' at an early age, and by now was a master at using it to control her mother and get her way.

The mother began asking Spence several personal questions like whether he was married, did he have kids, what type of job did he have. He realized she was measuring him against the 'husband material' yardstick. He decided the best way to deter her advances, and have a little fun in the process, was to begin by telling her that he never liked kids and was a strong believer in corporal punishment. Then he went on to say his father routinely beat him with a belt, but it made him the man he was today. Spence could tell by the startled expression, and the end of the interrogation, his plan had worked. Now if he only knew a way to get the kid to stop jumping around like a Mexican jumping bean. Just then, he had a sudden revelation, as he pulled his money clip from his pants pocket. He offered the little girl a dollar if she'd sit down and behave for the rest of the flight. She informed Spence that it would cost him five, which he gladly forked over for some peace and quiet. Why hadn't he thought of it sooner? he wondered.

The remainder of the flight was peaceful, and seemed to pass rather quickly. As soon as they exited the plane, Spence saw the little girl begin throwing a temper tantrum right in the middle of the airport. Apparently, she was ready to burst from being forced to stay so quiet for so long, and decided to get it out of her system. The poor mother tried ineffectively to placate the child, then, finally had to threaten to take her back home instead of on their trip before the girl would calm down. Spence felt sorry for the person who would eventually pass the mother's 'daddy test,' and wind up in the role of step-dad to that little beast.

He chuckled to himself, shaking his head, as he walked past the two of them still arguing in the airport. He headed to baggage claims, and once he retrieved his bag, went next to the rental car counter. Sherrie had reserved a full-sized car at his request, after Spence complained the mid-size she rented before was actually a compact. After all, he was now a millionaire and could afford to splurge every now and then. This was one of those times, he thought, as he approached the white Cadillac STS waiting for him in space twelve. He placed his bag in the trunk, sliding onto the soft leather seat for the short trip to the hotel. Sherrie had booked a king deluxe suite, with Jacuzzi, on the ninth floor of the Marriott overlooking the Atlantic Ocean. After all, Spence definitely wanted the trip to have all the appearances of a vacation.

He placed the key card into the slot, when the light turned green, he turned the knob and slowly entered the room. He walked across the small foyer into the main living area, gliding his hand upon the soft leather adorning one of a set of winged-back chairs. Then he made his way to the French doors opening onto a balcony overlooking the ocean. Stepping outside, he took in a deep breath of ocean air as he watched the waves roll gently onto the sand. After a couple of minutes spent basking in the peaceful sounds of the ocean, he went back inside, moved to the dining area, making note of the glass top table and four chairs. When he entered the bedroom, he saw a fruit basket and bottle of champagne placed carefully beside the Jacuzzi, which was on a slightly raised platform across from the bed. He opened the accompanying card and read, 'Compliments of the Miami Beach Marriott.' He wondered what the room rate was for all this, then remembered his newfound wealth and decided to relax and enjoy. He only wished Arlene were here to enjoy it with him.

After a short nap, he decided to take a stroll on the beach, something he hadn't done in several years. He silently thanked Sherrie again as he donned the shorts and polo shirt she'd packed in his other bag. She had even included some sunscreen, which he carefully smoothed onto his legs to prevent burning, just in case he decided to stay out a while. His arms stayed tan most of the year from his frequent golf outings, so he felt it was unnecessary to coat them with SPF 30. He grabbed his favorite Detroit Tigers cap, and the tourist ensemble was complete. If only he had a Hawaiian shirt, weighed twenty pounds less, and was better looking, maybe he would be mistaken for Tom Selleck. He laughed as he raised his eyebrows in the mirror emulating the familiar signature of Thomas Magnum.

Spence found a burger shack down the beach, where he ordered a cheeseburger, fries and a soda. It had been hours since the continental breakfast, and he was starving, quickly wolfing down the burger and fries, then decided to walk down near the water. Usually a breeze blew in off the ocean, and today was no exception. The salt air blowing in the wind felt good on his face, and he stopped at the water's edge to watch a sailboat in the distance, sliding gracefully across the water as the wind filled its sail.

He took off his shoes, and waded into the surf, just far enough to cover the top of his feet. Walking south, he admired the view of scantily clad sunbathers, and thong wearing women playing in the surf. A few boys were on surfboards trying harder to impress the girls, than actually riding the waves. Ah, youth is wasted on the young, Spence thought.

He figured he had walked about a mile when the early morning schedule finally caught up with him. Even with the nap, he was still feeling tired. The salt air had refreshed him at first, but now he was sweating in the heat, and needed a cold drink. A beach side bar came into view just ahead, so he decided to stop in for a drink.

"Just a cola," he ordered, needing the cool refreshment more than alcohol. The bar was crowded with many patrons getting an early start on their evening buzz. Most were drinking beer, he noticed, with an occasional umbrella drink among a few of the women. Since it was cheaper, beer was the typical drink for the younger crowd.

As Spence was relaxing with his cola, his eyes wandered around the bar, trying not to be too obvious as he admired the beautiful young girls. Spring break, he decided, since so many seemed to be of college age. He smiled in the direction of a cute red head, but she just turned to her friends and laughed. Ouch, he thought of her obvious aversion to older men. Just wait, he told himself, and one day she'll appreciate the experience and commitment an older man offered.

Watching the couples walk hand-in-hand along the beach returned his thoughts to Arlene. He imagined her in a two-piece bikini, considering she definitely had the body for it. He could not help but think that even though Arlene had a few years on these girls, she was still by far the prettiest.

He finished his drink and headed back toward the hotel,

walking along the water's edge again, just as before, splashing his feet in the cool salt water. He loved the feel of the wet sand between his toes as the water rolled over his feet. It reminded him of the walks he used to take with his mother along Lake Michigan when he was a child. So many reminders of her. He missed not having her in his life, as he grew older. It wasn't fair she'd left him at so young an age.

Spence tried to block out his sorrow as he continued his walk. After being in the hot sun, the water felt cool and refreshing, so he decided to wade further into the ocean. Since he'd left his valuables and jewelry in the hotel suite, he wasn't afraid of the salt water as it swirled around his waist. He stood there for a minute enjoying the ebb and flow of the tide as the water first pushed him toward shore, and then gently pulled at his body as it returned to meet the next wave. After about five minutes, Spence turned and headed back toward the shore and the hotel.

When he reached the boardwalk that crossed the dunes back to the hotel, he rinsed the sand and salt from his feet, then walked across the boardwalk and back inside, still carrying his shoes in his hand. He fumbled for the key card in the back pocket of his shorts as he rode the elevator to the ninth floor. Soon the doors to the elevator opened and he walked down the hall to his room, inserted the plastic key card, and pushed open the door. Everything appeared to be just as he left it, so he scolded himself for feeling paranoid someone might be following him. Ever since the night he returned to the estate to find someone had been there watching his father's tape, he felt like eyes were constantly watching his every move. He smiled, shook his head, and muttered, 'Spence, you better get a hold of yourself, or they're going to lock you up.'

He felt dirty and sticky from the combination of sand, salt, and sweat after his walk on the beach, so he decided to take a shower. He removed his clothes and stepped into the shower, standing there for a few minutes just letting the water run all over his body, before lathering up to begin a thorough cleansing from head to toe. He always found a nice hot shower to be very relaxing, and this time was no different. He could feel the tension in his arms and legs ease as the muscles unwound themselves. He hadn't realize just how stressed he was until now. Of course, it wasn't as if he didn't have a good reason to be, what with the past week's events. Spence thought how amazing it was how a few days could change a person's life in so many ways. It made the past seem almost like a dream or a past life that was only a faint memory now. Yet the future was still so uncertain that sometimes his current situation seemed like a dream. However, as soap splashed in his eye, causing it to burn, he realized he was very much awake.

Finishing his shower, he dried off quickly, pulling the complimentary hotel robe from the hook behind the bathroom door, and slipped it on. Spence walked to the mini bar and fixed a Jack and Coke, settling into one of the easy chairs in the living room and pressed the remote control causing the entertainment center to spring to life.

His cell phone rang just as he was drifting off to sleep. It was Sherrie, probably making sure he was okay.

"Hi Sherrie," Spence said sleepily into the phone.

"I didn't wake you, did I?" she asked, sounding bubbly as usual.

"No, I was just watching a movie. I had a nice walk along the beach earlier. It must be spring break with all the college students here."

"Duh, it's only been the main topic on the news for the past week," she teased.

"Well, I haven't had time to watch much news lately."

"Is everything okay?" Sherrie pressed on. "You sound kind of down."

"I'm fine," he responded. "Just tired from the past week's events, I guess. I hope this vacation helps me rest up and recharge my batteries."

"Well don't worry about anything here," she assured him. "I was just checking on you, everything here's in tiptop shape. Just relax and get some rest, but stay in touch so I'll know when you're coming back."

"I will," Spence said, knowing Sherrie would call him enough times he'd never need to dial the office number.

He said goodbye and closed the cell phone, slowly walking to the bedroom to get dressed. Once he had his clothes on, he took the robe back to the bathroom and hung it behind the door. He fixed another Jack and Coke, sat down on the sofa to watch some more television, deciding to wait until it was dark before he left the hotel. He drained the glass quickly, and got up to fix another drink. He would need some courage before the night was over.

Chapter Twelve

S pence pulled out of the hotel-parking garage at exactly seven-thirty. It was dark now, and he felt less detect-able just in case someone was watching him. He headed down Highway 1 toward Key Largo, a forty-five minute drive from Miami, as he glanced at a copy of direc-tions Sherrie had printed for him. Even though the informa-tion she was able to uncover regarding the death of an Agnes Morehead in Michigan seemed overwhelmingly compelling that she was dead, Spence had that familiar gnawing in the pit of his stomach telling him something was just not right about this. He felt he at least needed to locate the Agnes Morehead in Key Largo to confirm or deny the evidence at hand.

The air was still very warm, but Spence decided to ride with the windows down. He liked the feeling of the salt air blowing through his hair, soothing and calming in effect. He'd brought along a Rolling Stones CD to keep him com-pany during the short drive to Key Largo. Traffic was moving rather smoothly, as Mick was in the middle of 'Satisfaction.' Spence drummed his fingers on the steering wheel to the beat of the music, enjoying the guitar proficiency of Keith Rich-ards. He'd listened to this tape over a hundred times, and still never grew tired of hearing it. Some classics never go out of style, he thought to himself, singing along with Mick, convinced he was doing a good impression.

As the car rolled on toward its destination, Spence began to let his mind wander over the past few days. Why were there so many references to his father's fortune when the bulk of his inheritance seemed to be from a life insurance policy? What exactly did Joey VanWarner mean when he mentioned the possibility of Spence finding something of unknown origin, and his offer to help dispose of it? Why was Arlene snooping around the house? What was she looking for? Why was there a telescope in Arlene's sunroom? How convenient was it that she lived within eyesight of the estate?

He definitely felt attracted to Arlene, but did she feel the same way, or was she simply getting closer to him in hopes of finding something? Spence needed some answers, and since his father specifically mentioned Agnes in the will, she seemed the best place to start looking. However, if she were no longer alive, he certainly wouldn't have to worry about making sure she received her inheritance, but many unanswered questions may have died along with her.

Spence began mentally preparing his end of the conversation for whoever was on the other side of the door he would soon be knocking on. He'd start with an introduction, followed by inquiring if an Agnes Morehead lived there. If the answer were yes, he would ask to speak with her. Although it had been several years since he had last seen Agnes, he was sure he'd recognize whether or not this woman was indeed the Agnes from his childhood. He began to get nervous as his eyes focused on a sign that read 'Key Largo 20', only twenty more miles to go.

The directions Sherrie had provided for Spence were right on the money. He had no trouble locating Cabana Way, as he turned left onto the street from Highway 1. The addresses were well marked as Spence searched for 1257. When he reached the 1200 block, he noticed the numbers jumped from 1202 to 1282, so at the next intersection he turned the car around and headed back the way he came. He slowed down when he reached 1282, and realized there was an apartment complex taking up almost the entire block. It soon became apparent that the apartment numbers ran consecutively, much the same as if they were separate individual residences along the street. This was unlike the apartments he'd seen in Lexington. They typically had one street number for the entire complex, then separate numbers and letters for each apartment. He drove around the complex until he found a building with the numbers 1250-1259 on the side. Then he parked in one of the spaces adjacent to the building.

The apartments appeared to be nice, but definitely not new. As he neared the building, he noticed the outside was covered with vinyl siding, but the trim around the eaves and steps was wood, which was flaking and in need of a couple of coats of paint. Spence could tell from the security lights that every building was the same color, beige. He noticed that aside from the occasional nice import, most of the vehicles were typical middle-class autos. No junk cars were around, so he figured it was a well-kept establishment, just not the Ritz.

Spence entered the breezeway between the odd and even numbered apartments, and turned to climb the steps. Apartment 1257 was on the second floor, facing away from the parking lot and toward what Spence could make out in the dark as a common grassy area between buildings. As he started up the steps, he could hear a baby crying in the back downstairs apartment. He stepped in front of the door to Apartment 1257, grasped the knocker, rapping it firmly against the door three times. As he waited, he thought he heard someone stirring inside. Just as he was reaching for the knocker again, the door slowly opened just barely enough for whomever was inside to peak out.

"Who is it?" asked a female voice from behind the door.

"My name is Spencer Rawlings. Do you mind if I come in?"

"What do you want?" she asked, not opening the door any wider.

"I'm trying to locate Agnes Morehead, and was given this address as her place of residence. Is she home?" Spence asked more firmly.

The light from inside the apartment flooded the landing as the door to the apartment opened wider, revealing the occupant inside. He stared in amazement, unable to speak, as his eyes focused on the young lady in front of him. She was the most beautiful creature he'd ever seen, a perfect specimen of the opposite sex. She stood approximately five feet four inches as best he could judge. Another red head, Spence thought, but exquisite in color and design, as her tresses fell just past her shoulders, turning inward toward her face at the bottom. She had bangs along the front, disguising a part in the middle. She had beautiful emerald green eyes, full red lips, and a small attractive nose that turned up ever so slightly at the end. She was wearing tight-fitting black Lycra athletic bottoms, and a tight pink spandex top, much like you'd see in a gym. There wasn't an inch of fat on her body, as her clothes clung to her in all the right places. She wasn't wearing shoes, and Spence noticed red nail polish on her toes that matched her fingernails. He figured her to have a thirty-eight bust, based on experience. He was clearly awestruck as she smiled up at him.

"Are you with the FBI, too?" she asked, breaking the long silence.

"No. What do you mean by too?" Spence questioned.

"A lady was here last week asking about an Agnes Morehead, too. She said she was with the FBI, flashed a badge and everything," she gestured.

"What did she look like?" he asked, trying not to seem too eager.

"She was tall with brown hair, very pretty," the lady replied.

"Did she tell you her name?" Spence pressed.

"Let me see," she paused. "It started with an 'A'."

"Arlene?" he asked, almost shouting.

"Yes. That was it, Arlene. Real nice lady."

"Well, what did you tell her?" Spence continued.

"Same thing I'm going to tell you," she replied. "I'm Agnes Morehead. Now, what do you want with me? Oh, and by the way, I have never lived in Michigan."

"I apologize," Spence quietly answered. "I had you mistaken for someone else."

"That's funny," she said. "That lady from the FBI said the same thing."

Spence apologized again, and turned to go, when the lady whispered, "Wait!" She reached out to shake his hand, sliding a small folded up piece of paper into his palm in the process. "It was a pleasure to meet you, Mr. Rawlings," she said, adding, "even if it was only for a minute. I sure hope you find what you're looking for."

Spence placed his hand and the note in his right pocket, and turned as the lady gently closed the door behind him. He walked back to his car as if everything was normal, being careful not to take the note out and look at it. He rode in silence for twenty minutes, still in somewhat of a state of shock, after his meeting with Agnes Morehead. Instead of finding answers, he ended up with more questions. Maybe the note would shed some light on the situation, but it would have to wait until he returned to the hotel.

As he continued on his route back to Miami, Spence was suddenly startled from his thoughts by the familiar ring of his cell phone. The display read 'caller unknown,' so Spence opened the phone and quietly said hello.

"Spence, its George. How's the vacation?"

"Hey George," Spence replied. "Let's just say it's turning out to be one of the most intriguing trips I've ever taken. What's up?"

"I've found something about the item we looked at the other day that I believe you will find very interesting," George answered, being careful not to divulge too many details over the airwaves. "When are you coming back?"

"I can't say," Spence said. "But I'll call you when I have a better idea."

"That sounds fine," George replied. "I just wanted to let you know you were on the right track. We'll talk more after you get back."

Spence closed the cell phone, convinced now, more than ever, there was definitely something amiss with his father's taped will. He could imagine all sorts of scenarios, but finally gave up on settling on one in particular until he had more information. He was sure that in time there would be enough evidence pointing to a clear and obvious conclusion.

Spence turned the rental car into the parking garage at approximately nine-fifteen that evening, suddenly realizing just how brief his conversation with Agnes Morehead had been. He rode the elevator to the ninth floor, and proceeded straight to his room. Once securely inside, he suddenly felt the gnawing from his empty stomach, remembering it had been several hours since the burger he ate at the beach. He picked up the phone and pressed the button for room service. After a couple of rings, someone with a heavy Latino accent answered. He ordered nachos and a piece of cheesecake with strawberry topping. There was plenty of Jack and Coke in the mini bar for him to drink. The voice on the other end replied, "Twenty minutes," before quickly hanging up. He lowered the receiver into its cradle, and walked to the bathroom to splash water on his face.

Spence had turned the television on, and was flipping through the channels, when there was a knock at the door. Peering through the peephole, he noticed a young Latino man in a hotel uniform carrying a tray. He opened the door, and told the waiter to place the tray on the table, then quickly signed the room charge slip, and escorted the hotel attendant back to the hallway. Spence thanked him, stepped back inside the room and closed the door, making sure he locked the dead bolt and put the chain on. He felt rather silly about his sudden bout of paranoia, especially since anyone could easily break through both locks if they wanted to.

Spence decided to wait until he finished eating the nachos before he looked at the paper Agnes had placed in his hand. Then, if he still had an appetite after he read the note, he'd finish the cheesecake. He devoured the nachos in record time, eager to read the contents of the note. He took a long drink of his Jack and Coke, and settled into one of the chairs in the living room. He pulled the paper from his right front pocket and slowly unfolded it until it was completely open. It was a single piece of paper with a typewritten message. It read:

The answers you seek are in the tapes. They're watching and listening to you, so be careful. We will meet again, but not here.

That was all she had written on the paper. Spence sat there for a moment staring at the note, trying to discern what she had *not* written. At least he was sure about one thing. Someone was watching him. Why and by whom he was still unsure of, but he'd definitely need to be more discreet in his travel and communications. The last sentence assured Spence he'd at least see Agnes again, hopefully receiving more detailed information in the process.

He drained his glass, and paced to the mini bar for another drink. He decided he'd eat the cheesecake anyway, especially since the nachos were not very filling. As he slowly ate, he stared again at the note, then realized if someone was watching him, he didn't want him or her to know Agnes had given him a note, so he grabbed a magazine from the coffee table, opened it as if he were reading, and placed the paper inside against the page. He read it again ten times before it leaped out at him from the page. "Tapes," he muttered to himself. She said the answers are in the tapes, plural. Until now, he was aware of only one tape, the one that held his father's will. Apparently, there was at least one more tape with more information, but how would he know which tape it was? After all, his father had quite a collection of old movies, and some personal tapes that held family events. Spence wondered where he should begin to look.

After racking his brain for twenty minutes, he realized he'd have to wait until he was back at the estate before he could find any other tapes containing the information necessary to answer his questions. He fixed another Jack and Coke, and sat back down in one of the easy chairs to watch television. He found a comedy on one of the movie channels that was just starting, and decided it would be good to watch something he could laugh at. Maybe it would offer him an escape from the immediate questions torturing his brain, and distract him from the notion of running from the hotel and not stopping until he reached Michigan.

He sat up quickly, realizing he'd dozed off while watching the movie. That was three hours ago, and another movie was now playing. The combination of a hectic day and several Jack and Cokes had finally taken its toll. It was three o'clock in the morning, and Spence decided his short nap was enough sleep for the night. He grabbed a quick shower to refresh, tossing on a pair of tan slacks and golf shirt when he was done. He neatly folded the rest of his clothes, and packed his bag. He wanted to get to the airport early enough to book the first flight back to Kentucky. Since 9/11, airport security was extremely tight, so it would take a while to turn in the rental car and clear the checkpoints. If he left now, he'd have plenty of time.

Spence punched the necessary buttons on the television in order to check out of his room without having to stop at the front desk. The hotel automatically billed all room charges to his credit card, and he could simply leave the key card in the room. He decided to take the stairs to the parking garage; thinking nine flights of stairs down hill were a piece of cake. After four flights, he was sucking wind, and cursing himself for thinking this was more elusive than the elevator. James Bond he was not, and, as slow as he moved, if anyone wanted to follow him, it would not be very difficult. He decided that from now on, he'd simply take more time to become familiar with his surroundings, and look for signs that someone was following him. After all, he certainly was no expert in surveillance, and a professional would have no problem staying one step behind. He would just need to be more careful not to prematurely disclose his destination, and try to mix up his routes in order to keep anyone who was watching off balance.

Spence arrived at the airport at five o'clock, dropping off the rental car first before entering the terminal. The lines at the ticket counter were much shorter now than they would be later in the day. He was able to purchase a ticket on a flight to Lexington, once again changing planes in Cincinnati. By the time he passed the security checkpoints, it was an hour and a

half until his flight left. Finding a bagel shop on the concourse near his gate just opening up, he decided to grab a
large coffee. Still drowsy from so little sleep, he hoped the
coffee would wake him up. He picked up a newspaper someone had laid on the table beside the seats in the waiting area.
It was yesterday's, but he didn't mind. Since he'd heard very
little news in the last couple of days anyway, he hoped it
would catch him up on current events.

More passengers began making their way to the waiting
area where Spence sat as the scheduled time of departure
drew nearer. Finally, they began boarding the plane, and
since he had booked a first class ticket, he was one of the first
to board. Knowing it was too early for a real drink, he settled
for orange juice instead. The coffee he just finished had been
extremely strong, and now wanted something more refreshing.

As he sipped, he contemplated his next move. First, he
needed to talk to George and find out what he discovered on
the tape. Presuming the rest of the day would depend on that
information, Spence decided to settle in for the flight and try
to relax, his mind constantly returning to the note Agnes gave
him. What if he was unable to determine any other clues from
the tape? How many other tapes were there, and where were
they? Still too many questions, he thought, as he closed his
eyes and waited patiently for the plane to begin its ascent.

Apparently, he dosed off for a minute, because when he
awoke, the flight attendant was giving connecting flight information for when they arrived in Cincinnati. Since they
hadn't yet begun their descent, Spence swiped his credit card
through the slot on the in-plane phone, and quickly dialed the
lab. Failing to recognize the voice when someone answered,
he immediately asked for George. After about one minute,
Spence recognized George's voice through the receiver.
Spence quickly gave him his expected arrival time, and asked
they be able to meet in a secure room. George explained he
had already thought of that, and was ready as soon as Spence
arrived. He'd ask for George at the security checkpoint, at
which time the guard would escort him to the theater, as they
called it. There they would be able to speak in confidence.

Chapter Thirteen

The plane landed smoothly in Cincinnati, and there was just enough time to make his connecting flight to Lexington. Spence never liked long layovers, so this type of situation was perfect. Once on board, the plane soon took off, climbing steadily until it reached cruising altitude. The flight from Cincinnati to Lexington was short, so there was no need to call anyone else at this point. Spence was eagerly anticipating his meeting with George in hopes he'd find at least some of the answers for which he was searching. The flight was very pleasant, but much like a child waiting on Christmas, Spence felt it was unusually long this time. In fact, he never remembered it taking this long to fly from Cincinnati to Lexington, and he'd flown it many times. He was about to call the flight attendant to inquire as to how soon they'd be landing, when the fasten seatbelt light illuminated and the captain's voice came over the speaker informing the passengers they were beginning their descent into Lexington. Spence sat back in his seat, trying to wait patiently while the plane landed, arrived securely at the gate, and began letting passengers off.

He almost ran to baggage claims to retrieve his luggage.

Then it was off to the rental car counter, where another Cadillac awaited him. Since he had already made the necessary arrangements, it did not take long to pick up the rental car, and soon he was on his way to the lab. It was not quite noon, and Spence made good time before the lunch hour traffic would soon begin. The parking lot at the lab was rather full this time of day, but some spaces were open near the front of the building reserved for visitors. Since he was uncertain who might be following him, Spence decided to take one trip around the block, check for signs of a pursuing vehicle, and quickly turn into the lot and park in one of the back rows between two SUV's. Proceeding with his plan, he wound around different automobiles, carefully looking around to see if anyone was taking the bait. Unable to determine that anyone was watching, he walked through the main door and headed to the security checkpoint. He identified himself and asked to see George. The guard issued a visitor's badge, then picked up the phone and dialed an extension. After he hung up, the guard told Spence it would just be a minute and waved his hand toward some idle chairs inviting him to have a seat while he waited.

He'd been waiting less than a minute when George walked through the double doors on the left side of the security desk. He extended his hand formally, referring to Spence as Mr. Rawlings and asked how he could help him. Noticing his lead, Spence in turn referred to George as Mr. Merit, and told him the district attorney had referred him to the lab to review evidence samples the lab obtained from a crime scene implicating his client in a homicide. He pulled some papers from his portfolio that he claimed gave him the authorization to review the evidence on his client's behalf. George took the papers and pretended to read them for a couple of minutes, then reluctantly told Spence to follow him, disappearing behind the double doors.

Walking in silence down the corridor, they made a left turn at the end before continuing in silence until they finally stopped in front of the last door on the left. George swiped his security badge through the slot beside the door, the light changing from red to green, and he gave the door a push. Once inside, the door securely closed behind them, George finally spoke.

"Sorry about all the cloak and dagger stuff," he said with a grin.

"That's okay," Spence replied. "Are you sure we are secure here?"

"Don't worry, I swept the room for bugs myself just in case. I'm beginning to wonder what's going on to make you so paranoid."

"I can't tell you too much at this point. I need more answers."

"Well, I might just have some for you," George told him, moving over to a table where several machines were located with a large viewing screen on the wall behind. "You were right about the tape," he continued. "There were definitely two different recordings put together. Do you see the calendar in the first part of the tape? I was able to enlarge the image enough to see the year," he explained as he focused the image for Spence to see.

"Then, I did the same thing on the second part of the tape, and what do you know? This section of the tape is from some time this year. As you can see from the first calendar, the initial tape was recorded four years earlier."

"So, Agnes was already dead when he recorded the second part," Spence said almost under his breath.

George continued as if Spence hadn't spoken. "Anyone simply viewing the tape would believe it was all recorded at one time. Believe me, I had to work to reveal this, so your average Joe wouldn't know the difference."

"Anyone viewing the tape would simply assume it was recorded prior to Agnes' death, and not give it another thought," Spence concluded. "But if that were the case, then why did Arlene go to Key Largo to see the other Agnes?" he asked himself, muttering under his breath.

"I'm sorry, did you just ask something?"

"No," sighed Spence. "I was just sort of thinking out loud. Tell me this, George, why would my father go to such an elaborate ploy as to make a new addition to the tape when he knew Agnes was already dead?"

"I don't know, maybe it's some kind of clue."

"Maybe," Spence mused. "Anyway, I need some more help."

"Sure, what is it?"

"I believe I'm being watched and possibly bugged. I need a way to determine if there are any listening or recording devices in the various locations I'm at," Spence said.

"I'm way ahead of you," George laughed. "Ever since you first called me, I felt like you might need some equipment, so I took the liberty of procuring some top of the line counter surveillance devices."

George led Spence over to another table that held several devices all laid out in a row.

"First," he began, "we'll start with this RF Detector pen. It looks like an ordinary ballpoint pen, but can actually locate hidden cameras and wire taps. Simply press the button and the frequency of the flashing red LED indicator light will increase the closer you get to the bugs. It's also a functioning ball point pen with a PDA stylus for touch screen devices, so you can carry it with you anywhere you go," George finished.

Spence took the pen and placed it in his pocket. "What else do you have?"

"This next item is a pocket size personal radio frequency detector which locates transmitters or bugging devices in a room or automobile. It is compact enough to carry anywhere, and offers vibration and earphone for private detection," George explained as he handed the device to Spence.

"Next," George continued, "we have a wireless camera and cellular phone detector, which will enable you to detect all hidden cameras up to ten feet away and all cellular phones within four feet. Just in case you're afraid of someone discovering that you've been sweeping for these devices, this last item is to thwart their attempts to listen in on you. It is an Acoustic Noise Generator. This protects you against listening devices that aren't detectable by conventional methods by producing a security blanket of generated white noise completely covering your private conversations with undetectable sound. I thought one of these might work well at the estate.

"Great," Spence replied. "Hopefully I'll be able to speak freely without worrying about someone listening in on my conversations."

"Oh, I almost forgot," George interrupted. "Use this cell phone. It has a built-in scrambler that makes it almost impossible to listen in on. Even a remote microphone will only hear white noise when directed toward it. I had Sherrie establish service in your firm's name, so it's ready to use. The number is right here on this paper taped to the back of the phone," George said as he turned the phone over for Spence to read the number.

"How often do you recommend I sweep my surroundings for bugs?" asked Spence.

"At least once a week," George answered. "But you can do it anytime you feel the need. The great thing about them is they're mobile, so you can turn on the pen, leave it in your pocket, and know if there's a bug nearby."

"Sounds good to me, George," Spence said. "Thanks for the help."

"Don't mention it. One word of caution, though, you may want to leave some of the bugs in place. At least that way, you'll know where they are so you can control the amount of information they receive. However, if you remove too many of them, it might make them suspect you're on to them. They'll be more relaxed and prone to mistakes if they believe they're in control."

"I never thought about it that way," acknowledged Spence. "All of this spy stuff is new to me. I'm lucky to have a friend like you who knows about these kinds of things. I'm sure I'll be calling on you again."

George started to laugh. "I'll make an agent out of you yet. Hey, it's the least I could do after all you've done for me."

"Oh, I almost forgot," said Spence. "I need you to check out someone for me. Her first name is Arlene; last name either Hurst, her maiden name, or Davis, the high school quarterback's last name. She claims to be an accountant with the FBI, but I'd like to know for sure."

"I'll see what I can dig up," George replied.

Spence gathered the equipment and placed it in the bag, along with the videotape of his father's will. He would still need to watch it again, possibly several times, in order to uncover any more clues his father buried between the lines. George escorted Spence back through the building to the lobby. Spence thanked George again for his help just before they stepped through the double doors leading to the security desk. Once back at the desk, George retrieved the visitor badge, shook Spence's hand, and both said their parting words in the same stiff formality as when they greeted each other at the onset of their meeting. It was necessary for them to avoid suspicion by pretending to know each other only in professional circles.

Spence arrived back at his office at one o'clock. Sherrie was in the middle of drafting some documents for a client, when Spence walked through the back door. He held out a note to her that read, 'Follow my lead. Someone may be listening,' and proceeded to make small talk as he began sweeping the office for bugs with the new equipment George had given him. As they spoke, the red LCD light began flashing on the radio frequency detector as Spence passed it over each phone in the office. It blinked again at the lamp on his desk, and once more at Sherrie's computer. Whoever placed them hid them from the naked eye, a professional job, Spence thought. At a break in the contrived conversation spoken solely for the benefit of whoever was at the other end of the bugs, Spence asked Sherrie if she'd join him for lunch. She told him that was the least he could do for leaving her with all the work while he flew away for a vacation. They left the office and walked down to the corner cafe, the detector pen still on inside Spence's shirt pocket.

They grabbed a small booth in the back where it was a little more secluded and afforded a good view of the front door. Apparently, their conversation would remain private since the pen registered no reading of any devices nearby.

They both ordered a hot brown, an open-faced sandwich of turkey and bacon, covered in Mornay sauce and baked until the sauce becomes brown, topped with tomatoes, a popular dish throughout Kentucky, and a soda, eager for the waitress to leave so they could talk. The lunch crowd was gone, leaving only one other couple besides them. After the waitress brought their drinks and retreated to the kitchen, Spence began filling in the details for Sherrie from their last conversation. He wanted to make sure she knew about the bugs and his father's possible connections so she'd be more careful with her conversations. Although there was no evidence of imminent harm, Spence was concerned for Sherrie's safety, especially if he stumbled onto anything involving the Van-Warners.

As they talked, each told the other possible scenarios that would account for the unusual conversations Spence had since returning to Michigan. Based on his encounter with Agnes Morehead, Spence felt certain there was something he was missing. He knew he would definitely need to review his father's tape, but since he had watched it several times, he couldn't figure out what he missed. Sherrie told him that maybe the clues were in the words themselves, rather than the instructions. She told him to listen carefully to the words for key phrases he might possibly recognize from years ago, maybe even childhood. Sherrie offered to watch the tape with Spence but he refused, telling her the less she knew the better off she would be. Sherrie obviously believed him, since she didn't push the issue.

They finished their lunch and headed back to the office. Spence told Sherrie he needed to return to Michigan to continue with the settlement of his father's estate. It seemed there were still some things to do before he could completely execute the will and close the estate. He told her he also wanted to speak to some realtors regarding the property, just in case he decided to sell. For now, he was thinking of keeping it, but he wanted to consider his options. Sherrie winked at Spence as a way of letting him know she approved of the improvised conversation.

Spence decided to fly back to Michigan that evening, Sherrie immediately making the travel arrangements. Not needing a rental car upon his arrival, he parked in the long-term lot at the airport in Grand Rapids. Able to find an open seat on a flight leaving in two hours, Spence had just enough time to swing by his place and pack a few more clothes, before heading to the airport.

He quickly entered his home, and raced to the bedroom to begin packing, noticing the red LCD light on the pen in his pocket blinking. He'd forgotten it was still on, until he neared the phone on the nightstand in his bedroom. Obviously, his phone was wired. He didn't have time to sweep the entire house, but felt certain there'd be several more bugs hidden around his place. He turned the pen off for now to save the batteries, and locked the door behind him. He placed his bag in the trunk of the rental car and sped off in the direction of the airport, which was actually located between his house and the office ... he didn't have very far to drive.

Spence made it through the security checkpoint just as his flight began boarding, hurried to the gate, handing his ticket to the attendant. Once on board, he settled into the comfortable leather seat of the first class section and ordered one of the small bottles of Jack Daniels and a Coke, before the plane pushed back from the gate. The plane was less than half-full, so there was no one seated beside him. He was on his second drink as the plane taxied down the runway for take-off. Soon the plane sped forward and lunged upward suddenly as the wheels lifted off the ground. It took very little time to reach cruising altitude, and once there, Spence ordered his third drink. He wouldn't need to drive until he reached Grand Rapids, and wanted to be relaxed after a hard day. He decided he'd have no drinks on the flight from Cincinnati to Grand Rapids, in order to be sharp for the drive to Traverse City.

As Spence became more accustomed to these flights, they seemed shorter each time. Once again, the connecting flight departed just after he arrived in Cincinnati, no layover this time. Spence stuck to his plan, drinking only coffee on the flight to Grand Rapids. Once the plane landed, he rushed to baggage claim, and then to the long-term parking lot. Not wanting to waste time with a long ride still ahead of him, he hurriedly left the airport parking area, and headed north toward Traverse City.

In the solitude of the automobile as he drove along Highway 131, he suddenly realized he hadn't spoken to Arlene since he'd left Michigan for his trip. He wondered if she'd tried to call him at the estate, but since there was no answering machine, he wouldn't be able to tell once he returned. He definitely wanted to see her, though, since he had several questions for her, especially after his visit with Agnes Morehead. He wanted to wait until George checked her out before confronting her. That way he'd have the advantage of knowing more than she thought he did. Knowledge is power, he reasoned to himself.

Spence blew out a sigh of relief as he turned from Highway 131 onto the drive of his father's estate. Feeling weary from all the flying and driving, he was looking forward to a hot bath in the Jacuzzi. There'd be plenty of time to search for missing clues, but for now, he needed some rest and relaxation.

As he entered the house, he looked around for signs of anyone who might've intruded while he was gone. After a quick search throughout the first floor, he was confident no one had been there. Spence climbed the stairs, taking his bags to his room, dropped them to the floor and walked straight to the bath to turn on the hot water in the Jacuzzi. Once the tub was full, he stripped and stepped in, settling all but his head under the water, and turned on the jets. As the water pulsed over his body, he could feel the tension melting away. He decided to remain in the tub until the water began to cool before climbing out, wrapping himself in a robe.

Spence had just walked from the bath into the bedroom, when the phone rang.

"Hello," Spence spoke into the phone, still a little weary from his travels.

"Hello, stranger," Arlene cooed. "Where have you been?

I've been trying to call you since Monday."

"I had to fly to Lexington to meet with a client, and didn't have time to call you," Spence lied. "I just got back a few minutes ago."

"I was afraid you were trying to give me the brush off," she complained with a sigh. "Would you like for me to come over?"

"Not tonight," Spence told her. "I'm really tired from the flight and drive."

"Oh, so you are brushing me off," she said, trying to sound indignant.

"No, not at all, I assure you. I'm just afraid I wouldn't be very good company tonight. How about lunch tomorrow, say around noon at Antoni's? I really do want to see you," he reassured her.

"Okay," she whispered on another sigh. "I guess I can wait until tomorrow. See you then."

Spence placed the receiver back in its cradle, and pulled down the sheets on the bed. He was so exhausted he decided to wait until tomorrow morning to begin his search for other hidden clues. All he wanted now was some sleep. He climbed into bed and turned off the lamp. In five minutes, he was out cold, enjoying the best sleep he'd had in days.

Chapter Fourteen

Spence awoke feeling very refreshed, ready for another day of mystery. He picked up his watch from the nightstand, glancing at it to see what the time was. Just a little after six o'clock, plenty of time to look for clues before his lunch date with Arlene. He just hoped he'd hear from George before noon.

He climbed out of bed and headed for the bathroom, eager to get going. After a quick shower, he threw on an old pair of sweat pants and a t-shirt. There was no need to put on anything nice just to sift through videotapes. Of course, he planned to change into something more appropriate for lunch.

Breakfast was a toaster pastry and coffee, which he made himself. He'd brought the video downstairs from his bag, and placed it in the VCR. He listened to the tape again, straining to discern every word individually for some sort of hidden meaning. The first half appeared to contain nothing he could determine as anything other than what it appeared to be. As the tape began the second part, which his father recorded recently, Spence sat up on the sofa paying close attention to his father's words. His father once again mentioned Agnes and Key Largo, causing Spence to assume his father meant to lure him to the meeting with that Agnes. What kept nagging at him was the thought that having known the Agnes that was his father's maid was already dead, there was a possibility he'd never have made the trip to Key Largo. Could it possibly mean something else? he wondered.

He decided to continue watching the video. Nothing else stood out until he got to the end. Suddenly, as his father was telling him how he was 'always the best,' Spence noticed for the first time a quick wink of his father's right eye. How could he have missed it before? But then, he wasn't looking so intently for clues earlier. He remembered his father using those exact words when they played hide and seek, but what was his father trying to tell him? Then it hit him! His favorite place to hide was the tree house. No one except he and his father knew that, which would make it the perfect place to hide something. Spence decided he'd investigate the tree house, but not until after dark where he'd be able to maneuver under the cover of darkness.

Spence sat back on the couch with a smug look on his face, feeling confident he'd uncovered a major clue in this mystery. Suddenly the cell phone George gave him began ringing. He grabbed it from the coffee table and flipped it open.

"Hello," Spence said somewhat hesitantly.

"Spence, it's me, George. I've got the information on the lady you asked for."

"Great. What did you find out?"

"Well, for starters, she's definitely not just an accountant. I crossed checked her name against the accounting staff and came up empty. Then when I tried to enter her name in a system search, the database shut me out, stating it was classified information. I called a contact I have on the inside, and when he looked it up, I could hear a warning sound coming from his computer. All he said was, 'She's OCB. Don't call me again until you hear from me.' You should have been here," George continued. "It gave me the creeps."

"Thanks," Spence said solemnly. "I owe you big for this one."

"Let's just call it even. And whatever you do, be careful."

Spence flipped the phone closed, and sat back on the sofa. So, he thought, Arlene was an agent after all. 'What was she up to?' he wondered. The Organized Crime Bureau, or OCB as the insiders called it, was a covert operation within the FBI. He knew that was why George ran into roadblocks on his search, and it would explain the alarms and reaction of his contact person on the inside. Most OCB operatives were like ghosts, typically working under a variety of assumed names. What made no sense in all of this was why Arlene was using her real identity. Unless that was her cover and he was her target. Hide in plain sight, he mused. It was actually a brilliant idea, if indeed the FBI was investigating his father's business dealings. He'd never suspect an old high school friend of being anything else, especially if she became a love interest. Suddenly he felt saddened at the thought of Arlene using him in such a way. Although he was far from becoming serious, he definitely had feelings for her.

He began laying out a plan to expose Arlene during their lunch meeting, hoping she'd admit to her recent activities and provide some much-needed answers to some of his questions. He decided to first act nonchalant to allow her to relax in her self-confidence, believing him to be clueless. Then at the most opportune time, he'd strike, catching her off guard and more inclined to make mistakes and divulge information. He patted himself on the back for designing what he believed to be an excellent plan. Then he realized if she were really with OCB, surely she'd be too experienced to fall for such a simple plan. Unfortunately, it was all he had, so he had to give it a shot, even if it backfired on him.

Spence decided to check in with Sherrie while waiting until it was time to meet Arlene. He flipped open the secure cell phone George gave him and dialed the office number. Sherrie answered after the first ring, "Law Offices, how can I help you?"

"Well," Spence began, "you can start by telling me what you're wearing."

He occasionally liked to think he was catching Sherrie

off guard by doing a little flirting of his own, but it rarely surprised her.

"Nothing but a black lace teddy, stockings, and a garter belt, and of course, those black stiletto heels you like so much. I wore them under my coat this morning, and plan to jump the first man that walks through the door. Pity you're not coming in to work today," she responded in a low, sexy voice. Obviously, she'd already had her morning coffee, and was ready for anything.

"Even if it's Neil Waterston?" Spence replied, and they both burst out laughing.

Neil Waterston was the local newspaper reporter who covered the legal happenings in the community. He'd been with the Times for thirty years, covering everything from criminal trials to civil proceedings. He was in his mid-fifties, balding on top with a little gray hair on the sides that made him look as if he just got out of bed. He was five feet five, with a beer belly that hung over his belt. He wore the same blue seersucker suit every day, and smelled of beef and cheese. Despite all of this, Neil considered himself a ladies' man, even though he'd only married once at an early age, only to have his bride leave him for another woman after six months. He was constantly dropping by the office, flirting with Sherrie. Though a bit abrasive, Neil was an excellent reporter. He had a way of finding out more facts about some cases than the detectives who worked on them. Moreover, his style of writing often made the readers feel they were at the scene of the crime, pouring over clues and examining the evidence. Spence believed this was the reason the Times had kept him around for so long, in spite of his outward appearance.

"Well, somebody's certainly in a good mood today," chirped Sherrie.

"Let's just say it's been a good morning so far," Spence replied. "How about you? Is everything okay with you?"

"I'm fine as frog's hair," Sherrie quipped, delving into her little bag of Southern colloquialisms. "When are you coming home? I'm starting to get lonely here without you."

"Okay, I asked for that," Spence said, recognizing Sherrie was once again flirting with him. "I've got to go. I'm meeting someone for lunch, and need to get dressed."

"Ooh, you're not dressed," Sherrie teased. "Maybe I need to come up there, unless of course, you have a lunch date with another woman."

"I'm hanging up now, Sherrie," Spence replied, still smiling.

"Okay, but don't say I didn't offer," Sherrie said with a laugh. "Call me later."

He shook his head as he closed the cell phone. No matter what was happening in his world, Spence could always count on Sherrie to make him smile. It was a wonderful working relationship, and he felt extremely lucky to have her by his side.

He made his way back to his room to change for his lunch date with Arlene. He completed his grooming ritual by touching up his hair with a brush, and splashing on some Tuscany, one squirt for each side of his face, and a large one for the back of his neck. Then he gently massaged the fragrant cologne into his skin. He'd worn the same cologne since his first marriage. Greta bought a bottle for him their first Christmas together, commenting on how good she thought it smelled. Over the years, Spence had received many compliments on this fragrance. At least, Greta had gotten that one thing right during their relationship. He'd tried several other colognes over the past few years, many he received as gifts, but always came back to his Tuscany. It was just like an old friend that he'd known forever, familiar and trustworthy.

After he was completely ready to leave, Spence bounced down the stairs and out the front door to his car. Since he still hadn't disposed of his father's car, he decided to leave it in the garage for now.

It was a beautiful sunny day as Spence made his way to Antoni's and what he hoped would be a very enlightening meal. He arrived ten minutes before noon, and apparently ahead of Arlene. Spence parked the car and went inside. A few patrons were already seated, but the place was far from crowded. The hostess looked up at Spence from her station and asked if he was alone. He told her someone would be joining him soon, but preferred she seat him now. She smiled and led him to a booth just past her station on the right, but he insisted on a more private location in the back. He decided to wait for Arlene before ordering a drink.

It wasn't long before he looked up to see the hostess leading Arlene back toward the table. She was dressed in a black two-piece business suit, with a red blouse to add some color. The skirt was as short as the other ones she wore, revealing her beautiful legs. She wore a gold serpentine necklace, and gold dangling filigree earrings. Spence immediately recognized the smell of her perfume as she leaned over and planted a soft kiss on his lips. He decided it was still a little early for his usual, ordering a carafe of wine instead of his usual Jack and Coke once she was seated.

"It's so good to see you," she began. "I've missed you the past few days."

"Good to see you too," Spence replied. "Did I miss anything while I was gone?"

"Just me!" she exclaimed, smiling and throwing her arms open wide.

The waitress returned with the wine, which afforded Spence a nice distraction. He wasn't yet ready to surprise Arlene with what he knew about her. He picked up the menu as the waitress went into her spiel for the special for today. Chicken Parmesan. Arlene said she'd been craving that very thing for weeks, and had planned to order the dish before she ever sat down. Spence decided to follow suit, ordering the same thing.

The waitress turned and headed back to the kitchen with their order, while Spence and Arlene returned to their conversation.

"So, did you really miss me?" Arlene asked.

"Sure," Spence replied. "I just needed to take care of some business. It's hard to run a law office in Kentucky from Michigan."

"I understand," expressed Arlene. "I hope everything was okay there."

"Yeah, just a few odds and ends that needed to be settled. So how about you?" Spence asked, quickly changing the subject. "What've you been up to the past few days? Catch any hardened criminals?"

Arlene laughed somewhat nervously. "I told you I am just an accountant. I leave all of the criminal chasing to the experts."

Spence decided now was as good a time as any to begin his assault.

"Really?" he said, sounding surprised. "Since when does a field agent perform bookkeeping duties, or is the OCB setting a new policy trend?"

Arlene sat back in her chair as she reacted in just the way he hoped she would. That 'deer in the headlights' look shone in her eyes. He'd obviously struck a chord, catching her totally off guard. He was glad to see some of his suspicions were true, but it intrigued him by how easily he'd gotten to her. Maybe she wasn't as experienced as he first thought at undercover work.

Since Arlene still hadn't spoken, Spence decided to take advantage of the moment and continue to chip away at her facade until he was satisfied she was fully exposed.

"So, how is the investigation into my father's affairs progressing? I was sort of hoping we could compare notes to help each other. Why, I'll even let you see some of his papers, and you won't even have to sleep with me to get a peek at the information. How does that sound?"

His last statements had given Arlene a little time to recuperate, her eyes like daggers piercing back at him as she leaned closer to the table.

"Are you out of your mind?" she hissed across the table in a half-whisper. "You obviously don't understand who or what you are dealing with," she continued. "I could have you arrested for obstruction of justice before you could toss a tip on the table."

Spence deftly interrupted her tirade. "But you won't, because right now I'm the only one who can help you. So let's cut the crap, and you level with me about your little operation, or I'll burn everything my father owned, including the house, and leave you with a lot of questions you'll never find answers to."

"Okay," Arlene hissed, "but not here. I'll call you later and we'll arrange a meeting where we can speak more freely. In the meantime, I suggest you learn a little more tact. It may serve you well if you wish to continue a more healthy dialogue with me. Oh, and just so you know, I didn't sleep with you just to gain access to your father's house. That really hurt."

They finished their meal in silence, rather than arouse suspicion by leaving abruptly, just in case someone was watching. He'd never eaten a quicker and more awkward meal. Neither ordered dessert, as both were eager to finish the meal and leave. Arlene clearly wanted the time to regroup and organize her next move. Likewise, Spence felt a need to re-collect his thoughts and plan how he should proceed from here.

During the drive back to the estate, he played back the entire conversation in his mind. He was relieved that he was on the right track, but frustrated at not finding any answers to his questions. He felt certain that whoever was watching would now be more careful, considering he'd revealed to Arlene that he knew who she was and some of what was going on. He had the eerie feeling of many eyes watching his every move, and would need to be careful now more than ever when he made his night maneuver to the tree house. He wanted to stay one step ahead of whoever was watching in uncovering the clues his father left behind.

Chapter Fifteen

Spence stopped his car in the driveway, just short of the garage. He made sure to leave enough room to get his father's car out. He felt he should take it out for a drive, at least for a short one, to keep the battery charged. He opened the side door to the garage and reached for the automatic garage door button. The motor sprang to life as he pressed the green-lit square, causing the door behind his father's car to rise. The other bay of the two-car garage was full of boxed items, Christmas decorations, and various yard tools. He decided there was plenty of time for spring-cleaning later.

The Judge had bought a Porsche convertible one year ago this past Christmas. It was a present to himself. He rarely splurged on anything so extravagant, but for some reason he felt he might be able to recapture some of his youth by driving a sports car. According to James, the Judge loved tooling around town with the top down and the radio blaring. He listened to the more modern rock stations, hoping the young women would find him sexy. So much for the reserved father he knew, Spence thought. Of course, the Judge could spend his money any way he pleased, and live the same way. After all those years of hard work, he deserved to enjoy it.

Spence stood for a moment admiring the beauty of his father's prized possession. It was painted black, with a matching black soft top, and shone like a new penny. The Judge obviously kept it detailed, almost clean enough you could eat off it. He suddenly felt the urge to cruise through town with the top down, and quickly understood how his father could've felt the same way. There was something about a man and his machine that even Freud wouldn't understand.

Spence searched through his pants pocket until he retrieved the set of keys to the Porsche. He had located them while going through his father's desk, and decided to keep them with him just in case someone else entered the house and wanted to take a joy ride. He eased into the soft leather interior of the car, savoring the experience moment by moment. Sure, he'd driven many different and luxurious automobiles over the years, but this was a first for him. He'd often wondered what it would be like to own one of these, especially after watching the rich kids at college cruising around in their parents' cars, but he always seemed to err on the side of caution and prudence, opting instead for a more practical mode of transportation.

He inserted the key into the ignition and turned it clockwise. The engine awoke; running at what Spence decided was a purr. It was a fine specimen of automotive achievement, and seemed to be in top working order. He eased the car out of the garage and onto the paved drive, reaching up toward the visor and pressing the remote button, closing the garage door slowly behind him. Carefully, he drove the length of the driveway, trying to get a feel for the way the car handled, but by the time he reached the end, he realized the car practically drove by its self. It was the smoothest handling automobile he'd ever driven.

Since it was a beautiful day for a drive, Spence decided to cruise north up Highway 31 to Petoskey with the top down. It was about an hour drive, which would give him plenty of time to think and plan his next encounter with Arlene. Once on the open road, he punched the accelerator with his right foot to see what kind of power it really had. The Porsche didn't disappoint him as it quickly reached eighty miles per hour. He eased back on the gas, not wanting to attract the attention of local law enforcement personnel. The feeling of the wind blowing through his hair as he raced along the highway was rejuvenating. Suddenly, he realized how his father must have felt while in the driver's seat. It made him feel young again.

Highway 31 ran alongside Grand Traverse Bay heading northward toward Petoskey. Spence was actually able to see the bay in places along his route, which made the trip even more enjoyable. For a few minutes, he actually emptied his mind of thoughts about Arlene and all he had encountered in the past few days. Instead, he was simply lost in his admiration of the beauty before his eyes, beauty he believed only God could produce. This was church to Spence, because times like these were when he felt the presence and closeness of God.

Spence was enjoying his ride so much, it seemed like no time at all before he'd reached his destination. Deciding to stop for coffee at a small cafe and relax for a few minutes before making the trip back, he parked the Porsche in front of a row of brick buildings with green awnings. The sign over one of the shops read 'Cup O' Joe.' He climbed out of the vehicle and stepped onto the sidewalk. As he opened the door to the coffee shop, a little bell attached to the top of the door alerted the people inside to his presence. Several small tables and chairs were scattered about the inside of the place. Toward the back was a long counter where you ordered, and paid for your coffee. They carried many different and exotic blends, including espresso and cappuccino. They also offered a limited menu of sandwiches for the lunch crowd.

A few patrons quietly sipped their coffee and conversed amongst themselves. Spence walked up to the counter and asked for a cup of black coffee. The young girl across the counter seemed flustered as she asked, "What flavor would you like?"

"Coffee flavor?" Spence replied. "I just want a simple cup of regular coffee."

"I'm sorry," the girl continued. "But I'm not familiar with that flavor."

Just then a young man walked up from somewhere in the back, carrying a cup of coffee.

"The regular coffee is labeled French Roast," he informed the girl, as he handed the cup to Spence. "She's still in training," he continued.

"No problem," answered Spence. "Thank you for the prompt service."

"You're welcome," the young man said. "Will there be anything else?"

"No, just the coffee," Spence replied, raising the cup to his lips.

The young girl punched on the cash register and informed Spence of the amount of the bill. He reached into his pocket, pulled out a five, and told her to keep the change, giving her a wink. She smiled and thanked him as she placed the change in her apron pocket.

He made his way to a small table on the right away from the window. He wanted to be able to view the entire place without being seen from outside just in case someone was watching. Spying a newspaper on the table next to him, he reached over and grabbed it. He was reading the sports section when he heard the little bell on the door ring its chiming alert. He looked up in time to see one of the couples leaving the shop. He returned to his reading, slowly sipping his coffee. It was very good coffee, he mused, much better than what he could make.

He was so engrossed in reading the paper, he didn't notice the bell as the door opened again and someone entered the coffee shop.

He was turning the page of the newspaper when suddenly a young lady sat down in front of him. She was wearing sunglasses and a black scarf, very much in style so as not to stand out, but concealing enough to hide her identity. Spence couldn't help but think she was somehow familiar, but when she spoke, he remembered her voice.

"Hello stranger, I told you we would meet again." It was

Agnes Morehead. "Just act natural," she instructed. "I don't think you were followed, but it's better to be safe than sorry. Have any luck finding the other clues?"

"I think I figured one out," Spence answered. "But I'm having a hard time uncovering anything else from the tape. What am I missing?"

"I can't say, just in case someone is listening," she replied, as Spence quickly glanced down at the pen in his pocket. He'd forgotten to turn it on for it to be able to detect any bugs nearby, and doing so now would only arouse suspicion if someone were watching. He cursed himself under his breath for being too cheap to keep it on continuously for fear of running down the batteries. He decided he'd buy some on the way back and make sure he kept them with him so this would not happen again.

"Can't you at least give me a hint?" he asked.

"You've already been given enough hints. Besides, I'm confident you'll figure it out," she answered.

"Who are you?" he finally asked in a half whisper.

"All in good time," she replied mysteriously. "We must be very careful or we'll all be in a lot of trouble. Just make sure you watch your back and don't be too open about any of this with anyone."

"Why should I even trust what you're saying?" asked Spence. "For all I know, you could be on the opposing team as well, whatever team that is."

"Your father asked me to assume the identity of Agnes Morehead so you would find me. He wanted someone he could trust to help guide you during this time. Even though I cannot give you the answers for which you seek, I agreed to watch over you, so to speak, in order to be there when you find your answers. It is then that you'll need my help and guidance."

"Thanks a lot," he sneered. "I may never get all the answers."

"Patience," she whispered. "Your father meant a great deal to me, and I'm determined to see you succeed at your quest. Just listen carefully for anything that could be a clue, no matter how ordinary it may sound. The answers you seek hide in plain sight. That's all the help I can give you for now. Just remember, I'll be watching." With that, she rose from the table and walked steadily toward the door so as not to attract attention.

Spence remained seated for several minutes after she was gone. He wanted to rush out behind her and see which direction she went so he could follow her and confront her with more questions, but he knew that wouldn't be a wise move. He wanted so badly to know her true identity and what her role was in all of this, but realized it may be a long time, if ever, before he found out. Although the scarf and sunglasses concealed her face, he remembered clearly how she looked when he first met her in Key Largo. She was the most beautiful woman he'd ever seen. Another time and place, he'd have liked to pursue a more intimate relationship with her.

He became lost for a few minutes in a daydream of love and fantasy with a lady he'd now only met twice, then quickly snapped out of it to the realization that until he settled all of the questions surrounding his father's death, there'd be no time or energy to pursue romantic endeavors.

Spence let out a huge sigh as he stood and walked out the door of the coffee shop. Knowing Arlene would probably call soon to arrange a meeting, he decided to head back to the estate. Once inside the car, he switched on the pen device in his pocket, which began glowing immediately, flashing the characteristic red light. He just shook his head, thinking to himself that he now knew how secret agents must feel knowing they're constantly being watched and listened to. He wondered what was so important to have so many bugs, and possibly cameras, pointed in his direction. The bugs in the car didn't worry him, though, because he still had the cell phone George gave him, which should prevent anyone from listening in on his phone conversations. Other than that, no one else was in the car with him, so all they would hear would be the sounds coming from the stereo. He was apprehensive about singing along with the music now that he knew someone was listening, and felt somewhat embarrassed about his poor vocal performance on the way to Petoskey earlier. It's amazing, he thought, how much more careful you are about what you say or do when you think someone else is watching.

The drive back to the estate seemed longer, probably because he was aware of the listening devices in the car. It took the same amount of time for the return trip, but Spence was relieved to see the familiar entrance to the estate. He eased the car onto the drive and proceeded down the winding path until he reached the garage. Returning the car to its original position, he secured the garage doors as before.

When he walked into the house, Spence suddenly decided to sweep the house for bugs. He retrieved the small device George gave him and began upstairs first. He quickly found one in each lamp in his bedroom, the phone, and even the showerhead. Also bugs were in all of the other bedrooms, specifically in bedside lamps and phones. He was relieved not to find any hidden cameras upstairs, especially since he often walked naked from the bath to the bedroom. It wasn't because he was ashamed of his body he wanted no one watching, but rather self-conscious about the particular bulges that came with age.

He continued his sweep downstairs, finding bugs in every room, including the guest powder room. Someone went to a lot of expense to plant so many, making Spence wonder what information he could possibly have that was so important.

He decided to remove the bugs from his father's office. George explained that sometimes these devices malfunction, so it was common for whoever was listening to lose a few of them, as long as there were still several working. He decided that since he hadn't spent much time in his father's office, whoever was listening would probably believe the bugs in his father's office simply went out on their own, especially if he left the others in place. This would give him a secure place to talk to someone while at the estate, without raising suspicions.

After completing his espionage work, Spence decided it

was time for a drink. He mixed a Jack and Coke, moving on to the den to watch his father's tape again. Based on what Agnes said, he believed there was still something he'd missed, but had no idea what it was. As he watched the tape repeatedly, he became increasingly sleepy, mainly due to the boredom, until finally, he closed his eyes and began snoring. The tape ran all the way to the end, and then automatically rewound, leaving only a solid blue screen on the television set.

Spence bolted from the sofa, having been startled awake by the ringing of the telephone. He clumsily grabbed for the receiver, his heart pounding from the shock of a deep sleep interrupted by a loud ringing noise. It was one of those rare times when a person gets completely relaxed, sleeping the hardest he had slept in days, only to awaken abruptly. He had to think for a minute to remember where he was, then lifted the receiver from its cradle and mumbled a faint hello.

"Is everything okay?" Arlene's voice sang through the receiver.

"Yeah," Spence said, still trying to shake the cobwebs out of his head.

"I thought I'd cook for you tonight to return the favor from the other night," she continued, her tone sounding normal as if today's lunch had never happened. Obviously, this was for the benefit of whoever was listening in.

Spence decided he'd play along and follow her lead. "Sounds great! I can't wait to see you again."

"I'll see you around seven, then," said Arlene, as she reminded Spence how to get to her place. He'd already passed by her house before.

"I'm looking forward to it," answered Spence as he hung up the phone.

He sat for a moment staring at the blue screen on the television before pressing the button on the remote to turn it off. Then he stood up and walked out to his car, carrying the bug detection device George gave him. He quickly found a listening device mounted underneath the dash, and one under the passenger seat. Perfect, he thought to himself as he checked the gas gauge. He remembered filling his tank on the way back from lunch, and the gauge still read full.

Walking to the garage, he retrieved a small gas can and a short piece of garden hose. He removed the gas cap from his car and began siphoning gas from the tank. Once he filled the can, he placed the cap back on the tank and returned the can and hose to the garage. With nothing else to do, he went back inside the house to wait until time to get ready for his date with Arlene.

At four o'clock, Spence returned to the television to review the tape once again. As he listened, he still failed to discern any additional clues. Frustrated from finding nothing, he decided to see what was on television. The soap operas were over now, giving way to the usual fare of talk shows. Spence flipped through the channels until he found an old cop show on one of the stations that showed nothing but re-runs of older programs. He fixed another Jack and Coke and sat watching as the story unfolded. He remembered the show, but it had been so many years since he last saw it, he couldn't remember this particular episode.

When the show ended at five, Spence decided to call Sherrie to check in. Since the conversation was mundane, no news to report from either of them, he quickly ended the call and headed upstairs to shower and change before his evening with Arlene. He chose a nice pair of jeans and a green crew neck pullover sweater to wear. He completed the outfit with a pair of short hiking boots, for that rugged outdoor look. He also knew they'd come in handy before the night was over. It was already dark outside as Spence left the house just before seven. It would only take a few minutes to get to Arlene's place.

Chapter Sixteen

Spence started the car and eased down the drive toward the road. About three quarters of the way down, the car started lurching and hesitating until the engine went dead.

"Damn!" Spence shouted, "It's out of gas!" He was certain he said it loud enough for the microphones to pick up. He reached into his pocket and retrieved his cell phone. After two rings, Spence heard Arlene's voice.

"Arlene, this is Spence. I just ran out of gas coming down the driveway. I think I saw a gas can in the garage, so I'm going to walk back there and see. I just wanted you to know I'd be a few minutes late," he told her.

"Do you need me to come get you?" asked Arlene.

"No, that won't be necessary. If I don't find any gas in the garage I'll just drive my father's car," he returned, then closed the phone and climbed out of the car.

That sounded convincing enough, Spence thought to himself. He quickly darted across the driveway into the trees alongside the path. Making his way through the dark to the old tree house, Spence quickly climbed the ladder to the top and crawled inside the structure. He was amazed at how well it had stood up over the years, but his father had insisted the builder use the best, treated lumber he could find. They'd worked on it together, so it was always something special between them.

Spence crawled over to the back right corner and switched on the miniature flashlight he brought with him. He knew it wouldn't give off enough light to be detected should anyone be watching, but there'd be enough light for him to see with. He felt around the floorboards with his hand until he found the one he was looking for. He had made a secret compartment under the floor not long after they'd built the house, and covered it with a loose board. Since it was in the corner, no one would ever walk over it and discover it was loose, especially since it blended in with the rest of the flooring. He'd used the hiding place for special items when he was small, and then for girly magazines once he reached puberty. One day after school, he'd climbed up into the tree house to spend some quiet time with his most recent centerfold, only to find a note lying on top of his magazines. All it said was, "Now I know why you spend so much time out here." Neither he nor his father ever mentioned it, apparently because his father viewed it as some sort of right of passage. He was certain that if his father left anything special for him in the tree house, it would be in his old secret hiding place.

Spence removed the loose board and aimed the light down into the dark compartment. As the light passed back and forth across the dark wood, something sparkled suddenly, attracting his attention. It was a key, lying on top of a piece of paper. He retrieved them both from the hole, before making another sweep of the light just to make sure he hadn't missed anything. Satisfied the key and the note were the only things inside the cavity, Spence stuffed the key and note into his pocket, placed the board back in place, and crawled out of the tree house.

Quickly climbing down the ladder, he made his way back to the driveway, walking at an angle toward the house so it would appear the time he spent in the tree house was actually time spent walking back to the garage. Once in the garage, he grabbed the gas can from earlier and headed back to the car. He quickly emptied the contents of the gas can into the tank and placed the can in the trunk. He wanted to make sure everything appeared, as it seemed, just in case someone was watching. Then he drove the remaining length of the drive and turned right onto the highway.

It was seven-thirty when Spence finally arrived at Arlene's house. The drive leading from the road was not nearly as long as his father's was. The house was a two story English Tudor design he figured was roughly thirty-five hundred square feet. A two-car garage stood directly in front of the house on the right the driveway led into. Seeing no sign of Arlene's car in the driveway, he felt certain it was inside the garage. He wondered what else she kept in there, and was hoping for the grand tour. Considering the outcome of their last encounter, though, he'd be lucky to get past the dining room.

Spence rang the doorbell and waited patiently for Arlene to welcome him into her home. It took less than half a minute for her to make her way to the foyer and gently open the front door, flashing a smile as she welcomed her guest. He wondered if this, too, was for show, or had she calmed down since lunch. He felt certain it wouldn't be very long before he knew exactly what her mood was.

Arlene turned and walked back toward the kitchen, allowing Spence to close the door himself. The floors were finished oak hardwood, and very well maintained. The entry way opened to a great room that had a fireplace on the far wall at the rear of the house. Immediately to the right was a small living room, and to the right past the living room was the sunroom she'd showed Spence from his house. Between these two rooms was a half bath for guests. The dining room was on the left, with an arched doorway leading to the kitchen. The kitchen was rather large, and had a breakfast nook at the far end with a bay window. The master bedroom suite was located in the far left corner of the first floor, complete with a large shower and separate whirlpool tub. The second floor held three additional bedrooms and two full baths.

Arlene offered Spence a glass of red wine, gesturing towards the glass sitting on the kitchen counter. He felt his nostrils fill with the pleasant aroma of freshly baked bread as he stepped into the kitchen. He reached for the glass of wine, carefully taking a sip as if afraid she might have laced it with some sort of lethal drug. Noticing his apprehension, Arlene seized the moment to sneer, "Don't worry. It's not poison." Spence managed a little nervous laughter, but continued to eye the glass suspiciously.

He glanced down at his pocket every few minutes, checking to see if the pen George gave him was flashing. So far, it remained dark, indicating no listening devices or cameras were present. Perhaps she invited him here because she knew no one would be listening in on the conversation. Outwardly, he remained calm and patient, while his insides churned from anxiety brought on by his curiosity over what Arlene would reveal tonight. He carefully sipped the wine, hoping it would settle his stomach.

She had prepared a home cooked meal consisting of baked chicken, mashed potatoes, green beans, and made-from-scratch biscuits. Spence wondered where she had learned to cook like this, but decided his other questions were more important right now.

After placing each serving dish on the table, Arlene gestured toward the table with a sweep of her hand. "Dinner is served," she said in a fake British accent. Spence thought it sounded rather cute coming from her, but was still reeling too much from her dishonesty with him to feel romantic.

After about ten minutes of silent eating, Spence finally mustered up enough courage to speak. "Okay," he said. "Now can you tell me what's going on?"

"Let's wait until after dinner," she answered. "We can talk over dessert."

They continued their meal in silence, occasionally looking up and smiling at each other. It was obvious to Spence that their relationship would never be the same. Considering how fond he had grown of Arlene, he was saddened at the thought of losing her, but once the trust barrier was broken, it was almost impossible to repair the damage that results. It felt much the same as his first divorce, which caused Spence to realize how hard he had actually fallen for Arlene. He soon found himself wondering what might have been.

Under normal circumstances he would've found the meal very delightful, as it was apparent Arlene was quite the chef. However, all of the emotions boiling inside him denied his palate the satisfaction of basking in a blend of wonderful tastes. Instead, it was more a labor to toil through than a repast.

Once they finished, Spence helped Arlene clear the dishes from the table. She cut two slices of carrot cake and placed each one on a small dessert plate, refilled their wine glasses, handed one of the slices of cake to Spence, and led the way into the living room. She sat down on the large leather sofa, placing her wine glass on the end table to her left, then motioned for Spence to sit beside her, as she lifted a portion of cake to her lips. He placed his wine glass on the right end table, and took the offered seat.

With her mouth still partially full of cake, she began, "So, you want to know the truth, do you? Well, okay. But don't shoot the messenger if you don't like what you hear." She paused a moment before continuing. "A lot of what I told you is the truth. I am, or was, an accountant for the FBI. The Bureau has been watching the VanWarners for several years now, hoping to find a link between them and the Gregorio crime family in Chicago. There's a rumor that Joey has been running money from his illegal gambling operations to Chicago and laundering it through some of the Gregorio's businesses along with his own. So far, everything looks legitimate. We've even tried to subpoena the records from Joey's various bars and other companies, but the Judge said we didn't have enough evidence. Then we got a tip that your father might have some damaging evidence against Joey and his family. Rumor has it that one of the attorneys in your father's firm was making a money-run for Joey when suddenly he vanished, along with ten million dollars. We began watching your father very closely to determine if he was actually involved as well, or just happened upon some incriminating information. We were unable to locate the attorney or the missing money, so we contacted your father, hoping he would cooperate with us and offer what information he had. He refused, stating he had no idea as to what we were referring. I transferred from accounting as an agent when your father died. I had wanted a chance to prove myself, so I told my superiors I went to high school with you. They asked me to work undercover to see what information I could get from you. We were hoping you'd stumble onto something while going through your father's estate that would cause you to seek my help in finding out what it was; something I'd recognize as crucial evidence in our case against Joey but something you'd never have to become involved in. Spence, I'm sorry, but we feel certain your father was involved, or at least knew of, Joey's operations," Arlene finished. She paused for a moment to give Spence time to digest everything he'd just heard. He sat quietly staring at the piece of cake on his lap, carefully processing the information before responding to Arlene's accusations.

"What makes you so sure my father was involved with Joey?" he finally asked. "Where's your proof?"

"Spence, the man who disappeared with Joey's money worked for your father. Do you think your father wouldn't know if one of his staff was missing? Besides, there was no missing person report filed, no concern from your father, nothing at all when we questioned him. It was as if the attorney just vanished into thin air, and your father didn't seem to care at all," Arlene concluded.

"Just how much involved do you think my father was?" He continued with his line of questioning.

"We believe he not only knew about the missing ten million, but possibly had some very incriminating evidence of Joey's illegal activities. We contacted him on several occasions, but if he did have any such documents, he refused to disclose it. At first we thought his death might not have been from natural causes, which is until we received the coroner's report."

"Who was your source for all of this information?"

"We don't know. We received emails that we could only manage to trace to different public libraries in the state, but each time the person used a different I.D., and never used the same library twice. At first, we thought it was your father using this method because he was still afraid to come forward, but now it appears we've been chasing a ghost. Since your father died, we've received no more emails from our source."

"So it was you who entered the house that night and watched the tape of my father's will?" Spence seethed in accusation.

"Yes," she answered, lowering her head as if she were embarrassed or ashamed. "We had to know for certain exactly what was on that tape. I even tried to locate Agnes Morehead to see if she knew of any records your father may have kept regarding any of the VanWarner business, but that was a dead end. We were hoping the information regarding her death was false and that she was actually living and hiding out in Key Largo, but it wasn't her," she added with a sigh.

Spence decided not to reveal the fact he'd also had made a trip to Florida in search of Agnes Morehead. At this point, he felt it was better to limit the amount of information he disclosed. "Let me get this straight, the FBI believes Joey Van-Warner and his pals are involved in illegal activities, and you believe my father was involved, but yet you have no proof. You're relying solely on a few emails sent by God knows who, but you've decided they're legitimate. How am I doing so far?"

Arlene simply nodded her head.

He continued, "What exactly did you say to my father, and what exactly was his answer?"

"We offered him immunity for his testimony against Joey, along with our witness protection program. He responded by telling us he'd seen how the witness protection program failed in the past. Then told us to go to hell. The fact that he didn't specifically deny any knowledge of Joey's operation led us to a stronger feeling he was involved." She hesitated as if weighing her next words. "Spence, if you have this information, or know where it is, we can offer you the same deal as we did your father. Of course, I'm speaking solely of the witness protection program, since there's no evidence linking you to Joey VanWarner."

"Thanks for the vote of confidence," Spence sneered. "But I assure you I've uncovered nothing that would be of any use to you. In fact, aside from a few loose ends regarding property and the like, I'm just about finished executing my father's will."

"Spence, please, if you've found anything at all, I need to know," Arlene pleaded.

"Sorry, Arlene." His reply was swift. "But I don't have anything you. I hope this won't affect your job."

"Forget it," she returned, brushing it off with a wave of her hand. "If you don't know, you don't know. I'll be okay. Worst case I'll still have my old job in accounting."

Spence couldn't help but feel a little sorry for Arlene, but then she did put herself in this position. After all, it wasn't his place to look out for her. Telling himself that still didn't ease the guilt pangs, especially since there were things he was keeping from her. At this point, though, he felt it was in his best interest to remain quiet regarding anything he uncovered from his latest adventures. He reasoned that if his father was unwilling to cooperate with the Feds, there must be a good explanation.

After a few moments of silence, Arlene finally spoke. "So, where does all of this leave us?"

"What do you mean?"

"Well granted my job was to pump you for information, but as I told you before, I was sincere when we made love. I'm very interested in pursuing our relationship."

"I don't mean to berate you," Spence said. "But as far as I'm concerned, this relationship began on lies and broken trust. I can be as forgiving as the next man can, but I cannot forget. I need time to sort through all of this and make my peace with it, before I can even consider pursuing a relationship with you. Can you understand that?"

"Actually, I do," Arlene answered. "I can only say again how sorry I am for ever deceiving you," she whispered, wiping away a tear.

Spence thanked her for dinner as he walked toward the front door. He turned his head just as Arlene leaned over to kiss him, causing her lips to fall on his cheek. He cursed himself under his breath for being so cold, knowing he wanted nothing else but to sweep her into his arms and carry her to the bedroom, but he was still hurting too bad from her deception. It had been so long since he had a meaningful relationship that he wondered if he would ever trust again, as he walked out the door.

Chapter Seventeen

Spence waited until he was securely inside the estate with the doors locked before he pulled the key and paper he discovered in the tree house from his pocket. The paper displayed the name of Paul Boyle scrawled across the front, along with the number 1115. The key was typical except for a logo engraved on one side, a large letter G with the letter H to the left and the letter C to the right.

He racked his brain, searching for an old discarded memory of a Paul Boyle that perhaps his father had mentioned once in conversation, until he could think no more. He poured himself a Jack and Coke and collapsed on the leather sofa in the den, rubbing his forehead as if all of that thinking had unleashed a migraine on his brain. Leaning back, he pushed the button on the remote control, bringing the television to life. Deciding he needed a break from reality, he tuned in to watch an old "Magnum PI" episode. Having seen Tom Selleck recently in a television movie role, he suddenly realized how much younger Thomas Magnum looked than Jesse Stone, the character Selleck played in the movie. Age has a way of finding us all, he thought.

Spence suddenly sat up on the edge of the sofa, as if a

light bulb illuminated above his head. He remembered seeing the same logo that was on the key while looking through his father's papers. He walked to the office and began searching through the desk until he pulled out an invoice for an annual membership to a health club. There at the top was the same logo as the one on the key and the name Paul Boyle listed as the member. Perhaps, either this Paul Boyle was an unknown acquaintance of his father, or his father had joined a health club under an assumed name. Either way, it was a hunch worth following, since he'd come up empty for other explanations of the name and number scrawled on the piece of paper. He decided that since his father left a key behind, his theory about his father using an assumed name seemed more logical, and this key must be to his locker. The question now was where the health club was located.

Spence rose from the sofa and walked into his father's office. He retrieved a Detroit area phone book from a desk drawer and began rifling through the yellow pages until he came to the listing for health clubs. The Genesis Health Club & Resort was one of the finer health clubs in the Detroit metropolitan area. It was actually located in Pontiac, a suburb north of Detroit proper.

He dialed the number, and when a lady answered, he made up a story about being an old college roommate of Paul Boyle and was trying to locate him, asking her if they had a member by that name. At first, she was hesitant to give out any information, but Spence was able to convince her that this was a matter of life and death, so she confirmed they had a member by that name.

Deciding to wait until tomorrow so he could map out its exact location using a computer at the library, rather than exposing his itinerary to whoever was listening by asking Sherrie to pull the directions on the Internet, he settled in. All he could do for now was to wait until morning.

Morning came slowly, as Spence tossed and turned all night. His mind was racing with thoughts of the next day's journey. It seemed he'd just fallen asleep when his alarm sounded at six o'clock. However, Spence leapt from his bed as if he'd slept ten hours. He was still obviously running on adrenaline from the night before, and was anxious to get the day started. He showered and dressed, before descending the stairs to the kitchen.

He wore jeans and a grey pullover sweater, but packed a change of clothes in his overnight bag. He also tucked an old jacket from the closet, and a baseball cap inside. It was now eight o'clock ... time to begin his plan.

He phoned the office, eagerly waiting for Sherrie to answer. It took only one ring before her sweet voice radiated through the receiver. He couldn't help but smile as he heard her familiar southern drawl.

"Sherrie, it's Spence," he greeted. "How's everything at the office?"

"Under control, just like I told you it would be," she answered.

"Listen, I need you to book a flight for me to Vegas from Detroit for this afternoon. I'm going to run by my father's firm to finish that part of the estate settlement, then I'm going to Vegas for a couple of days to enjoy myself."

"Do you want me to book a hotel for you too?"

"No. I'll do that myself. Just call me with the flight times."

"Will do, shug," she drawled. "Just win enough for us both while you're there." She laughed as she hung up.

The doorbell rang just as Sherrie ended the call. Spence peered through the front door to see a delivery guy standing on the front porch. He barely cracked open the door, when the delivery guy said, "Package for Mr. Rawlings."

Taking the package, he signed the electronic tracking machine. As he turned to go back inside, he heard a faint 'Have a nice day' from the deliveryman. Spence could tell from the return address that the package contained the stuff he asked George to send him. The cover was set. Now it was time for stage two.

He left the estate and drove to the town library. He accessed one of the public computers and quickly entered the location of the health club into the driving directions program. The map and detailed directions appeared almost instantly, as Spence pushed print and logged off the computer. He grabbed the paper from the printer, handed the librarian a quarter for the copy, and walked quickly out the door to his car. Glancing at the directions, he sped off on his way to Detroit. Knowing it was a little over two hundred fifty miles from Traverse City to Detroit, he had plenty of time to perfect his plan as he drove.

Spence was barely on his way when his cell phone rang. He knew it was Sherrie without even looking at the caller ID.

"Hi, Sherrie. What have you got?"

"Well, I'm impressed at your psychic abilities," she cooed.

"Never mind that," he ordered. "Let's have it."

"Keep your shirt on," Sherrie countered. "I know there's no way you could be anywhere close to Detroit by now. Besides, I booked your flight for seven o'clock. That way you'll have plenty of time to finish your business, and still get to Vegas by two o'clock in the morning, Vegas time."

"I'm sorry if I sounded a little short with you," Spence apologized.

"I understand. You can make it up to me when you get back," she teased, unable to resist flirting with Spence again. "By the way, I checked availability at Caesar's, just in case you changed your mind and wanted me to book you a room, and they have plenty of rooms still open."

"Thanks, Sherrie. I appreciate the info."

"Be careful driving, Spence," she cautioned.

"Don't worry. I'll be fine. Just call me if you need me." With that, Spence ended the call.

He turned on the radio, put in a Queen CD, and settled in for the long ride to Royal Oak. It had been a long time since Spence set foot in that building, but he still remembered how to get there. Finding it to be a great day for a drive, Spence suddenly found himself enjoying the solitude of the open road.

The trip didn't seem very long, he thought as he pulled into the parking lot of his father's old firm. Little had changed since he'd last seen it, aside from the usual landscaping alterations. Stepping inside, he approached the front receptionist, whom he perceived as a definite improvement over Gladys Pender, the lady who worked for his father for years. Gladys was one of those matronly types whose requests sounded more like orders barked out by an army sergeant. This receptionist, however, was very polite, petite, and pretty ... a winning combination, in his book of feminine attributes.

Spence asked to see Ed Harris, as the receptionist picked up the receiver and punched at the numbers. A man's voice came on the other end, obviously Mr. Harris, as she announced his arrival. She quickly hung up, and proceeded to escort him to an empty conference room, asking if he would like something to drink. He declined her invitation; seeing how he'd just finished a large soda he'd bought at the convenience store where he'd topped off his tank thirty minutes earlier.

The receptionist informed Spence that Mr. Harris would be a few minutes, then closed the door to the conference room and returned to the front desk. Spotting a Wall Street Journal on the table, he occupied the time scanning for recent events in the world of corporate enterprise. After about ten minutes the door to the conference room opened, and in stepped Ed Harris.

Ed was in his early fifties, a wiry build atop a six foot three inch frame. He had wavy hair, mostly on the sides and back since he was balding on top. He had a pleasant smile, and a boisterous voice, usually the life of the party, always telling jokes. However, when it came to business, he was a tough negotiator. He was always well prepared, often knowing the answers before he asked the questions.

Ed extended his hand, smiling as he welcomed Spence. Spence shook his hand, dispensing the same typical pleasantries. Ed offered him a tour of the recently renovated interior of the building. As they walked, Ed caught Spence up on the latest office news, disclosing details of who had left the firm, who had died, and who were still there from the old days. As they walked past his father's old office, Spence could see that Ed had already moved in, assuming the leadership role of the firm. That was what his father wanted, though, and Spence was glad not to be the successor.

Spence asked Ed if he'd received the insurance company settlement from the key person life insurance policy his father had. Ed told him he'd received it a couple of days ago, and had already taken the liberty of having his secretary prepare a check to give to Spence made out to the estate. Stepping into his office, he retrieved an envelope, handing it to Spence when he returned. Spence could almost hear the 'I believe that concludes our business' line in Ed's smile, sensing the man's eagerness to move on to other pressing matters. He took Ed's cue, thanked him for his time, and offered to let himself out.

Spence easily made his way back to the lobby and out the front door. Now that he was finally finished with the firm, he could concentrate on why he really made the drive today. Pulling out of the parking lot, he headed in the direction of the interstate. He still had to make his way south through the evening rush hour traffic if he was going to make the flight on time.

He took Woodward Avenue South to 696, going west around Southfield and Farmington Hills. He knew the traffic would be easier to navigate this way than if he went south on 75 to 94. 696 would become 96, and then 275 as Spence passed Livonia. Once past the 96/275 Interchange, traffic lessened considerably as most of the commuters were heading in the opposite direction from the way he was going. He'd take 275 to 94 and head east to the airport exit. He was making good time, so he wasn't worried about missing his flight.

Spence soon arrived at the airport, driving toward the long-term parking area. He parked, grabbed the bag he brought with him, and hurried toward the main terminal. Sherrie booked the flight through Northwest Airlines, with one stop in Salt Lake City, Utah before continuing on to Las Vegas. He checked in at the ticket counter but advised the clerk he had no luggage to check. Instead, he planned to carry his bag on the plane. The clerk instructed Spence which direction to go, writing the gate number on the envelope that held his ticket.

Spence headed in the direction of the gates, and soon found himself in a long line waiting to go through the security checkpoint. He shifted his weight from one foot to the other as he stood for what seemed an eternity while other passengers passed through the post 9/11 security counter measures. On more than one occasion, he found himself exhaling a rather large sigh, unable to contain the frustration at having to wait so long. Once he finally made it to the metal detector, Spence emptied the contents of his pockets into the little basket that security provided. Placing the basket and his bag onto the conveyor belt to run through the X-ray machine, he stepped through the metal detector. Suddenly a loud beep alerted security Spence had something metal on his person. The security guard motioned Spence over to the side and began sweeping his body with a wand. When he reached his shirt pocket, the wand beeped.

"What's that in your pocket?" asked the guard, causing Spence to freeze in terror. He'd forgotten about the pen.

"Oh, it's just an ink pen," Spence hurriedly assured the guard, carefully removing it from his shirt pocket, while pressing the off button at the same time. "I forgot I was carrying it."

"Okay, you can go," the guard told him, handing the pen back. Spence grabbed his belongings and moved quickly away from the checkpoint toward the gates.

As soon as he passed a restroom, he ducked inside, found an empty stall, and secured the door behind him. He proceeded to remove the clothes he'd packed in the bag and exchange them for what he was wearing. He put on the old jacket he brought with him and a baseball cap. Finally, he retrieved a larger black duffle bag from inside the brown one he was carrying, and placed all of his belongings into it. Then he opened the stall door, slung the bag over his shoulder, and exited the restroom.

Spence turned in the opposite direction from the gates, taking the down escalator to the baggage claim area. Once there he searched for a car rental counter, approached the counter clerk and asked to rent a mid-sized car. The lady smiled and asked to see his driver's license and a major credit card. He pulled two cards from his wallet and handed them to her. She punched in some information, swiped the credit card through a machine, and handed them back to Spence.

"Thank you, Mr. Miller," she said.

The documents from George worked, Spence thought with relief. He now had a second identity he could use, Walter Miller. The clerk handed him the keys, along with his paperwork and gave him directions to the rental car parking area. Leaving the terminal, he headed toward space number fifty-one where a black Chevy Lumina was waiting. Complete with different clothes and a new identity, Spence turned out of the airport parking garage and headed toward the interstate.

Looking at the directions again as he drove north toward Pontiac, he felt he'd have no problem locating the health club since he was somewhat familiar with that area. He remembered going to see the Lions play at the Silverdome many times when he was still a resident of Michigan. Spence had tried to get his father to go with him, but he always had something else more pressing to do. Actually, to be fair, his father really didn't understand the game that much, but was too proud to admit it, preferring to watch a golf tournament instead.

Spence arrived at the health club at exactly eight o'clock. Most of the regulars were already gone, so the parking lot was almost empty. He walked through the front door and headed directly toward the locker room. There was a counter to the left where a woman was busy writing in a notebook. As Spence passed the counter, she looked up and said, "Hey! Can I help you?" stopping him in his tracks, his mind frantically searching for some sort of story he could lay on her that would gain him access to the club. Then a thought crossed his mind. If it had been a long time since Paul Boyle had visited the club, maybe this lady wouldn't know what he looked like.

"I'm sorry," Spence said, a slight shrug lifting his shoulders. "I've been out of town for a few months and haven't been able to come here to work out."

"Let me see your card," the lady insisted skeptically.

"Well, here's the thing. I had it before I left town, but when I got back, I couldn't find it anywhere. Can I get a replacement?"

"Sure. No problem. I just need to see your I.D."

Spence paused then said, "I left it at home. I don't like leaving my wallet in the locker. But my locker number is 1115," he said, flashing a smile and showing her his key.

She checked the member records to verify the locker number. "Well, I can't issue you a new card without proper I.D., but since you know your locker, and have your key, I believe you're who you say you are, so I'll let you work out tonight," said the lady, smiling back at him.

He thanked her and walked quickly to the locker room before she changed her mind. He was glad he thought to pack a nylon jogging suit in the bag he had with him. Spence searched the lockers until he found number 1115. When he opened the locker, he found two rather large black duffle bags stuffed inside. Since there was no room to put his other bag in the locker, Spence pulled the two bags out and replaced them with the bag he brought. After all, he could afford to buy more clothes.

He grabbed his cell phone and quickly punched in the number to the health club. He recognized the voice that answered as the lady at the front counter. Spence disguised his voice, and made up a story about missing his house keys and wondering if he left them in the racquetball court. He asked if she'd be a dear and go check for him. Spence cracked open the door to the locker room to see if she would leave her post. She agreed to go check while he remained on the line. Spence watched her walk down the hallway to the left, disappearing from sight when she made another right turn. He seized the moment, hurrying across the lobby and out the door. He remained on the line until she returned to inform him that she didn't find any keys in the court. He politely thanked her and said he must have left them somewhere else. Then Spence ended the call and drove out of the parking lot toward the interstate.

Once back on the highway, Spence headed back toward the airport. He knew no one would be watching his car now. They would have someone waiting for him to arrive in Las Vegas, so he had a few hours before they realized he hadn't made the trip. It should be enough time to retrieve his car and make it back to the estate. He pressed the accelerator more firmly, pacing the car as fast as he could without drawing attention from any members of the local law enforcement.

Spence checked the rental car back in with the clerk working the parking area as part of their easy drop-off service. Then he walked quickly to the long-term parking lot, carrying the two black duffle bags, placed them in the trunk, and settled in his seat for the ride back to Traverse City. Suddenly a thought came to him. He had almost enough time to make it to Versailles before anyone knew he wasn't in Vegas. He could lay low there while everyone was looking for him in Michigan. By the time they figured out where he was, he would have whatever was in the bags securely stashed away where no one would find them.

He left the airport and headed down 275 in the direction of Toledo. He would take Interstate 75, drive south to Lexington, and continue from there to his home.

Traffic had thinned out considerably since early afternoon, and Spence was able to make good time. He arrived at his house and parked the car in the garage, preventing anyone passing by from knowing he was home. He entered the house very quietly carrying the bug detector George gave him. He swept the entire house, finding devices in the bedroom, living room, and kitchen. He carefully carried them out to the garage, opened the trunk of his car, and once the bags were removed, he placed the bugs in the trunk. Now he was free to move about the house free from detection, as long as he stayed away from the windows. He always left a living room lamp on whenever he was gone, so that, along with his small flashlight, would have to suffice for tonight. He didn't want to turn on other lights in the house and alert anyone who might drive by to see someone was home.

Spence carried the two black duffle bags into his bedroom, carefully unzipped the first one and opened it, shining his light into the bag. It was all he could do to remain calm as he stared down at the largest amount of cash he had ever seen. He quickly opened the other bag, revealing its contents to be the same. Two large bags crammed full of money, all neatly strapped in large denominations. Spence carefully removed each band of money, counting as he went. When he learned that the first bag contained five million dollars, he realized this must be half of the missing ten million and the other bag held the rest. Somehow, his father had obtained this money, and obviously, by the pains he had taken with it, had no plans to return it to Joey.

He placed the money back inside the bags and stowed them in his closet. He lay down on the bed, trying to get some rest, but his mind was racing from his discovery too much to sleep. He started planning his next move. He didn't want to leave the money here unprotected. However, if he took it with him, there was a risk Joey, or even Arlene and her agents, would find a reason to search his car and find it. His only alternative was to stash the money somewhere safe where only he knew where it was. Then he would have to play innocent, and not reveal he had found anything.

He wished his father were here now, more than ever. He wanted ... and needed ... some answers that only his father could give, and all but cursed the Judge under his breath for placing him in such a precarious situation. Finally, after what seemed like hours, sheer exhaustion overcame Spence, and he drifted off to sleep.

Chapter Eighteen

S pence awoke suddenly to his body's need to relieve itself from all of the soda he drank during the long drive home the night before. He could tell it was light outside, and quickly checked his watch. Eight o'clock.

He walked to the bathroom and after relieving himself, washed his hands and splashed cold water on his face to help clear the cobwebs from his brain. He'd developed a plan before falling asleep, and needed to be fully alert for it to work. Spence found bread that had not yet molded and strawberry jam in the refrigerator. He spread jam on a slice of bread and grabbed a bottle of water from the fridge. This would have to suffice for breakfast until he could unload the money at a safe place.

After gulping down his meal, Spence walked to the garage and retrieved the bugs from the trunk of his car, carefully placing them as best he could remember, then loaded the two bags into the trunk. He drove into Frankfort to one of the larger commercial banks where he was sure no one would recognize him. He took one of the bags with him into the bank, leaving the other one securely hidden in the trunk.

The lobby was very large and open, with only a view of

the teller windows upon first glance. A check-writing table used for filling out deposit slips, or endorsing checks before they approached the windows, sat in the middle of the lobby. As Spence walked in, one of tellers called to him asking if she could help him. He walked toward her and informed her he wanted to open a safe deposit box. She asked him to wait, motioning to a group of chairs to her left, while she summoned a customer service representative. He barely reached the waiting area when a young lady in her twenties came out of an office and walked toward him.

She was wearing a cobalt blue blouse and black pants. Her nametag read 'Amy.' She had short blond hair and large green eyes, and a very pretty smile. Spence believed most banks must screen employees not only by their abilities, but by their looks as well. At least his last several banking experiences were all with beautiful women.

"Hello, my name is Amy," she said needlessly. "How may I help you?"

"I need a safe deposit box."

"Certainly," she responded in a polite tone. "Do you have an account here?"

"No. Is that a problem?" Spence asked.

"Not at all. It's just that without an account there is a fee. We have many different types of accounts if you're interested," she continued.

He quickly cut her off, not having time to listen to a banking spiel. "Not today, thank you. Just the box."

Amy pulled out a chart showing the different sizes of safe deposit boxes and costs associated with each one. Spence asked to see one of the largest boxes available. Amy told him several of these were available since most people had no need for a box that size, and didn't want to pay the one hundred twenty-five dollar annual fee to have it.

She led Spence into the vault area and opened one of the bottom boxes. It appeared large enough to hold at least one of the bags of cash, so Spence told her it would do. She closed the box and led Spence back to her office, where she began punching keys on the computer. When she asked for his I.D., he handed the Walter Miller documents to her George had sent him. After a few minutes of typing, the printer behind Amy started humming as sheets of paper came streaming out.

She handed back his cards and placed the papers in front of him, pointing to where he needed to sign his name. He signed Walter Miller as if he'd been signing his name that way for years. Amy explained to Spence he could access his box anytime the bank was open, simply by walking in the vault with his key. She explained how many banks still require a bank employee with a guard key to carry one of the two keys needed to open a box, and the customer would sign in each time he entered the box. This bank, however, had opted for self-entry safe deposit boxes a few years ago, so there was no need for him to sign when he needed to access the box. Spence found this to be very well suited for his needs, and asked if other banks were using this method. Amy told him the only other bank in town that had these services was State Street Bank, just three blocks up the street.

Spence followed Amy back to the vault, where she showed him which box was his. He expressed his desire to go ahead and place important documents in the box at this time. Before politely excusing herself, she advised him once he was finished to simply lock the box and leave.

He waited until she was completely out of sight before opening the duffle bag. Quickly placing the contents of the bag into the box, he locked it securely, then walked out of the bank, waving to Amy as he passed her office. One down and one to go, he thought as he tossed the empty bag into the back seat. Next stop… State Street Bank.

Spence pulled into the parking lot, climbed out of the driver's seat, and retrieved the second bag from the trunk. He walked through the glass double doors of the bank into a lobby even larger than the one he'd just left. It seems, Spence thought, that every time a bank builds a new building, they always try to make it larger than the other ones in town. A competition to see whose will be the biggest, he supposed.

An information workstation was strategically located in the middle of this lobby, with another very attractive female placed behind it. She was wearing a navy blue business suit, with a nametag that read 'Carol.' She had dark hair and deep brown eyes. On his approach, she flashed a beautiful smile, asking if she could help him. He inquired about their safe deposit boxes, and she retrieved a sheet, much like Amy's, listing the different sizes and costs. He quickly scanned down the page until he recognized the description as being the same size as the one he'd just rented from Amy.

Pointing at the list, he indicated which one he was interested in. Carol told him several of those types of boxes were still available, giving him the same information Amy had—many people had no need for boxes that large. As before, his driver's license and social security card were needed. Once again, Walter Miller made an appearance.

Carol punched on her keyboard, and after a few seconds, produced some forms for Spence to sign. She asked if he was familiar with self-entry safe deposit boxes, and he nodded he was. Handing him the keys, she waved a hand in the direction of the vault. He was amazed at the efficiency of her being able to take care of him immediately, instead of being passed on to someone in an office. Banking had sure come a long way from the good old days.

He proceeded to the vault, located his box number, and inserted the key, turned it in the lock and pulled open the door. Pulling the large box out, he stuffed it with the contents of his duffle bag, looking around to make sure no one was watching. Once the bag was empty, he closed the lid, returned the box to its safe, and locked it securely in place. Then he removed his key and headed back to the lobby. He thanked Carol for her help as he walked by the information stand and out the front door. He paused for a minute to breathe a sigh of relief, then moved on to his car and got in. At least for now the money was safe, he told himself, but there were still many unanswered questions.

He turned the key in the ignition and headed off toward his office. Although Sherrie was excellent at her job, there may be a need for his appearance after being away for so long.

Spence arrived at the office around eleven o'clock. As he entered the back door, he jumped back quickly to avoid Sherrie wielding a Louisville slugger baseball bat.

"Hey! It's just me!" he shouted as the air swished around his head.

"What are you doing here?" Sherrie gasped, still clutching the bat.

"I was in the neighborhood and thought I'd check in," he answered smartly.

"Well, next time call first. I almost decked you."

Spence waited a few seconds while they both caught their breath before continuing the conversation. "So, how are things going here?"

"Just fine; we've only had a couple of inquiries lately, so I referred them to Bill, just as you asked me to do. Although, they were only traffic violations, I probably could have handled them for you myself. Then again, I guess you don't really need the income," Sherrie said, clasping her hand over her mouth when she realized listening devices were still planted in the office.

"Yeah, that insurance policy Dad left me was certainly a nice surprise," added Spence without missing a beat. That statement should be sufficient to keep anyone from suspecting he had found any large fortune. At least he hoped it would.

"How about some lunch?" he asked.

Sherrie quickly agreed, so they locked up, placed the 'will be back in one hour' sign in the front window, and left out the back way, securing the door behind them.

After some discussion in the car, they decided on Mexican for lunch. Spence drove to a quaint little joint he often took clients. Arriving a little before noon, they were well ahead of the regular lunch crowd.

Spence had the bug-detecting pen on, just in case, but decided not to tell Sherrie about the ten million dollars. It was for her safety as well as to avoid the many questions he was already asking himself. He opened the door for her, and she walked through with Spence in tow behind her. Although she was a very attractive lady, Spence mused at how he didn't look at Sherrie the same way as he looked at the waitresses, or Arlene, or even the mystery woman he knew only as Agnes Morehead.

The hostess led them to a small table, placed menus in front of them, smiled and turned back toward the front. Before they could open the menus, a gentleman appeared wearing black pants and a white polo shirt with the restaurant logo embroidered on the left breast. Just underneath was a name-tag that read 'Juan.' Juan spoke in broken English with a heavy Latino accent, as he asked for their orders. Spence ordered his usual fajita nachos, while Sherrie ordered the chimi-changa. Both decided on water for their beverage, as Spence was not in the mood for anything stronger.

As they waited for their food, Spence carefully controlled how much and what he told Sherrie as he filled her in on the latest information. He did tell her enough about his conversation with Arlene to evoke a concerned look on her face. She told him she was worried he may be getting in over his head, but he assured her that most of what the FBI had was conjecture without solid proof. Besides, he still wasn't sure whether his father was involved to the extent that Arlene believed. He confessed to Sherrie, though, that he felt he was at a dead end, and wasn't sure what his next move should be.

The food came quickly, and they began eating as they resumed their discussion.

"You know, that Agnes gal told you to look in the tapes for your answers, tapes as in plural, as in more than one. There must be something else recorded on at least one, if not more, of the tapes in your father's house," Sherrie reasoned.

"Yeah, I thought of that," Spence agreed. "But I just don't know where to start. I mean, how do I figure out which tapes have any hidden clues, and which ones do not? My father probably had close to one hundred different tapes. It will take weeks to go through all of them," he said, shaking his head in dismay.

"Maybe it's not as hard as you think," Sherrie replied, smiling as she sat up on the edge of her seat. "Maybe there is something on the original tape to lead you to the next one."

"I've looked at that tape so much that I know it backwards and forwards. There just aren't any more clues."

"Tell me exactly what he said," she insisted, moving a little closer to the table in her seat, her eyes widening in anticipation.

"Well," Spence began, "he started with the typical legal jargon that you see in every will. There certainly were no clues there. Then he mentioned Agnes and Key Largo, but I've already been to Key Largo and…"

"That's it!" Sherrie gasped, catching herself before she shouted and leaped from her seat. "The next tape must be Key Largo. Does he have a tape of that old movie?"

"Probably. He had a lot of old movies on tape."

"Did he mention anything else that might lead to another tape?"

"No. Those were the only words that really stuck out," Spence said. "Everything else was typical for a will."

"Well then, I'd say your next move should be to look for a copy of Key Largo in your father's collection," Sherrie concluded.

"You seem very intrigued by all of this, Sherrie. Would you like to join me in my little adventure?"

"I can't. My husband would kill me. Besides, it might get a bit hairy, what with mobsters in the picture. No, I'm content to sit on the sidelines as long as you keep me in the loop and allow me to practice my sleuthing over the phone, or here in Kentucky. Just make sure you play it safe yourself."

"I'm perfectly capable of handling myself," he said, throwing a few fake punches that caused them both to laugh.

Juan came back to ask if they would like dessert, but they declined his invitation, asking for the check instead. They lingered over their water with some polite casual conversation as Juan processed Spence's credit card for the meal. Before too long he returned to the table, handing Spence both copies of the tab, one for him to sign and one to keep. Spence quickly scrawled out his name on the slip, and stuffed the copy into his left front pants pocket. After that, he and Sherrie leisurely walked out of the restaurant to Spence's car.

They continued the small talk on the way back to the office. As they turned into the parking lot, she told him he should just go home now and rest before heading back to Michigan. He agreed it was a good idea, letting her out of the car and driving away.

He always enjoyed their conversations, and today was no exception. On the drive home, Spence thought about what Sherrie said about looking for a tape of Key Largo. He marveled at how he hadn't thought of something that seemed so simple to her. Then he did a rather poor Bogey imitation saying, "Here's looking at you, kid," as if to say thanks to Sherrie, glancing at himself in the rearview mirror as he tried to twitch his mouth like Bogart.

He sat quietly for the remainder of the ride home. He pulled the car into the garage, entered the house, and locked the door behind him. Inside, he poured himself a Jack and Coke, draining the glass in one long gulp. He sighed deeply as he moved on to the bedroom and began undressing. He decided to take a long bath in the Jacuzzi to relax his muscles, especially since the last couple of days' stress had tied him in knots. He poured another Jack and Coke, then eased himself into the tub. The water was very warm and inviting, as he turned on the jets, causing the water to roil. He lay back against the end of the tub and closed his eyes.

Too soon, the water in the tub began to cool down, so instead of running more hot water, Spence decided to get out and lay down for a nap. Since he was alone, he went to bed naked. There was no need to set the alarm, since he had no set schedule to follow. As soon as he rested, he would head back to Michigan, he decided. The hot bath and alcohol soon took effect, as Spence drifted off to sleep.

Spence woke to the sound of the doorbell, along with pounding fists against his front door. Bolting out of bed, he frantically grabbed his jeans, pulling them on hurrying to see who was trying to beat down his door. He finished zipping his fly closed, just before sliding back the deadbolt. A bright flashlight in his eyes greeted him as a gruff voice asked, "Are you Spencer Rawlings?"

"Who wants to know?" Spence shot back, obviously annoyed at whoever had roused him from a deep sleep.

"Lieutenant Jack Malloy with the Lexington Police," said the voice behind the light. "We'd like to ask you a few questions. May we come inside?" he asked, gesturing toward the door.

"What's this about, Jack?" Spence asked, somewhat puzzled.

"We'd rather discuss this inside where it's more private, if that's okay with you. Alternatively, we can take a ride downtown. We just thought you'd be more comfortable here," said Malloy, shrugging his shoulders as if he didn't care in the least where they talked.

"Okay," Spence relented, opening the door wider. "Come in."

He turned on the living room light so they could see, and motioned toward the sofa to make themselves comfortable and take a seat. Meanwhile Spence settled into one of the wingback chairs, angled beside the fireplace facing the sofa.

"This is my partner, Detective Cole," Malloy said. Then he began...

"Do you lease an office building located at 103 Vine Street in downtown Lexington?" he asked, exchanging glances from his notebook back to Spence.

"Yes, why do you ask?"

Malloy pressed on. "Do you know a Mrs. Sherrie Barbour?"

"You know she works for me, Jack. What's this all about?" Spence asked, growing more agitated.

"Well, I hate to be the bearer of bad news, but Sherrie is dead," Malloy stated, placing a stern emphasis on the word *dead*.

"How... how did it happen?" Spence asked as he suddenly grew dizzy.

"It looks like someone entered your office from the back door, because when we got there, the front door was locked. From what we've been able to ascertain, the person, or persons, surprised Mrs. Barbour, shooting her at point blank range in the back of her head with a .38 caliber revolver. Of course, we have ballistics checking the slug to make sure. After the suspect shot Mrs. Barbour, the perp tossed the office as if he was looking for something. Can you tell me where you were this afternoon between one and three?" Malloy asked in a rather accusing tone.

"I was here, alone," answered Spence, suddenly realizing he was probably their prime suspect. "Sherrie and I had lunch around eleven-thirty then I dropped her off at the office, and drove straight home. I wanted to rest before I returned to Michigan, so I had a hot bath, and afterward I laid down for a nap. I was asleep when you guys woke me up. Whoever did this must have been waiting outside somewhere, and followed Sherrie inside before she could lock the door."

Malloy and Cole exchanged raised eyebrows. "Michigan? Why were you going to Michigan?"

"My father passed away a few weeks ago, and I still have some things to take care of in settling his estate," answered Spence.

"So, you're telling us that no one can verify you were here this afternoon, and you were planning a trip out of state to Michigan. And you expect us to believe that?" Cole accused.

"Wait a minute," Spence objected, raising his voice. "You're not suggesting I had anything to do with Sherrie's murder!"

"Well, here's the thing," Malloy began, "Mrs. Barbour was found slumped over her desk, so whoever shot her didn't follow her in the door. There was no sign of forced entry, so if she locked the door when she went in, they had to have a key. Now we're not accusing you of anything, yet. Just don't leave town until we've cleared you. The CSI guys are processing the scene, so we'll know soon enough whose prints are there. You understand, we have to rule you out as a suspect, especially since you have access to the crime scene."

"I understand. But if you think I had anything to do with this, you're barking up the wrong tree."

The detectives stood up and began walking toward the

door. Then Malloy paused and turned back toward Spence.

"One more thing, Mr. Rawlings," he began. "Do you have any idea what you might have that is so important someone would come into your office, kill your secretary, and toss the place?"

"I have no idea," answered Spence.

"Thank you, Mr. Rawlings. We'll be in touch," said Cole.

They walked briskly out the front door and back to their unmarked cruiser. Spence noticed two other marked police cars with uniformed policemen inside were parked at the road in front of the house. He assumed they came for added backup, in case he was the murderer. Spence wanted to go straight to the office to look around, but knew he wouldn't be allowed access. The reality of Sherrie's death suddenly gripped him, as he closed the door and sank to the floor behind it. He felt very alone as his thoughts turned to when he was a child and how his mother would hold him in her arms and rock him when he was sick. How he longed for her comfort now. He began to cry, shaking all over, wondering who could've killed such an innocent person and why he was still alive.

Chapter Nineteen

Spence awoke early the next morning to the sound of the doorbell and fists pounding the door the same as the night before. He walked sleepily to the door and peered through the side window, immediately recognizing Lieutenant Malloy and Detective Cole. When he opened the door, Malloy stepped past him into the house, shoving a paper into Spence's hand.

"We have a warrant to search the premises," Malloy stated.

"And, we're going to need a DNA sample," said Cole, as he motioned for a forensic team member to join them. "It's all in the warrant," Cole explained, still smiling.

Spence read the warrant carefully, although he'd seen enough of them to know they were telling the truth. He compliantly opened his mouth, while the forensic officer took a cotton swab and ran it around his gums. That was usually sufficient for the DNA test.

The police tossed his house from top to bottom confiscating any items they thought were pertinent to their case. There was also a team searching his car, but they found nothing of value to them inside the Mercedes. When they finished

Malloy gave Spence the same speech about not leaving town again, then turned and was gone. They left Spence the mess to clean up after them.

He began putting things back in order when he suddenly reached for his cell phone and began punching in the office number, before realizing Sherrie wouldn't be there. He decided to get dressed and head into town for a newspaper and a bite to eat. He threw on a pair of jeans and an old sweatshirt, then hopped in the car and headed for Lexington. As he was driving, he decided to call George. George answered on the first ring, as if he were expecting the call.

"Hey man. How are you holding up?"

"How did you know it was me?"

"Caller ID. Besides, you've become a hot topic," George told him.

"What do you mean?" Spence asked cautiously.

"I mean, you're the number one suspect in your assistant's homicide. I hope you have a damn good attorney."

"Actually, I don't. Not yet. I was thinking about calling Josh Treadway. I watched him a few times in court. He's well known for winning the impossible cases."

"Well, you better call him quick," George urged. "The DA is hot on this one, and definitely has his sights on you."

"How do you know so much about this?" asked Spence.

"You know me," answered George. "Ear always to the ground."

"At least I can always count on you for reliable info."

"Just be careful," warned George. "And call Treadway."

He closed the phone and began searching through his briefcase. The cops had left it in such a mess, it was hard to know where anything was now. Treadway had observed Spence during an important case, and when it was over, he introduced himself and handed him a business card. He offered his services should Spence land a difficult case that would require assistance from someone well versed in criminal law. He remembered thinking how arrogant this man was, and yet couldn't help but admire his nerve, approaching him just after winning a major criminal case. Cockiness is often mistaken for confidence, and right now Spence could use some confidence. He remembered tossing the card in his briefcase on his way back to the office that day. After fishing around for a few minutes, he retrieved the card from the mass of other paper items that were now one large pile in the bottom of his briefcase, thanks to the Lexington police.

Spence dialed the number and waited as it began to ring. A young lady announced the firm name, then, offered her assistance. He asked to speak to Mr. Treadway, stating it was an urgent matter. She asked his name, then placed him on hold. It was a matter of seconds before a man's voice came on the line.

"Mr. Rawlings," Treadway began, "I was hoping you would call."

"Good news really travels fast," replied Spence. "Then I guess you know why I am calling."

"Certainly. Moreover, I must say I'm very flattered you called me. After all, I'm sure you know a lot of attorneys."

"Well, since you seem to know so much about my situation, do you think you can help me?"

"Of course. In fact, I cleared my calendar for the remainder of the day. If you can come by my office immediately, we can grab some lunch and dive right in."

"It just so happens, I'm only ten minutes from your office. I'll see you shortly," Spence finished, then close the phone. In less then ten minutes he parked outside Treadway's office.

Josh Treadway came to Lexington from Memphis, where he was a high-powered defense attorney. He became bored with the usual suspects Memphis had to offer, relocating to Lexington where he hoped to uncover many wealthy clients that a horse farm rich environment might produce. He believed where there was money, there was motive, and he was right. In the three short years since he hung out his shingle, he had become a living legend among the town's gossipmongers. He quickly gained a reputation of being a strong litigator, and penetrating examiner. He had the ability to make the most assured witness question his own identity.

Treadway tried every case in the press, giving him more exposure to the public and strengthening his position as the best defense attorney in Fayette County. He stood a mere five feet six inches tall, but carried himself as if he were seven feet. He had dark wavy hair and hazel eyes that seemed to sparkle, especially when he was working a jury. Treadway had a winning smile that revealed dimples on both cheeks. Only thirty-seven years old, he looked like an all-American boy next door, but could destroy a witness in five seconds.

Spence climbed out of his car and headed toward the entrance to Treadway's five-story testament to his greatness. The law offices of Josh Treadway had grown to a staff of ten lawyers, specializing in both criminal defense and tort actions. In his second year in Lexington, and after establishing his winning reputation in the area of criminal defense, he brought in a partner by the name of Alexandra Fontaine, or Alex for short. Alex specialized in tort actions, having gained a rather exalted reputation in Louisiana, especially in New Orleans, having successfully represented clients in class actions against large drug companies. Treadway had coaxed her away with the offer of partner and full control over all tort actions at Treadway Law Center. Together they made a rather formidable pair, each educating the other in their own expertise. Now they sometimes co-counseled on special cases. Adding the tort section to Treadway Law Center turned out to be a lucrative endeavor for Treadway. After all, he could earn the most money in the legal arena defending criminals with deep pockets, and suing large corporations that kept cash in reserves to make problems disappear. Alex was an extremely talented negotiator, often settling claims before they ever made it inside a courtroom.

Equally as impressive as the outside, the inside of Treadway Law Center was a vision of luxury and grandeur. The floor and chair railings in the front lobby and reception area were a beautiful mahogany, with soft leather sofas and chairs for clients to relax in while waiting. The receptionist served coffee and tea on a silver tray, with English biscuits to enjoy with your beverage. Treadway had a vast collection of

Thomas Kinkade art that adorned the walls of the lobby and offices.

Spence approached the receptionist, but before he could speak, she welcomed him by name and ushered him to the sofa to wait for Mr. Treadway. She apologized for not offering coffee or tea, but Mr. Treadway had informed her they'd be leaving immediately for lunch. Just then, Treadway stepped off the elevator and walked briskly toward Spence, extending his hand.

"Mr. Rawlings. Nice to see you again."

"Please, call me Spence," he replied, grasping his hand.

"I made lunch reservations for us at the club," Treadway stated, as he led Spence back out the front door to his Cadillac Escalade parked in its reserved space at the front left side of the building.

Since it was a short drive to the country club, Treadway used the time to give Spence a little history lesson regarding his background. Once inside the club, the maitre d' immediately recognized Treadway, and ushered them to a table in the back. It was Treadway's usual table he used when discussing a sensitive case with a client. He had another table, closer to the front, he reserved when he wanted society's elite to be aware of his presence.

The waiter arrived just after the maitre d' and began to give his spiel about the daily specials. Treadway informed the waiter he would have his usual working lunch, which meant a seven-ounce filet mignon, cooked medium rare and served with garlic mashed potatoes and asparagus. He also took the liberty of ordering the same for Spence, who by all indications was on another planet and not at the moment concerned with food. Besides, his stomach was churning and twisting in so many knots that it would be a struggle to keep anything down. After returning with some wine, the waiter left them alone. Now it was time to get down to business.

"Well, Spence," Treadway began, "it seems you've become the main topic of conversation this morning. Why don't you tell me your side of the story?"

"What story?" asked Spence.

"Well, for starters you can tell me about what happened to your assistant."

"Well, Mr. Treadway..." Treadway held up his hand stopping Spence.

"Since you prefer being called by your first name, I insist you do likewise and call me Josh. Besides, it will make us more of a team if we're on a first name basis. Please continue."

"Well, Josh," Spence began again, "Sherrie, my assistant, and I had lunch yesterday. I dropped her off at the office around one, and went straight home. I was exhausted from being up late the night before, so I decided to take a nap before heading back to Michigan to continue settling my late father's estate. Later that evening the police came to inform me that someone killed Sherrie at the office, and asked me a few questions. Then this morning they showed up again with a warrant to search my place. They also had a warrant for a sample of my DNA. It appears they're considering me their prime suspect. That's why I called you. I felt I should be prepared in case they arrest me," Spence finished.

"Umm ... interesting," Josh mused. "Rumor has it that you and your assistant were having an affair. Is that true?" he asked.

"No way!" Spence replied, almost shouting. "Sherrie was a good friend, and a good assistant, but that was as far as the relationship went. It was strictly professional."

"Well, if that's true, then why do you believe the police suspect you're the one who killed her?" Josh asked.

"That's just it. I have no idea. But based on their actions so far, I feel they suspect me," replied Spence.

"Okay. Let's say, for arguments sake, they decide to charge you with her murder. What evidence do you think they'll use against you?" queried Josh.

"Of course my fingerprints will be everywhere," Spence said. "But that's to be expected since it's my office. They told me there was no sign of forced entry, and I have a key. However, someone coming through the front door, locking it, killing Sherrie, and exiting through the back door, could explain that. I just don't see where the cops will have any concrete evidence against me," declared Spence.

"Yet you feel they're planning to arrest you," mused Josh.

"Based on their questions and attitude, it looks that way. I've represented too many clients who were questioned the same way, and wound up in an interrogation room at the station."

"Did they test you for gun powder residue?" asked Josh.

"Yes. They also searched my house and car for a gun, but I don't own one."

"Well, it appears to me they have no case against you, but you're right about them suspecting you. At least that's the talk going around town this morning. In fact, my sources tell me they're planning to make an arrest this afternoon. Why don't we go back to the office after we finish lunch, and I'll place a few calls to the local authorities. If they're planning to charge you, I will take you to surrender. That will avoid a big scene involving them leading you away in handcuffs, which might play bad in the press," Josh said, folding his hands in front of him.

Spence nodded his head in agreement, taking a bite of his filet. They finished the rest of their meal discussing trial strategies just in case the police charged Spence with Sherrie's murder. Once they finished, they left the club and headed back to Josh's office.

The office of Josh Treadway was located on the fifth floor of the Treadway Law Center. He had a large corner office, complete with the usual fine office furniture plus a wide screen TV, a treadmill, and a wet bar. The walls displayed his law degrees and several paintings Spence considered fine art.

Josh motioned for Spence to sit at the conference table while he made his way behind his desk. As he sat down, Josh picked up the phone and punched in a number. After a brief pause, he asked for Jill Henderson. Ms. Henderson was a detective in the special victims unit, and had many good contacts in all departments. She had been there long enough to garner the trust of almost every officer in the precinct, allowing her to obtain information on almost everything that went on inside those walls.

Josh first met her when she testified against one of his clients in a rape case. After a couple of dinners, they decided to remain friends, and thus Jill became an earpiece for Josh.

Spence couldn't hear the conversation, as Josh spoke in low tones. After about a minute, he quickly hung up, letting out a loud whistle.

"What's wrong?" asked Spence, sensing trouble from Josh's gaze.

"You're definitely their number one suspect," Josh said. "In fact, they're on their way to your house to arrest you as we speak."

"They still don't have any hard evidence, right?"

"I know I've already asked you this once. Were you and Mrs. Barbour romantically involved?"

Spence stood staring at Josh in disbelief. "I told you there was never anything sexual between us," he said, raising his voice.

"Well then, you'd better sit down," cautioned Josh. "Because the DNA they took from you matched the DNA of semen found in Mrs. Barbour. That, along with rumors of an affair, is pretty damning evidence. I'm afraid we're in for a fight," Josh said.

Spence dropped his gaze to the floor as he wrestled with this new piece of information. He couldn't understand how his DNA could possibly have been a match with semen left inside Sherrie. They'd never kissed, let alone had sex. He just shook his head, trying to make some sense of it all. Finally, after a few minutes, Spence mustered enough courage to speak.

"I swear to you, Josh, we never had sex," Spence insisted.

"I believe you, but it's the jury we've got to convince," Josh reminded him.

"I'm being framed. But I don't know by whom or why."

"Well, we'd better figure that out soon, because proving that may be our only way to win this one. In the meantime, you're going to have to turn yourself in. I'll arrange for bail, and have you out as soon as possible. Then we can plan our trial strategy, and find out who is behind this."

They left the office together, climbing into Josh's vehicle for the ride to the police station. Josh had already told Jill to spread the word that Spence would turn himself in soon, so there was no need for police theatrics.

Spence tried to calm his nerves, as he racked his brain for an answer. He'd been with many clients on this same ride, but never before as the defendant. It felt unnatural, and for the first time in years, he wished he were in Michigan.

Chapter Twenty

Josh led Spence into the police station, then waited while they processed him through booking. Once they brought him to an interrogation room, Josh rejoined them for questioning. Detectives Malloy and Cole were present, along with Tom Fiedler, the District Attorney. Normally one of Tom's assistants handled the prosecution for the state, but this case would be too high profile for Tom to pass up the spotlight, especially when he felt the evidence was so compelling.

"We're ready to begin," Malloy said, as he pressed a button on the recorder on the table in front of Spence. "Okay," he began, "why don't you tell us about your relationship with Sherrie Barbour, Mr. Rawlings."

Josh leaned over and whispered in Spence's ear. Then Spence sat upright and replied, "Mrs. Barbour was my assistant. Our relationship was strictly of a professional nature."

"Come on," Cole snapped back. "We found your semen inside Mrs. Barbour. How do you explain that?"

Again, Josh whispered into Spence's ear before he answered.

"I don't know," replied Spence. "Maybe you fabricated it."

Cole slammed his hand down hard on the table and walked to the back of the room. Meanwhile Malloy eased closer to Spence, obviously taking the role of 'good cop.'

"Look Mr. Rawlings," he began. "We're just trying to make sense of this. We know you and Mrs. Barbour were having an affair. What happened? Did she threaten to break it off, or tell her husband about the two of you, or was she black mailing you by threatening to go public and create a scandal? I know I'd be very upset if that happened to me. I can understand why you'd want to keep her quiet," Malloy paused, allowing the words to sink in.

"We were *not* having an affair," insisted Spence.

"Spence," Tom spoke up, "I'll make you a deal. Manslaughter one, ten to twenty-five. If you take this to trial, you're looking at life, or possibly the death penalty."

Josh whispered in Spence's ear again. Then Spence jerked away from him and said, "No deal!"

"Josh, talk some sense into your client," Tom ordered.

"I'm sorry, Tom, but Mr. Rawlings is adamant about his innocence. It appears we're going to trial."

After that, they led Spence away to a holding cell. Once there, they allowed Josh to meet with him as his counsel.

"Spence," Josh began, "I have to tell you this looks pretty bad for you. Are you sure you don't want to take the plea?"

"I told you I was innocent, and you said you believed me," hissed Spence.

"I do believe you, but is it worth risking your life?"

"I just can't admit to doing something I didn't do," said Spence.

"Okay. Then help me figure out how we're going to get you out of this mess."

Spence felt he had no choice but to tell Josh about his father's possible involvement with the VanWarners, and the missing ten million dollars. Spence decided not to tell Josh he had actually found the money. For now, it was probably better if everyone believed it was still missing. Josh listened intently, scribbling notes the entire time. When Spence finished, Josh sat back in his chair, folded his hands in front of him, and let out a big sigh.

"So you think this Joey character may have something to do with this?" Josh inquired. "If that's the case, how do we link him to someone on the inside of the police department that had access to the DNA test?"

"I don't know," answered Spence, "But I think it's where we should start. Do you think your friend inside the department might have some information about this?"

"Maybe," said Josh, rubbing his chin thoughtfully. "I'll ask her over to my place for dinner. She can talk more openly there. In the meantime, I'll get your bail hearing pushed up so we can get you out of here tonight. Since this is your first offense, I'm hoping the judge won't set it too high," he finished, shaking Spence's hand as he turned to leave the conference room.

They moved the bail hearing up to four o'clock just as Josh hoped.

"Mr. Rawlings," the judge began, "you're charged with murder in the first degree. How do you plead?"

"Not guilty, your honor," Spence stated emphatically, standing behind the defense table.

"Mr. Fiedler, what does the prosecution recommend for bail?"

"Your honor, the defendant brutally murdered his lover in cold blood by shooting her in the back of the head while she was working in his office," Tom stated. "We believe Mr. Rawlings recently inherited a large sum of money from his deceased father's estate, making it easier for him to travel. Given these facts, we consider the defendant to be a high flight risk, and ask he be remanded without bail until trial."

The judge turned to look at Josh. "Care to respond, Mr. Treadway?"

"Your honor," Josh entreated, "Mr. Rawlings is a well-respected member of this community who has been unjustly accused of a crime he did not commit. He's never been guilty of any crime, not even a parking ticket. Considering this is his first alleged offense, and given his contributions to the community, we respectfully request he be released on his own recognizance."

"Nice try, counselor," snapped the judge. "Bail is set at one million dollars," he concluded, pounding his gavel.

Spence had already given his account information to Josh to arrange for bail. The officer led him back to the holding cell, while Josh contacted the bank. Within twenty minutes, he walked out of the police station with Josh, into a throng of reporters who were throwing questions at him. Even so, he remained silent as Josh paused for a brief moment in front of the cameras.

"My client is innocent," shouted Josh. "He is the victim of police malfeasance in an attempt to railroad my client while the real murderer is free to roam the streets in search of his next victim. My client is grieved by the death of his legal assistant, Mrs. Barbour, and has vowed to help me fight to uncover the true identity of the perpetrator who committed this horrible act of atrocity against his friend and co-worker."

With that, Josh turned away from the reporters and ushered Spence through the crowd to his vehicle. They returned to Josh's office where they began mapping out a strategy for Spence's defense.

"Why the big speech to the reporters?" Spence asked.

"Just hoping to influence the potential jury pool," answered Josh. "A case like this where the evidence seems to be overwhelming is best tried in the press. Now, let's focus on the task at hand," he continued, "which is uncovering sufficient evidence to get you acquitted."

"Where do you suggest we start?" asked Spence.

"I'm going to have my investigators do a little snooping around the VanWarner camp, see if any of their people can be placed near the scene of the crime yesterday. I suggest you contact your FBI friend to see if there is any way she can help."

Suddenly Spence realized he hadn't thought about Arlene in all of this. If the bugging devices in the office were the FBI's, maybe they'd have a recording of what actually went down during Sherrie's murder. If so, they may have the voice, and possibly the identity of the killer.

Spence decided not to share this speculation with Josh, but felt it best he deal with Arlene himself for the time being. He hoped she'd be cooperative, considering what was at stake, especially if she really did have feelings for him.

He retrieved his briefcase from Josh's office and left the building on his way back home. He had left the bug detecting pen, his cell phone, and other personal effects inside his briefcase, secured away inside the office, so the police wouldn't be nosing around them when he turned himself in. He felt relieved he'd fooled the detectives into thinking the pen George had provided was simply that, an ink pen, when they first searched his house. Now he needed to get back home and call Arlene.

The judge ordered Spence not to leave the county, so a trip to Michigan was out of the question, at least for now. Perhaps he could get Arlene to come to Lexington.

Spence made sure he drove the speed limit all the way to his house. He didn't want to give the police any reason to arrest him again. Once he returned home, he parked inside the garage and entered the house, making sure he turned the pen back on. The blinking red light assured him someone some-where was still listening. He almost felt glad someone was monitoring him so closely.

He opened the cell phone and punched in a series of numbers. After a couple of seconds, a voice came on the line, but it was a recording of Arlene's voice. He had received her voice mail, so he decided to leave her a message to call him. Just as he was beginning to say his number, the doorbell rang. He closed the phone, deciding he could call back later, and walked toward the front door to see who was there. The bell rang once again before he reached the foyer. Easing back the curtain on the front window just enough to see who was standing on his doorstep, he was amazed, and glad, to see Arlene standing there, realizing he still had feelings for her.

He tugged the door open, as Arlene smiled back at him.

"Hello stranger," she began. "I heard you were in trouble."

"With a capital 'T'," he joked. "But I'm glad you're here."

"I came as soon as I heard about it on the news," she said, as Spence ushered her inside and led her to the sofa.

Sitting beside her, Spence again said, "I'm sure glad you're here."

"I'm here to help. Just say the word."

"I was hoping in your zeal to link my father to Joey you had planted some sort of listening devices in my office that would have recorded Sherrie's murder, and hopefully, reveal the identity of the killer," Spence remarked earnestly, but Arlene began shaking her head.

"I'm sorry Spence, but I'm not aware of any bugs. I came to offer my help as a concerned friend. We know you found the ten million dollars. Just give me the money and we can make all of this go away."

"I don't know what you're talking about," insisted Spence caustically.

"Look! This is no time to play games, Spence," Arlene argued. "Your life is on the line here! I'm just trying to help."

"What makes you think I have the money?" he asked in a cautious tone.

"Well, we assumed since you went to such great lengths to conceal your whereabouts for the last two days, you must have stumbled onto the money and needed time to find the right hiding place for it. Am I right?" she asked.

"Suppose I have the money," began Spence, "You're saying that all I have to do is hand it over to you, and you can guarantee I'll walk away from this a free man?"

"You have our word," said Arlene, nodding in agreement.

"I thought you were looking for a way to tie this money to Joey. I thought my father was supposed to have some kind of evidence that would help you put Joey away. Why all of a sudden is the money the main motivator?"

"Because we feel certain the money will eventually lead us to not only Joey, but the Gregorio family in Chicago as well. But we need the money to put the final pieces in place."

Spence knew the money was his ace in the hole, but something just didn't feel right about this, so he decided to save it for now.

"Well, I just don't have it," Spence lied. "I wish I did, because it would really come in handy now."

"Spence, don't lie to me," Arlene pleaded. "We know you have it..."

He suddenly cut her off. "How do you know I have it!" he barked, staring intently into her eyes.

"Look, you know I can't reveal confidential sources. Just trust me on this. We know," she claimed, returning his fixed gaze.

"And just how did you plan to make all of this go away?"

"Trust me; you don't want to know the details. Let's just say we have many good friends in high places," she answered, smiling knowingly.

"I'm sorry, Arlene, but I can't help you," Spence told her.

"You mean you won't help me," she hissed, "Fine! It's your neck. Just don't say I didn't offer to help." With that, Arlene bolted from the sofa and raced for the front door.

Spence stood for a moment, unable to speak, and then blurted out the first thing that came to mind. "So that's it! You're just going to leave like that? What happened to being here for me?"

"I'm sorry, Spence," she replied. "But I refuse to support anyone who has the ability but refuses to help himself." Then she slammed the front door behind her and with quick strides hurried to her car.

He could tell by the way she gunned the motor, spinning her tires in the process, that Arlene was very upset. The question was whether she was actually upset for him, or because she failed to coax him into handing her ten million dollars. He needed a drink now more than ever, so he mixed a Jack and Coke and collapsed in his easy chair in front of the television. Before turning it on, he decided to call Josh and inform him of Arlene's visit. They certainly weren't going to get any help from the feds.

Josh had given Spence his cell phone number in case he needed to get in touch with him any time without having to wade through the office barrage of administrative assistants and endless voice mail. He punched in the numbers and sat back in his chair, bracing for the expected defeat in Josh's voice when Spence told him the bad news.

"Josh Treadway."

"Josh, its Spence. I'm afraid I have some bad news. It looks like the FBI can't help after all. I just spoke with Arlene, and she said they didn't bug my office, so they don't have Sherrie's murder on tape," Spence said in a rush, letting out a huge sigh at the end.

Josh was silent for what seemed an eternity, as Spence prepared for the pep talk that a good defense attorney always gives his client immediately following such bad news. "Spence, I don't have to tell you how unfortunate this is," he began, while Spence thought, 'here it comes.' "But I have my investigators in the field as we speak, and I feel confident they will uncover the truth that will lead to your acquittal," he finished, trying to hide the disappointment in his voice.

Spence had been there too many times in the same place Josh was now, so he decided to let Josh off the hook. "It's okay. I know you're trying your best. Obviously whoever orchestrated this charade was professional enough to cover all the bases, along with their tracks, but I'm not giving up."

"Good," replied Josh, obviously relieved to have a client who knew the ropes. "I'll let you know what my team finds." With that, Josh ended the call.

Slowly, Spence closed the cell phone and reached for the remote since there was nothing more he could do at this point. As he turned on the television and began surfing the channels, he was suddenly overwhelmed with a heavy feeling of hopelessness. He downed his drink and quickly mixed another. After he finished the can of Coke, Spence began drinking straight from the bottle. Eventually he succumbed under the weight of alcohol and depression, drifting off to sleep, the remote still clutched in his hand.

He slept through the night and late into the next morning

before he awoke to the sound of his cell phone ringing. Still groggy from the self-inflicted mugging the night before, his first thought was that Sherrie was phoning from the office before realizing he'd never again hear her voice. Fighting back tears, he answered the call.

"Hello," Spence rasped into the phone.

"Spence? Are you okay?" asked Josh.

"Yeah," Spence yawned, "I'm fine. Just a little hung over."

"Listen, Spence," Josh warned. "I understand you're going through hell right now, but you've got to stay off the booze. I need all of your faculties on full alert if we're going to prove your innocence. I just got the okay from the prosecutor's office to examine the crime scene. I was hoping you could meet me there, but from the way you sound, I'd better come get you."

"Fine," Spence mumbled, closing the phone without letting Josh finish his train of thought.

He knew Josh would be ringing his doorbell soon, because he would have done the same thing for a client. Reluctantly climbing out of the easy chair, he stumbled to the shower, hoping the water would wash away the cobwebs from the night before. Spence grabbed a pair of jeans and a sweatshirt from the closet, then, proceeded to get dressed. His head was about to explode, so he grabbed a few aspirin and washed them down with a little 'hair of the dog.'

He really didn't expect to find anything helpful at the office, especially considering the CSI folks probably went over the entire building with a fine-tooth comb. Nevertheless, he recalled a few cases where he was able to find evidence the police overlooked, evidence which helped him establish reasonable doubt in the minds of the jurors, and earned him a couple of acquittals. Besides, he didn't have anything better to do.

Josh rang the doorbell almost on cue, as Spence was already reaching for the knob. They walked back to Josh's vehicle and climbed in, heading for Vine Street. As they pulled into the back parking lot, Spence could see the familiar yellow tape indicating a crime scene. Josh asked him if he was okay, to which Spence merely nodded his head. He had wanted to come here the night Sherrie died, but now found it difficult to walk the few steps necessary to enter the office, afraid of what awaited him just behind the door.

Josh grabbed Spence by the arm, as if to steady him. Then he took the key from Spence's right hand and inserted it into the lock. With a quick turn, the door opened and the two men stepped inside.

The first thing they noticed was a sea of papers strewn about everywhere. Then as they proceeded toward the front, Spence stopped in his tracks for fear of what lie ahead. Josh waited while Spence composed himself, then, assisted Spence toward the front office. The sea of papers continued into the front as well. Then as they reached Sherrie's desk, they saw it. A huge pool of crimson blood remained on top of Sherrie's desk, just as the crime scene investigators had left it. Spence could tell by the amount of blood that the shot must have ruptured a major artery in the head. Death was surely instantaneous. It reminded him of crime scene photos he had viewed many times over the years, yet this all seemed so surreal. Suddenly feeling sick to his stomach, he raced out the back door, vomiting onto a shrub.

Josh walked toward the back of the office, but Spence returned inside before he reached the door. Assuring Josh he was okay, he began looking around the office, not sure yet exactly what he was looking for. Josh started looking at files that were on top of the desks, just in case the suspect spared them from the piles of papers on the floor for some specific reason. Spence remembered Arlene's denial of bugging the office, so he started looking immediately for the bugs he'd found before. Since whoever planted them hid them well, he knew the police probably wouldn't have located them. Luckily, he brought the pen with him, so he quickly turned it on, smiling as it began blinking.

He located the two bugs in the desk lamps. Next, he would have to maneuver around Sherrie's blood to retrieve the one from her computer. He cringed as some of Sherrie's blood smeared onto his palms, but the spatter had covered her computer, and there was no other way to retrieve the bug planted there. The one he found inside her computer before was still there. He placed the bugs in his front pants pocket. No one had removed the bugs, yet why had Arlene denied they were there? After he was satisfied they'd find no help there, Josh called an end to their search. They drove back to Spence's house in silence. Spence remained quiet about finding the bugs, as Josh dropped him off. It was time to call George.

Chapter Twenty-One

George had a cell phone completely secure and untraceable by anyone. He'd given Spence the number just in case he was ever in trouble and needed his help without alerting anyone who may be monitoring both Spence's and the lab's phone calls. Spence remembered calling George paranoid at the time, but now was certainly glad George had been so cautious. When his phone began to vibrate, alerting him to a call, George quickly retreated to a small office with no windows and fished the phone from beneath his lab coat.

"Yes," George said into the phone, not identifying himself.

"The porridge is too hot," whispered Spence.

"Try baby bear's," answered George, quickly ending the call.

He'd developed this code for them to use in case either needed to meet with the other in a secure environment. Knowing the feds were probably still watching him, Spence didn't want to lead them straight to George. George had established a meeting place where they could go, and talk in private. The trick would be eluding anyone who might be following before reaching the rendezvous point. No one probably was watching George, as the friendship between he and Spence was a secret. Spence, on the other hand, would need a couple of disguises and some crafty moves to lose the eyes that were upon him.

Not long after darkness fell, Spence opened the garage and ventured out onto the main road headed toward Lexington. He stopped at a local bar along the way, where he knew the owner quite well. A quick nod to the bartender and Spence disappeared into the back room. Twenty minutes later, two men walked out the back door into the alley behind the bar and climbed into a white Camaro. Ten minutes later, someone wearing Spence's clothes walked out the front door and climbed into Spence's car, drove back to Spence's house and parked in the garage. Then he got out and went inside, being careful not to turn on the light. After about five minutes, the television illuminated the den, as a man sat watching a movie and drinking a Jack and Coke.

The Camaro drove out of town, and when it was apparent no one was following, turned around and headed back into town. It stopped in front of a movie theater, one man got out, and the Camaro drove away. The man purchased a ticket for the movie that had started ten minutes before, and sat down beside a dark figure in the back of the theater.

"Good to see you, Goldilocks," whispered George.

"Funny," Spence whispered back, handing the envelope containing the bugs to George. "Check these out for me."

"Am I looking for anything in particular?"

"Everything," he whispered low, then remained quiet for the rest of the movie.

When the movie finished, George got up and left as the credits were rolling. Spence remained seated until the theater was empty. Heading out the side exit, he climbed into the waiting Camaro and headed back to the bar. Once back at the bar, Spence crashed on a cot in the back room. Ten minutes before closing, he walked out the front door and climbed into his car, which he found conveniently returned to the space he'd parked in earlier.

Returning home, he parked the car in the garage, and entered the house, glancing through the living room window to see the undercover surveillance car parked in place across the street. He mixed a Jack and Coke and settled into his easy chair, reaching for the remote. After surfing the channels for five minutes, he settled on an old Cary Grant movie, while he mixed another drink. An hour later, he was asleep, while Cary was still going strong.

Spence slept in the next morning hoping to make up for the lost sleep the past few nights. It was ten-thirty before he roused from his slumber and groped his way to the bathroom, still recalling his last dream about a beautiful woman leading him through a dark tunnel. He never was a believer in psychic phenomenon, so he dismissed her as an apparition brought on by too much alcohol and too little sleep. He showered, dressed, and headed to the kitchen to fix a pot of coffee. Grabbing a bagel from the freezer, he toasted it, placed it on a small plate when it popped up, poured a cup of coffee, and took it all to the den to catch up on the latest news.

There was no mention of his case, since the news channels opted to report on stories that were more current. Besides, Lexington was not New York, and he certainly wasn't famous enough to warrant a CNN news crew. He watched as the pre-season baseball scores appeared, wondering how George was making out with the bugs. At this point, there was nothing to do but sit and wait.

Deciding it was time to check in with Josh to see if he had uncovered any new evidence, he picked up his cell phone. Before he could punch in the number, his phone rang. He recognized Josh's number, pressing the send button to answer the call.

"Spence, its Josh. I just found out the trial date is set for six weeks from now. That doesn't give us a lot of time, so we need to start working on your defense."

"Six weeks!" exclaimed Spence. "Boy, they sure are in a hurry on this one, aren't they?"

"Tom's pushing this really hard," Josh told him. "It seems this may be his ticket to the Governor's mansion."

"Well, I hope for my sake he's unsuccessful."

"Are you able to come to the office now?"

"Sure. I've got nothing better to do."

"Good. We can grab some lunch and start planning our strategy. See you in a few," said Josh, ending the call.

Spence tossed the half-eaten bagel in the trash, grabbed his jacket, and headed to the garage. He noticed the surveillance car was still parked in the same spot as last night, as he pulled onto the street and headed toward Lexington. He eyed his rear view mirror as the unmarked police car fell in behind him a few yards back. Our tax dollars at work, he thought to himself, chuckling under his breath.

Josh met Spence at the front door of the office building, ushering him to his car. They climbed in and drove to the club, where once again Josh demanded his table in the back. He ordered the usual for them, making small talk until the food arrived. Once the waiter brought their meal, he asked they not be disturbed until he signaled them. It was now time to get down to business.

"Okay, Spence," Josh began, "here's what we're up against. I've had a chance to review the discovery from the prosecutor's office, and quite frankly, I'm a little worried."

"Why's that?" asked Spence.

"Well, as you are aware, the positive DNA test that matches you to the semen found inside Mrs. Barbour is very damaging. So far, I haven't been able to find any trace of evidence tampering, and I've called in most of my markers on this one. My investigators have drawn a blank with the Van-Warner angle, and unless something big breaks soon, stick a fork in us, cause we're done," Josh exclaimed, sighing as he shrugged his shoulders.

"What about witnesses?" Spence asked. "Were there not any witnesses near the office at the time of the murder?"

"The only people we could find who saw anything around that time only remember seeing you leaving for lunch with her. No one seems to have seen you return. Look, I believe you're innocent, but maybe you should reconsider the deal. At least you'd still be alive and eligible for parole after a few years. Don't get me wrong, but..."

Folding his arms in defiance, Spence cut him off. "Look! I'm only going to say this one more time! I was *not* having an affair with Sherrie, and I certainly did not kill her. No deal! End of story."

"Then tell me this," Josh queried, "how you would build this case if you were in my position?"

He blew out a pent-up breath. "Well, I guess all we have now are character witnesses that can at least make me look like a human being instead of a cold-blooded killer. Besides that, I'm as much at a loss as you. Is there any way we can compel the FBI to testify about the bugs and what they heard?"

"You already know the answer to that," said Josh matter-of-factly. "They would simply deny there ever were any listening devices, and without proof, you'd look like a desperate man trying to pull a defense out of thin air. A jury would see right through that."

"You're right," Spence said. "I just don't understand why I'm being framed for this."

Although he was beginning to see the picture, he was afraid to divulge too much information to Josh, at least until he was certain he could fully trust him. He could tell Josh was growing weary from the conversation. Spence suddenly realized that Josh had never tried a case from this weak of a position, instead convincing clients to take a plea bargain when the odds were against them. He could sense the fear in Josh's face, as he struggled with the realization that he might actually lose a case. He couldn't help but feel sorry for the man, but sometimes humility made a man stronger.

"Okay," Josh said, breaking the silence. "I'll keep my people digging on this end. Let me know if the FBI decides to have a change of heart, or if you can come up with a plausible defense."

"Don't worry," Spence said, taking hold of his shoulder. "We're going to be okay. I can just feel it."

The problem was he didn't feel it at all. He felt the same despair that Josh was feeling, but had to remain as positive as he could. He had to maintain his focus, and stay sharp, if he was going to be able to piece this puzzle together. There was still hope that George would be able to uncover something they could use. As a last resort, he could always give Arlene the ten million to secure his freedom. Spence didn't trust Arlene, though, so he thought it best to keep the money a secret for now.

During the drive back to his house from Treadway Law Center, Spence kept thinking about the other tapes at his father's estate, and what they may lead to. The police had him on such a short leash, he was afraid to gamble on taking a trip across state lines.

He immediately noticed the unmarked patrol car parked across the street from his house as he pulled into his driveway. Pulling into the garage, he entered the house, carrying his briefcase. Once inside, he turned on the bug-detecting pen, staring as it blinked its warning in bright red. He knew someone was listening, but since Arlene told him the FBI wasn't the culprit, who could it be? Then again, Arlene was probably lying. In fact, she just might have the necessary evidence on tape that would clear him of Sherrie's murder. Perhaps, Spence thought, Arlene felt she could easily get lost with ten million dollars, and decided to execute her own little covert operation of helping him out in exchange for the money.

Suddenly Spence realized his mind was wandering off in all directions, so he reminded himself that he needed to stay focused. He almost jumped when his cell phone began to vibrate.

"Hello," Spence whispered into the phone.

"Baby bear has a new bowl of porridge," said a voice.

"Is it just right?" asked Spence.

"Just right," replied the voice on the other end.

Spence hung up the phone and grabbed his jacket, heading out the garage, with the surveillance unit in pursuit. They followed him to the same bar, where they parked a few cars away to conceal their presence. He knew they were there, so he took his time walking into the bar. He walked up to the bar and ordered a beer, then walked toward the back where the restrooms were. The bartender kept serving the other patrons, ignoring the request for a beer. Two men exited the bar in the back alley and climbed into a Camaro. Both had on hats and sunglasses to hide their faces, but no one was watching. They drove away, heading west out of town.

Once the Camaro drove ten miles out of town and no one appeared to be following them, it turned around and headed back toward Lexington. Once again, the car stopped in front of a movie theater. This time the driver got out and walked up to the cashier. He ordered a ticket, paid the cashier, and returned to the vehicle. The passenger then got out and entered the building. He entered the theater room where the movie had already begun, and made his way to the back row. He sat down beside a figure he recognized and settled back in the seat.

"Good to see you're still in one piece, Goldilocks," said George.

"Can't we use some other names?" asked Spence.

"Maybe next time. I examined the things you gave me last time. Standard Government Issue, complete with serial numbers. I was able to hack into their database and confirm they were indeed FBI items. Apparently they're the ones listening in on you," finished George.

Spence sat silent for a moment. "You're absolutely sure about this?"

"Positive," George whispered, handing an envelope to Spence. "It's all in there."

They sat in silence for the remainder of the movie. Once the movie was over, they left separately, just as before. Spence returned to the Camaro, where it left the theater and traveled outside of town again. Then it circled back and found its way to the bar. The passenger got out and walked back in the bar while the Camaro drove away. As Spence walked toward the bar from the back, the bartender opened a beer and placed it beside two other empties on the bar. Spence sat down and began sipping the beer. He noticed a suit was sitting in a corner booth, so he motioned for the bartender and leaned across the bar.

"How long?" Spence mumbled, motioning to the booth.

"Just came in before you," he replied. "I already had the empties out, so he don't suspect a thing." Spence sat back on the stool, and continued to nurse his beer.

After another twenty minutes, he stood up, tossed a few dollars on the bar, and walked out. As he climbed into his car, Spence noticed the suit heading straight for the unmarked patrol car. He shook his head, marveling at the poor surveillance work. He turned the ignition and drove out of the parking lot toward his house. Once there, he parked in the garage again and entered the house through the garage entrance. He walked to the living room in time to see the unmarked car stop in its former place. It became obvious to Spence that the police did not care if he knew they were following him. They were probably hoping he'd let the pressure get to him, causing him to make a mistake they were sure to witness. However, considering his life was on the line, Spence did not intend to tip his hand.

Removing the envelope from inside his jacket, he sat down to review its contents. George had returned the bugs along with some hand written papers. He read the information, which detailed the individual serial numbers for each bug, along with the date shipped to the FBI. George was right. These were government issued. So why did Arlene lie to him? What could she hope to gain by saying the FBI were not listening. She could have revealed the truth and still demanded the money in return for tapes confirming his innocence. Suddenly his cell phone began to vibrate.

"Spence, I'm sorry I lost my temper with you." It was Arlene. "I decided to give you one last chance to give me the money so I can help you get out of this mess."

"So you did have my office bugged," accused Spence.

"No. I told you there were no bugs," she replied.

"Then you'll have to tell me how you were planning to fix things in my favor if you want me to cooperate."

"Fine!" she said, "We have access to the DNA evidence. That's their whole case, and we can make it disappear. Now will you tell me where the money is so I can help you?"

"I'm sorry, Arlene, but I already told you I don't know anything about any money. I found nothing in my father's possessions that even resembled ten million dollars," answered Spence.

"Keep my number handy in case you change your mind." She smirked. "The clock is ticking."

Spence closed the phone and leaned back in his chair, still puzzled by Arlene's refusal to admit to the bugs. Maybe, he reasoned, she wasn't aware they were there. That would explain her ability to act as if no one was listening when she was at the estate. That had to be it, he thought. She didn't know about the bugs.

Satisfied for now, Spence began putting the pieces of evidence together in his mind as he tried to formulate a defense strategy. Finally, he came to the realization there was only one option left. Now he must wait.

Chapter Twenty-Two

The package arrived early the next morning as Spence was sipping his first cup of coffee. He could always count on George, especially when he needed him most. He ripped open the package and placed the contents onto the kitchen table. This had to work. He kept telling himself that as he examined the contents of the package. He carefully made note of each item as he poured a second cup. Once he was finished with his coffee, he made his way to the shower, placing the items from the package on the vanity.

Spence took a long, hot shower, dried off, and proceeded to shave. He threw on a pair of jeans and a long-sleeved t-shirt bearing the Detroit Tiger's emblem. Now he was ready for the transformation. First, he tried on the blonde wig, making sure he tucked away all remnants of his darker hair. Next, he applied bleach to his eyebrows from a tube George sent. As the bleach was working, he carefully applied the fake mustache that matched the wig. Then he rinsed the bleach from his eyebrows, revealing a much lighter shade that would pass as a match for the rest of his hair. He stood there for a moment admiring his creation; much like a painter admires his art. The wire-framed glasses made the disguise complete.

In fact, for a moment he hardly recognized himself. Now to get past the unmarked police car that was watching his every move.

Spence decided he better wait until dark to leave so the watchers wouldn't see him in his disguise. This gave him a whole day to kill, but he had nothing better to do at this moment. He grabbed the driver's license that came in the package with the other items. George had used the same assumed name, but altered the photograph to match the hair, wig, and glasses. Walter Miller was now a near-sighted blonde man from Panama City, Florida. It seemed as good as any place to live, he thought.

He made one phone call around noon before whipping up a tuna fish sandwich. The plan was in place, so he flipped on the television as he ate. He found an old movie he hadn't seen in years, and settled in for the afternoon, making sure he stayed awake, not wanting to miss his appointment. As soon as it was dark enough to conceal his transformation, Spence opened the garage and eased his car onto the street. The unmarked patrol car fell in behind him for their usual game of follow the leader.

Once again he parked at his favorite watering hole, and walked inside, ordered a beer as before, then walked to the back room, exiting the building through the rear door, climbing into the Camaro waiting outside. As before, the car drove off, heading out of town a few miles to make sure no one was following, before turning back and making its way to the airport. In a repeat of earlier episodes, after thirty minutes, a man resembling Spence's description left the bar, climbed into his car, and drove back to his house, parking in the garage and entering the house.

The Camaro stopped in front of the departing passenger-loading zone, the passenger door opened, and out stepped Walter Miller. He walked through the automatic double doors into the terminal. Remembering the ticket counter was upstairs, Spence made his way up the escalator, took his place in line, and waited for his turn. When he reached the counter, he told the clerk he wanted a one-way flight to Grand Rapids,

Michigan. The clerk typed on the keyboard in front of him, then looked up at Spence and informed him they had a flight leaving in one hour that would take him to Grand Rapids with one stop in Cincinnati. He handed the clerk his license and credit card, indicating that flight would be fine. The clerk resumed typing, retrieved a ticket that he handed to Spence, thanked Mr. Miller and wished him a good flight.

So far so good, Spence thought, still checking over his shoulder every few minutes to make sure no one was following. Although he looked completely different with the disguise, he knew inside who he was and couldn't help but feel others may see through the facade as well.

Proceeding through the security checkpoint, having secured the bug-detecting pen inside his carry-on bag, he walked through the metal detector. Relieved that the alarm did not go off, he quickly retrieved his bag from the conveyor belt and walked toward his gate, blending into the crowd as much as possible. Though it was only a matter of minutes before his flight began to board, it seemed like an eternity to Spence. He was taking a big risk to leave Kentucky while out on bail, but he just had to know what other clues remained in the tapes at his father's estate.

Spence tried to relax a little during the flight, but he kept looking around at the other passengers. The feeling of paranoia was almost overwhelming, as he realized how the FBI's most wanted must feel. Then again, he reasoned, most of those people are sociopaths with no conscience to bother them. He almost caught himself wishing he were more like them, but rational sane thinking prevailed, and as the flight continued on, he began to relax.

Changing planes in Cincinnati would provide an ego boost for Spence, as he was able to blend in well with the crowd, and seemed to go about his business unnoticed by the throngs of passengers around him. One lady actually complimented him on his mustache, explaining how she wished her husband would grow one, but that he never considered her feelings when making his personal grooming choices. Spence smiled and thanked her for the compliment, taking time to engage her in a rather brief conversation. He was growing more confident in his disguise, which helped to ease his anxiety. It was a short wait for the flight to Grand Rapids, and soon he was in the air again.

When the plane touched down in Michigan and began to taxi toward the gate, Spence reviewed the plan he'd developed in his mind. Once the plane stopped, he grabbed his carry-on bag from the overhead compartment and walked from the plane, up the ramp, and into the terminal. He headed straight for the rental car counters, once again using his assumed identity to rent a vehicle. This time Spence requested an SUV, so the clerk told him the price would be much higher than the average cars, since the only SUV they rented was a Cadillac Escalade, typically reserved for VIPs. He indicated his acceptance by handing the clerk his credit card. After a few strokes on the keyboard, the clerk handed him the keys with a map of Grand Rapids and the parking space number for the rental car. Exiting the terminal at the rental car parking lot, he located the rental. Then he climbed into the Escalade, tossing his bag into the back seat.

He used the quiet time from Grand Rapids to Traverse City to replay his plan repeatedly in his head, feeling certain he'd be safe for now since his disguise had worked so well up to this point. The hardest obstacle would be getting into the estate without detection, especially since he felt certain someone was watching him. At the moment, his only recourse was to relax and enjoy the rest of the trip, turning on the radio to search for a good station. As the radio was blasting out one of those alternative rock tunes, he wished he'd brought his Stones CD with him.

As he neared Traverse City, he began looking for a hotel along the way. He spied a Holiday Inn Express just ahead, and turned into the parking lot. It was rather late with little traffic on the road. Parking in front of the entrance, he climbed out of the Escalade, and walked into the lobby. A short skinny man with black hair and a mustache was standing behind the counter. Judging by his appearance, Spence believed he was of middle-eastern descent, probably from

Pakistan or India. As Spence approached the counter, the man asked if he could be of help, speaking broken English with a heavy middle-eastern accent.

Spence asked for a room, handing him the Walter Miller license and credit card. George had established a fifteen thousand dollar limit on the credit card for Walter Miller, including two keys to a post office box in Lexington where Mr. Miller received his mail. He was glad his friend had been so thorough in his planning and preparation. It certainly was paying huge dividends for him now.

The man handed Spence back his cards along with the key cards to his room. Spence had reserved the room for one night, feeling that was long enough to stay in one place. He parked the rental in one of the spaces in the back of the hotel, and walked back into the building at the rear entrance, using his key card to gain access. Once inside he quickly walked to the elevator and pressed the third floor button. The hotel had only three floors, and he'd requested a room on the top floor. He exited the elevator and strode quickly to the room. Once inside, he searched the nightstand drawers until he found a phone book. It was a few minutes before two in the morning, as Spence dialed the number of a local cab company. Exiting the room, he headed downstairs to the front to wait outside for the cab.

Fifteen minutes later, the taxi pulled up in front of the hotel. Spence quickly climbed in and barked an address to the driver. The cabbie was a short round man with a five o'clock shadow. He wore a plaid flannel shirt and a red toboggan. The cabbie gave him a suspicious look in the rearview mirror, then drove off toward his destination. As they neared the address, Spence made up a story about he and his wife having a big fight and preferring to stay alone in the hotel tonight, yet he'd called her and she asked him to come back home. He told the cabbie to stop at the road in front of the house and let him out, handing him a fifty-dollar bill, which was much more than the fare. The taxi sped away, leaving Spence standing in the dark. The address he used was about three hundred yards down the road from the driveway to his father's estate.

He walked the rest of the way, entering the woods once he reached the drive, making his way through the trees until he was within a few hundred feet of the house. Running across the yard, he hunched in a crouching position, glancing around as if checking for anyone who may be watching, then turned his key in the lock and quickly stepped inside. He left the lights off, as he closed the door and locked it behind him.

Bringing his small flashlight with him, he made his way upstairs to his old room, retrieving an old army duffle bag his father had given him to use at college from the closet, and then carefully walked back downstairs, making as little noise as possible. He didn't want to announce his presence to whoever may be listening.

He headed to the den, searching the tape collection his father had carefully assembled. Deciding not to waste time by trying to figure out which tapes were important, he filled the duffle bag with all of the tapes. Luckily, the bag was large enough to hold them all, as there were probably close to a hundred tapes. He walked steadily down the hall and back out the front door, making sure he locked it. Once he reached the trees, he opened his cell phone and punched in the number of the cab company, requesting a cab for the same address he'd just been dropped off at, and then made his way back through the woods to the road and back in front of the house to wait for his ride. He squatted down in hopes no one would see him, as he waited for the taxi.

About ten minutes after he reached the house where the cabbie had dropped him off, a taxi pulled up and stopped in front of Spence. He reached quickly for the door, opening it to announce his presence so the cabbie wouldn't honk the horn. He recognized the same cabbie who'd driven him out there from the hotel.

Spence tossed the bag into the back seat, climbed in, shrugging his shoulders. He asked the cabbie to take him back to the hotel, explaining the reunion with his wife did not go well, so he grabbed some extra clothes as it looked like he'd be staying on at the hotel longer than he hoped. The cabbie shot another suspicious look back at Spence, shaking his head as he drove off. He made some small talk with Spence on the way back to the hotel about his second wife, women in general, and how he'd never figure them out. Although the two trips seemed suspicious, the cabbie wasn't about to offend a good tipping customer.

When he let Spence out in front of the hotel, he told him to call him any time he needed a ride, handing him a card from the cab company with the name Dominick scrawled across the bottom of the card in ink.

Spence returned to his room carrying the duffle bag full of tapes. It was now three-thirty, so he decided to try to get some rest before morning. He carefully removed the disguise, and stretched out on the bed. The mattress was actually comfortable for a hotel, and soon he was sound asleep, exhausted from the day's activities. Checkout wasn't until eleven that morning, so he had seven and a half hours to sleep. At nine o'clock, his cell phone began chirping, causing him to nearly jump out of bed.

"Spence, it's Josh. Where are you?"

"Good morning to you too," Spence yawned into the phone.

"Listen," Josh hurried on. "The cops called me because they followed you home from a bar but they haven't seen or heard a peep out of you since then. I told them you were staying home for a few days to rest, but I don't know how long they'll be satisfied with that. They think you skipped town. Don't tell me you left the state."

"Okay, I won't tell you," answered Spence.

"Are you okay?" Josh asked.

"I'm fine. I'm just trying to find anything I can to help my case," replied Spence. "Don't worry about me. Just concentrate on the case."

"We're following every lead we have," Josh told him. "But I know I don't have to tell you what kind of trouble you'll be in if they learn you violated the conditions of your release."

"I won't tell if you don't," Spence smirked. "Besides, you don't really know for sure where I am, so you don't have to lie."

"Look, I don't know, nor do I want to know, where you are or what you're up to," Josh informed him. "Just get back home as soon as you can." With that, the phone went silent.

Spence sat on the side of the bed for a few minutes, still groggy after awakening from a deep sleep. He walked to the bathroom and took a nice hot shower. After he dried off and got dressed, it was time for the transformation to Walter Miller. He felt he was actually getting better at donning the disguise, as it didn't take nearly as long as it did yesterday for him to complete the transformation. Once everything was in place, he carried his bags down to the Escalade and went to the counter to check out. He felt it was better not to stay in one place too long.

Spence grabbed a biscuit and coffee from a local drive-thru restaurant, as he headed in the direction of Detroit. He wanted to locate a hotel where he'd go virtually unnoticed, as he took the time to view the tapes he retrieved from the estate. Key Largo was the first movie he was going to watch from the collection since Sherrie felt it was a clue his father left in the will. He continued his journey until he reached Livonia. There he found a nice hotel he felt would surely have a VCR available to rent for an added charge to his room.

As he entered the lobby, Spence noticed several people milling about. There was some sort of conference going on, he thought, noticing several people with nametags displayed on their clothing. He walked up to the counter where three ladies seemed busily punching keys on their computers. Two of them were assisting customers, while the third was talking on the phone. He patiently waited until one of the ladies was free to help him. She had the features of an oriental woman, but spoke excellent English. He assumed she'd been educated in America. She wore her hair in a ponytail, and was wearing a navy blue skirt with matching vest and a white blouse. Apparently, this was the uniform of the day, as all three ladies were dressed alike. Her nametag read 'Kim.'

Spence requested a suite with a king bed and Jacuzzi tub. When he inquired about a VCR, Kim informed him he could rent a VCR for an extra charge. He nodded his understanding, requesting one be brought to his room. He pulled a roll of bills from his pocket and informed Kim he'd pay cash for the room and all additional charges. She smiled as she punched a few keys on her computer, and told him what the charges totaled. He paid for two nights, hoping he would find the answers he was looking for by then. She handed him two key cards, then showed him the best place to park and enter for his room on a diagram of the hotel. He thanked her and headed back out the entrance to the Escalade.

He drove around to the entrance Kim circled on the map and parked as close to the door as he could, using the key card to enter the building, then made his way to the elevator, carrying his bags. On the tenth floor, he stepped off the elevator and turned left, walking to the end of the hall before locating his room. He inserted the key card into the door, and turned the handle. Once inside he locked the door securely behind him and placed his bags on the bed.

After about five minutes, there was a knock on the door. Spence peered through the peephole to see someone in uniform holding a VCR. He opened the door just enough to reach out and take the VCR from the man, handing him a five dollar tip and closing the door, securely locking it again.

He had no trouble connecting the VCR to the television. Then he dumped the tapes onto the bed, searching through them until he found Key Largo. He shoved the tape into the VCR and pressed play. The video started to play, then stopped abruptly.

Spence pressed buttons on the remote, but the tape appeared to be jammed. He ejected the tape from the machine and turned it repeatedly examining the outer casing. The tape appeared to be in working order, so he pushed it back into the VCR and pressed play. The tape still would not play, so Spence removed it again from the VCR. This time he decided to pry apart the case to see if he could determine why it was jammed. As Spence pried the case apart, something caught his eye as it fell out of the case and onto the floor.

It appeared to be a small brown leather case a little larger than the size if a business card. It had a closed zipper on the top. Spence tugged on the zipper, opening the pouch to reveal its contents. Inside was a key, and a small piece of paper with an address hand-written on it in black ink. He recognized the address as the same apartment building in Detroit where his father kept an apartment to use when he needed to stay in town on business. The apartment number was different from his father's, though, which made Spence wonder who lived there and why his father had a key.

Obviously, this was the next clue to the puzzle, but after removing the bag, the tape still refused to play. Spence realized the bag was the only clue from this tape, which left him feeling lost, not knowing which tape to look at next.

Spence watched each one, fast forwarding through most to see if his father had hidden any additional clues within the recorded movies. He worked for hours, stopping only to eat dinner he ordered from room service before continuing his mission.

By fast forwarding through most of the tapes, he was able to finish in eighteen hours. Since he found no other clues, the apartment must hold the remaining answers he was seeking. He was into his second day at the hotel, and scheduled to check out in the morning. He decided to wait until then to find the apartment building and see what was waiting behind the door this key would possibly unlock.

Filling the Jacuzzi with hot water, he climbed in for a relaxing bath. Then he placed a call to the front desk for a seven o'clock wake up call for the morning and retired for the evening, completely exhausted from the hours he spent combing over the tapes. Tomorrow offered a lot of hope, Spence thought, but he was too tired to think about it as he drifted off to sleep.

Chapter Twenty-Three

The phone rang precisely at seven o'clock, rousing Spence from a deep slumber. He vowed that when all of this was over he'd find a secluded beach somewhere and sleep for a week. That would have to wait, though, as there was still a lot of work to do. He ordered room service for breakfast, then carefully mapped out his route to the apartment building address he found in the Key Largo tape. He was unfamiliar with the area, seeing his father had never invited him for a visit when he was staying overnight in town. He was good with directions, though, so it should be easy enough for him to find. The question was what he would discover once he got there, and would it prove to be useful in his defense.

As Spence was drawing a crude map for his route, someone knocked at the door. He peered through the peephole, spying another Latino gentleman in uniform carrying what appeared to be a food tray. He'd already wrapped the complimentary hotel towel around him when he got out of bed, so he unbolted the door, opening it slightly. The gentleman announced he was from room service, and Spence opened the door wide enough for the man to enter, gesturing to the table to show the man where to place the food tray. Spence handed him a five-dollar bill, which brought a large smile and a thank you, then closed and locked the door once the man returned outside to the hallway.

He took a break from drawing his map long enough to eat, flipping the television on to the news channel to catch up on the latest events. He paid little attention to the lead-in about a manhunt underway for a murder suspect who appeared to have fled jurisdiction. That was until his picture suddenly flashed upon the screen. He reached for his cell phone just as it began to ring.

"Where the hell are you?" Josh shouted through the phone.

"Why? What's going on?" asked Spence.

"The police just found the gun that was used to kill Sherrie hidden in a dumpster a few blocks from your house. It turns out your fingerprints are all over it. The judge revoked your bail based on this new evidence. The police have reason to believe you've skipped town and have put out an all-points bulletin for your apprehension. I'm surprised it hasn't made it to where you are, considering they're not certain where you could be," said Josh.

"Actually, it has. I just saw a terrible picture of me on CNN. You'd think they could have at least shown my good side," he said with a laugh.

"Oh, you think this is funny do you? Well let me tell you, they've listed you as armed and dangerous, which I'm sure I don't have to tell you what that means."

"Every John Wayne with a badge or a bounty hunter's license will be looking for me. Shoot first and ask questions later," replied Spence lightly.

"You got it, pal. Now tell me where you are so I can bring you back in safely," Josh counseled. "If you come back now, I'm sure there's not enough concrete proof to get a judge to find you in contempt. But if they find you out there, they'll throw away the key."

"Thanks for the vote of confidence," Spence returned in a sarcastic tone. "By the way, how's the investigation going? Any luck yet?"

"None. I'm at a dead end, and I haven't been there in a long time. I know you're innocent, but whoever wants you to go down for this covered all the bases. There's still the plea—"

Spence interrupted Josh in mid-sentence. "I'm not telling you again, no plea! There has to be something we missed. Keep looking."

"Okay, but will you at least come back until the trial? You know, the longer you run, the guiltier you look."

"At this point I think it's better if no one knows where I am. If we can't come up with some evidence to keep me out of prison, I may need to get lost for good. I'll be in touch," Spence finished.

He closed the phone and stared back at the television. The reporter had already moved on from his story, but the words 'armed and dangerous' kept circling through his head like a flock of vultures waiting to pick his dead bones.

He began pacing around the room, trying to formulate a new plan based on this information. He was afraid Michigan would be one of the first states they would look considering his ties here. The visit to the apartment building would have to wait. He felt certain there would be people watching all places associated with his father.

With Sherrie dead and Arlene no longer an ally, he suddenly felt all alone. Unexpectedly his cell phone sprang to life again, as if on cue.

"You're a hot item again, my friend." It was George.

"You can say that again. Have you heard the latest?"

"I assume you're talking about the missing murder weapon that just happened to appear based on an anonymous tip? Yeah, I heard about it. Boy, someone really wants to nail you to the wall. Still no idea who or why?" asked George.

"Nothing I can prove, but I have an idea," replied Spence.

"You realize everyone is looking for you. By the way, how's the stuff I sent you working?"

"So far, so good. At least I can remain mobile, but I've become so hot now, I'm afraid to chance going out, even like this. I need to lay low for a while until I can figure a way out of this mess, if there is one," he added as an afterthought.

"Try not to worry too much," suggested George. "In fact, that's why I called. I want you to go to Grosse Pointe. Look for the East Bay Marina on Lake Shore Drive. Park in the main lot among as many cars as you can so you won't stand out. Then go straight to slip thirty-two. There will be a boat named 'Hole in the Water.' Climb on board, go downstairs into the cabin, and wait. Don't worry, Spence. Just be careful," George warned.

Spence vaguely remembered Grosse Pointe from his old college days when some of the Pi Kappa Alpha fraternity boys invited him on one of their rich father's yachts. The food and drinks were good, but the company was too stuffy for his taste. He'd enjoyed the trip as best he could, but vowed never to hook up with that crowd again.

He packed his bags and checked out of the hotel, frustrated at finding another clue, only to have to wait and wonder what it would reveal. However, he had to stay focused on the task, which was getting to the marina at Grosse Pointe without the authorities identifying him. The disguise George sent him had worked up to this point, but it would only take one person seeing through the facade to cause major problems for him. He kept reminding himself to stay calm and focused, all the while wondering what awaited him at Grosse Pointe.

As he drove east on I-96 from Livonia, Spence felt assured the Escalade would fit in well with the other vehicles of the elite at the marina. Others just like it would blanket the parking lot, so it should blend in well. He rehearsed his plan repeatedly until he was certain he could pull it off. After all, how difficult would it be to casually step out of his vehicle and walk the short distance to the docks and onto the ship? Obviously, there should be no harm awaiting him once on board for he trusted George with his life. He double-checked his briefcase to make sure he still had the bug detectors, just in case. Then he settled back in the seat and tried to relax, tuning the radio to a classic rock station.

Spence navigated his way through the traffic, as the highway became I-94 East, until he reached the exit that would take him from the interstate to Lake Shore Drive. He turned left onto the main highway and began immediately searching for East Bay Marina. Immediately, he saw what appeared to be a marina to his right and slowed down enough to read the sign out front. The words East Bay Marina shone in bright red letters on a white background with a large anchor insignia overlaid in the middle of the words. The sign had a gold border in a rope design that wove all the way around it. The sign was attached to two sturdy posts at the entrance to the marina, and appeared well-maintained. Of course, given the fact that many rich people frequented this place, it had to be in pristine condition.

He turned the Escalade into the marina drive and parked in the front lot between two other SUVs. Several people were milling about, so he was certain his presence wouldn't arouse suspicion. He quickly scanned the docks from his car hoping to spot slip thirty-two, but they were too far away to make out the numbers. The main office was located to the left of the parking area, but he could reach the main causeway without having to go through the building.

Double-checking his disguise, he adjusted his sunglasses, and stepped out into the open, gently closing the door to the Escalade, strolling casually toward the main causeway, his bag flung over his shoulders, with his hands thrust into his pockets. He thought about whistling, but decided that might draw more attention than he wanted. He walked purposefully along the docks, casually making note of each slip number he passed. He arrived at slip thirty-two, looking as if he knew exactly where he was going.

The 'Hole in the Water' was far from resembling its name. It was an average-size yacht, new, but not flashy enough to stand out in the crowd. Other than the name scrawled across the back, the boat had basic trimmings. He was glad it wasn't the type of vessel to attract much attention. On approach, he boarded the vessel as if he owned the joint, and quickly headed downstairs into the cabin, unable to see for a few minutes until he remembered to remove his sunglasses. As his eyes adjusted, he realized he wasn't alone. The beautiful redhead he knew only as Agnes stood at the far end of the cabin.

"I've been expecting you," a familiar voice spoke from across the room.

"Ah, the mystery lady appears again," he said. "To what do I owe this pleasure?"

"As I told you before, I'm here to help you," she replied.

"And exactly how do you intend to do that, considering I'm currently in the middle of a rather peculiar quandary?"

"You make a valid point," she said, laughing lightly. "But I prefer to see the glass as half full rather than half empty."

"That kind of thinking can set you up for a lot of disappointment in life."

"Or provide a lot of untapped motivation," she retorted. "But, we have more pressing matters than a discussion on positive thinking."

"What did you have in mind?" asked Spence.

"Patience. First we must take a little trip."

"Where to?" he asked, suddenly wondering what her plan was.

"You'll see soon enough," she said, smiling. "Just trust me."

"Trust you? I don't even know your name."

"Of course you do. It's Agnes Morehead." Her smile was mysterious.

"No, I mean your real name," he said with a sigh.

"And just what makes you think that's not my real name?"

"Well, for starters, you don't look like an Agnes to me."

"Oh really! Then tell me, what do I look like to you?"

He felt like jumping overboard after the words came out of his mouth, but he couldn't help himself. "You look like the most beautiful woman I have ever seen."

He blushed hard as he heard the words echo from his lips. She couldn't stop herself from blushing either after receiving such a wonderful compliment, which appeared to Spence to be something she rarely heard from anyone, judging by her reaction. Although given her stark beauty, he could not imagine why men weren't tripping over their tongues in front of her every day. But then again, maybe they were for all he knew. He reminded himself he still knew virtually nothing about her. Yet for some unexplained reason, he felt drawn to her, as if he had known her all of his life. He wanted desperately to know more about her. He decided to press on.

"You're blushing," he said with a grin. "I thought you would be used to hearing those words every day from that special someone." Spence wondered if she would take the bait.

"All I'll say is thank you for the compliment and leave it at that," she replied, still somewhat rosy in the cheeks.

"Okay, okay, I'll stop pushing for now," he said. "But I'm not giving up that easily. Changing the subject, is there anything to eat in here? I'm starving. I haven't eaten since this morning."

"Wait until we shove off," she answered. "Then I'll fix us something."

She excused herself and went up on deck. Spence heard her speaking to someone in what appeared to be Spanish, before she returned to the cabin, heading straight for the galley. Spence could feel the engine come to life, and soon the boat began moving.

"I hope you like hamburgers," she said.

"At this point, I'd eat almost anything," Spence joked, rubbing his stomach.

"Who's piloting the boat?" he asked.

"Well, I could tell you, but then I'd have to kill you," she answered, unable to control her laughter. Spence thought even her laugh was beautiful, as he smiled back at her.

"His name's Frederique, but I call him Freddie," she said. "He sort of came with the boat you might say, but he's a good captain."

"Well, now I definitely feel in good hands," he said, and smiled.

"How do you like your burger?"

"Medium, with everything you can put on it."

As she continued with the meal preparation, Spence sat and watched, admiring her graceful movements. He was amazed at how well she knew her way around a kitchen, and soon found himself staring helplessly. He decided to avert his gaze before she realized what was happening. His attraction to her was unmistakable, but he wondered if she felt the same way toward him. Moreover, there was still the small detail that he knew nothing about her, including her identity. He let out a long sigh as he told himself to be patient and play this out. It was the only way for him to learn more about her. He continued to observe her as she placed the cooked meat on the buns, added the necessary condiments, and tossed a small individual-sized bag of potato chips on each plate.

"We're far enough away from shore that it's safe to eat up on deck, if you want to," she said, gesturing toward the steps.

"Sounds good to me; I could use a little fresh air," he replied.

"How about grabbing us a couple of beers on your way up?" she asked as she disappeared up the steps.

Spence pulled two long necks from the fridge and followed up the steps behind her. She sat at a table on the deck toward the back of the boat, one plate in front of her, the other on the opposite side of the table. He placed a beer to the left of her plate, and the other one next to his own. He made note as she reached for the bottle, moving it to her right side, revealing that she was obviously right-handed. He sat down, ripped open the bag of chips, and took a big bite from the burger. He nodded his approval as he gulped down the first bite.

"I take it the food is prepared to your liking," she said.

Spence simply nodded again as he crammed another bite into his mouth. Beautiful and a great cook, he thought. What a winning combination. In four bites, his burger was gone, as he munched on what was left of the chips. She was barely half-finished with hers, so she offered her other half to

Spence. At the risk of looking like a selfish pig, he gladly accepted her offer, considering he was still somewhat hungry. She couldn't stop the smile that curved her lips as he gulped down the remainder of the food.

"Boy, you were hungry," she joked.

"I'm sorry. I'm usually much better mannered."

"No problem," she said, waving her hands. "I love to watch a man enjoy a good meal. Especially one I cooked," she beamed.

"How about another beer?" she asked, as she headed back toward the cabin.

Spence said that sounded good to him as he leaned back in the chair, suddenly feeling very full and satisfied from his meal. She returned quickly holding two beers in each hand by the bottle necks. She handed two to Spence, placing one on the table while opening the other. Then she sat down and took a long pull from the bottle. He could sense she was more relaxed, but felt he should continue to remain on his toes. So many unanswered questions were still spinning in his head that he felt like he would explode. However, he had to take it one step at a time.

"So, where are we headed?" he finally asked after a few minutes.

"Somewhere you can lay low for a while without fear of being arrested, at least until the heat is off."

"How long will we be gone?"

"As long as it takes," she replied curtly.

"How many beers will it take to get you to loosen that tongue of yours and give me more information?" he asked, smiling.

"More than we have on board tonight," she answered tartly, smiling back.

The sun was beginning to set over the water, painting a beautiful mural upon the landscape. Spence grabbed his chair and moved it around beside hers so he would have a better view, at least that's what he told her. It all felt surreal to him as he sat on a boat in the middle of the ocean beside a beautiful woman watching the sunset. It would have made for a great movie scene, he mused. Just as he opened the second beer and settled back in his chair, her head gently leaned to the side, resting on his shoulder. He could definitely feel the electricity between them as it surged through his body, but he remained calm, enjoying the moment. Suddenly she sat upright, pulling away from him.

"I'm sorry," she stammered. "I don't know why I did that."

"It's okay," he said in a half whisper, reaching his arm around her, pulling her back close to him. "I don't mind. Besides, a beautiful evening like this is meant to be shared."

She leaned her head back onto his shoulder as they basked in the moment. Spence closed his eyes, listening to the gentle hum of the boat cutting through the water, a gentle breeze upon his face. Neither spoke a word for several minutes, as each became lost in their own serenity that comes from believing for a single moment in time all seemed right with the world. Being out on the open water together made them both feel safe and secure in each other's company. It was a comfortable silence, the same as between a couple who have been together so long that words are not required to convey the depth of their feelings for one another. Yet these two souls really did not know each other at all, at least not yet. It was getting late when she broke the silence.

"I need to retire for the night. You should think about getting some sleep yourself. Tomorrow could be a long day again."

"What are the sleeping arrangements?" he asked expectantly.

"Easy tiger," she responded. "There are two bedrooms on either side of the front of the cabin. Since I already stowed my gear in the left one, you can have the one on the right."

"And if I get cold during the night?" he asked, flashing a grin.

"Grab the blanket from the top of the closet, Romeo," she charged lightly.

"Sorry. I just couldn't help myself," he said. "You go on ahead. I think I'll stay up here for a little while longer. Goodnight Agnes, or whatever your name is."

"It's Macy," she replied. "And goodnight to you too, Spence."

She turned quickly and headed down into the cabin. Spence took another pull from his beer as her name rolled repeatedly through his mind. Macy is such a cute name, he mused, and it suited her well. He was glad she felt comfortable enough to tell him her true name; at least he hoped it was true. After his encounter with Arlene, it was hard to know whom he could trust. Even though he knew nothing about her, Spence believed Macy was someone he could trust. After all, she had led him in the right direction several times, even now risking her own safety while helping him elude the authorities.

He eased back in his chair, soon drifting off to sleep to the soft hum of the motor, the spray of the waves, and sweet happy thoughts of what life could be like with Macy.

Chapter Twenty-Four

S pence opened his eyes to find he was lying in a strange bed. He felt like he had the mother of all hangovers as he tried to sit up on the side of the bed. Smelling the aroma of bacon wafting up from the cabin, he slowly stood up and made his way to the door. As he walked from the room, Macy turned toward him from the kitchen, a beautiful smile on her face.

"I thought you might want some breakfast, seeing as how hungry you probably are," she said, setting a plate in front of him.

"Coffee," he mumbled, managing a half smile, while she poured a cup and sat it in front of him. "How long have I been out?"

"Eight days," said Macy, biting her lip. "I added a special ingredient to your burger so you would sleep until we reached our destination," she confessed. "It was for your own protection."

"Eight days?" he asked, holding his head.

"Freddie and I got you up long enough to feed you and relieve your bladder, but I'm sure you don't remember any of it with what we gave you. I guess I don't have to ask how you slept," she said.

"Are you always this cheerful in the morning?"

"Sorry. I guess I'm just one of those morning people. I take it you're not?" she asked, shaking her head.

"Well, most mornings I'm fine, but I don't usually sleep eight days either. Of course it's still better than jail."

"Spence," Macy said, taking hold of his hand, "you're not going to jail. I know you're innocent, so please don't give up."

"And just how do you know I'm not a cold-blooded killer?" he asked, making an evil face as he spoke.

"Well for starters, a guilty person wouldn't have taken the time to look for evidence to clear them. They would have simply run the first chance they got. Also, my brother George believes you, and that's good enough for me," she said.

"Whoa, time out! You're George's sister?" asked Spence in amazement, as Macy nodded her head in agreement. "George never told me he had a sister. Thank goodness you don't look like him, but don't tell him I said that."

"Don't worry," she laughed. "My lips are sealed."

Macy placed scrambled eggs, bacon and toast on each of their plates. Then they began eating, stopping long enough to smile at each other every few minutes between bites. Spence enjoyed the feeling of sharing time with someone, and realized what he'd been missing in his life for so long. Unable to get that nagging voice out of his head that kept screaming 'Be Careful! Remember Arlene?', he decided he should slow down and play things more cautiously. He decided to make a little small talk instead.

"Where exactly are we?" he asked, noticing they weren't moving.

"At the moment we're docked in a small private marina in Bermuda," she replied. "We should be safe here for as long as it takes."

"As long as it takes for what?" he asked, raising his eyebrows.

"You know, for your trail to become cold enough that you become one more in a stack of too many cases the police cannot expend enough time on to worry about where you might turn up."

"What makes you think they'll put me on the back burner?"

"Don't flatter yourself. You know as well as I do that Mrs. Barbour was not famous enough to keep this case on the hot list. This will become another unsolved homicide like the many others every year, and your face will end up in the post office."

"But I don't want to have to live life constantly looking over my shoulder, and having to wear a stupid disguise," he protested.

"I understand," she comforted, lightly touching his shoulder. "And you will clear your name one day. But for now there's too much attention focused on you for you to be able to effectively work to uncover enough evidence to prove your innocence."

"So what do we do in the meantime?" he asked, tossing up his hands.

"Well, I thought today we might do a little fishing," she responded with a grin. "Freddie knows a place not far from here that's very secluded, and an excellent fishing spot. We can relax here. No one is looking for you here."

Spence nodded his head in agreement, as they finished their meal. Macy climbed out of the cabin and made her way to where Freddie was doing his daily boat check. After a brief discussion, he smiled and waved at her as she headed back toward the cabin.

Freddie released the ropes from the dock and started the motor. They began moving away from the marina, as Macy made her way back down into the cabin. She grabbed Spence by the hand and led him up on deck into the bright sunlight. Freddie had already placed two deck chairs near the rail, with a couple of rods and two Styrofoam coolers between them. One cooler held nothing but water in case they decided to keep any fish they caught. The other held bait Freddie had already sliced and prepared.

Macy had retrieved a couple of wide brimmed straw hats from below for each of them to keep the sun from burning their faces and necks. She crammed one onto Spence's head, laughing as she pushed it down over his eyes. He instinctively reached over to do the same to hers, but she successfully dodged his grasp. After a few minutes of horseplay, they each settled into their chairs and waited for Freddie to steer the boat to their final destination. The trip took just a few minutes before he shut off the engine and dropped anchor. They could still see the shore, but were far enough away that Spence didn't feel eyes staring at him. Maybe now he could relax for the first time in days.

Freddie brought up a cooler of beer packed in ice and placed it between them as well. Then he headed off in the direction of the helm, probably to give them some alone time, and probably to watch an old western on the portable DVD player. Macy said Freddie was a huge John Wayne fan, so she brought several DVD's to keep him occupied during their trip. Obviously she wanted some alone time with Spence as well, he thought, then the nagging voice came back warning him to take it slow, so he shrugged his shoulders as if to say 'cool,' then cast his line into the water and sat back in his chair.

Macy cast her line out also, then grabbed two beers from the cooler, handing one to Spence and opening the other. Spence had never been a beer man, and could almost kill for a Jack and Coke, but decided to be a gracious guest. Besides, by now he was actually able to halfway enjoy them. Maybe by the end of their trip, Macy would have converted him to a beer man; then again—maybe not.

After a few minutes, Macy placed her rod in the holder attached to the rail and headed back toward the cabin. Spence thought she probably needed to use the restroom, so he made no comment in her direction. Instead, he stared out into the ocean watching his line as he slowly cranked the bait through the water. The beer Macy had opened for him still sat untouched. After a few minutes, she reappeared, handing him a tall glass.

"What's this?" he asked, catching a faint odor of bourbon.

"I decided not to torture you any more with the beer. Don't you recognize your favorite drink, Jack and Coke?"

"But how did you?" Spence began, then, realized. "George. I'm almost afraid to ask what else George told you about me," he told her, as he took a long swig from the glass.

"Don't worry," she said, smiling. "Nothing that will embarrass you."

Spence quickly downed the drink, savoring every drop. Macy retreated to the cabin and mixed another, then she sat back down beside him and picked up her fishing rod. After a couple of hours, he was beginning to think this wasn't a hot fishing spot, but instead something to keep them occupied. His assumption proved to be correct when Macy started to speak.

"Well, it's obvious the fish aren't biting, so let's talk."

"Okay," he grinned, playing along. "What would you like to talk about?"

"Now don't take this the wrong way." She hesitated. "And if it starts to upset you, we'll change the subject. But I'm curious; do you have any theories on who might have killed your assistant, and what the motive could have possibly been?"

Surprisingly, Macy sounded less like George's sister, and more like a detective. That eerie 'spider sense' went off in his head, but he decided to play along … at least for now. Besides, if Macy was a cop, he could only uncover that fact through conversation.

"Well," he began, "without going through a lot of boring details, my first thought was that Joey VanWarner had something to do with it. But he has nothing to gain if I go to prison."

"Maybe he's just trying to make you sweat it out, thinking you'll eventually crack and give him what he wants," she said.

"Maybe." He shrugged, a slight lifting of his shoulder, scraping a thumb across his chin thoughtfully. "But how could Joey help me beat this murder wrap, unless he has a contact on the inside? Someone who could tamper with the evidence, or better yet, make it disappear? Then again, who knows how far Joey's reach is?"

"And what exactly does Joey want from you anyway?" she asked.

"I'm not sure I know you well enough to confide in you with all the details. Let's just say for now he believes my father had something that belonged to him, and he might think I stumbled upon it when I was going through my father's estate."

"And did you stumble upon this something?" she pressed.

"Possibly," he answered tentatively. "But there's no way he could know for sure that I did. Besides, the FBI is looking for the same thing, and Arlene assured me she could make this all go away if I hand it over to her."

"Who's Arlene?" Macy asked, raising an eyebrow questioningly.

"Oh, I left that part out. She and I went to high school together, but haven't seen each other in years. All of a sudden, I'm dining in a restaurant in Traverse City, while I was there to settle my father's estate when in walks Arlene right out of the clear blue. After several meetings and a little investigative work of my own, I learned she's an agent with the FBI. Then she tells me she's working on a case involving my father and Joey, and wants to know if I came across anything that might help her when I was going through my father's stuff. I told her no, but ever since Sherrie's murder, she seems convinced I'm holding out on her, and has promised to make all the evidence against me disappear if I give her something she and Joey have both been looking for."

"Well, it sounds to me like you should hand it over, that is, if you actually have it. That way you'd be in the clear and could resume your life where you left off, free from prison," reasoned Macy.

"That may be true," Spence agreed. "But after some of the things Arlene has said and done, I'm not sure I can trust her. I mean, what if I give her what she wants, and then she still hangs me out to dry. I've got no guarantees with her."

"Well, tell me this, if I'm not being too nosy, what were you doing in Michigan when you weren't supposed to leave the state of Kentucky?"

"I was following up on another clue my father left in his will. I was hoping it would somehow give me something to help aid in my defense of these murder charges. Besides, after all of the conversations with Arlene, I'm curious as to exactly how much my father was involved with the VanWarners."

"Sounds like you and Arlene spent a lot of time together recently. Maybe even more than just conversations." Macy winked at him.

"Well, since you and I are still just getting to know each other, I really don't need to defend myself. But honestly, I was starting to have feelings for Arlene, until I figured out she was just using me for information," he admitted, shaking his head.

"How do you know I'm not doing the same?" quipped Macy. "After all, we haven't even slept together yet."

"I don't." Spence glared at her, then suddenly smiled and added, "But I like the way you finished that statement with 'yet.'"

"I apologize if I'm asking too many questions," Macy expressed. "It's just that when I first met you I could tell you were looking for answers. However, the other day when you came on board the boat, I could tell there was much more weight on your shoulders. I guess what I'm trying to say is that I'm here whenever you need to talk about anything. I want to help you get through all of this," she said, touching his hand.

He let her hand linger on his for a moment before pulling away. "Why are you so interested in helping me?" he asked. "What's in it for you?"

"Fair enough," she countered. "George has been trying for months to set me up with you, you know, as a favor to you for introducing him to his wife. He knew I'd been in and out of several relationships, mostly bad ones, because most men can't handle what I do for a living. He showed me a picture of you which quite frankly, displayed a very handsome man—"

"Who was in that picture with me?" Spence interrupted.

"No one but you," she said. "Now do you want to know

the rest of the story or not?" she demanded, crossing her arms.

"Oh, I apologize for the interruption. Please continue," he urged.

"Well, I was about to give in and agree to let him set us up, just before your father died. Once I heard about that, I knew you would have your hands full, and would find it difficult to think about starting a new relationship. Therefore, I decided to wait until things got back to normal for you, then all hell broke loose, so to speak, and George really needed my help. Little did I know until after I agreed to help, that it involved you. Since I had already committed to George, I decided getting involved in your situation might actually give me some insight into you without having to go through all the first date crap that most couples wade through. I know this doesn't make a lot of sense right now, especially with everything you're dealing with. However, if you don't believe anything else, believe this. Yesterday took care of all that 'first date' crap, and I'm still here. You have enough on your plate as it is, but I just wanted you to know that once everything is back to normal, I am very interested in pursuing a relationship with you. Let's just keep it professional for now, though, considering we both need to keep focused."

Spence sat silent for a moment, trying to process everything Macy had just laid out in the open for him, taking a huge risk in revealing her inner feelings so early in the game. He knew she was right about not getting involved until after everything was back to normal, whatever normal would be from now on. He certainly did not have the mental strength to enter into a new relationship while juggling the issues of his current dilemma. The fact that Macy was so open with him, and still willing to explore a relationship at some point, offered Spence a ray of hope in a soul filled with utter darkness. He could not find the words to express his gratitude for her honesty and help in his time of need, so he simply took her hand and gave it a squeeze as he stared out into the ocean. He could feel the pressure as she closed her fingers around his like a security blanket wrapping a crying child, comforting him when he needed it most. It was the most secure he'd felt since his mother died. They sat for an hour in the same position completely silent, not looking at each other, until Spence finally choked back his emotions enough to speak.

"You said other men couldn't handle what you do for a living. Can you tell me what it is that you do?"

"I'd rather wait for a more appropriate moment, not that I don't want to tell you, or am afraid it'll drive you away. I just think there are still some issues you need to work through yourself before laying anything else on you," she said.

"I understand. Life's too complicated lately anyway."

Freddie reappeared to inform Macy they should be heading back. He made some comment in Spanish, laughing as he flipped open the lid to the cooler that held only water and no fish. Obviously, he'd said something to her about their fishing abilities, because Macy fired back a string of what Spence took to be Spanish profanity, judging by the way Freddie was smiling and shaking his head. Once Freddie was out of sight, Macy turned and burst out laughing herself.

"Care to include me in that little interlude?" asked Spence.

"Oh, Freddie was just saying that we must have found something else better to do than fish, considering we hadn't caught anything. Then he made a comment similar to what most guys do when they think two people have been making out. I just let him know, along with some colorful language, that he was out of line," she said.

"I see," said Spence. "Protecting your honor, or something like that."

"Yeah, something like that."

Freddie pulled up the anchor, and headed back to the marina. Once he secured the boat, he mumbled something in Spanish to Macy before leaving the boat. Macy asked Spence if he would like to take a shower before dinner, which seemed like a good idea, considering he didn't have one that morning. He spent a long time letting the water run over his body as he mulled over Macy's earlier comments. He too was definitely interested in pursuing a relationship with her, but not if he ended up in prison. No, she was right. He had to get through this first, then, get on with his life. The problem was he didn't know what to do next. After he finished his shower and dressed, Spence put on his confident face. He didn't want Macy to see how worried he really was.

Before much time had passed, Freddie returned with some fresh fish he'd obviously bought at a local market, uttered something in Spanish to Macy, then, began searching around in the kitchen. Macy took Spence by the hand and led him up on deck and out of harm's way.

"What's up with him?" asked Spence.

"He feels bad about the comment he made earlier, so he wants to make it up by cooking dinner for us," she replied. "Actually, he's an excellent cook, so this should be a treat."

Spence hoped she was right, because the food they had earlier had long left him, causing his stomach to rumble in protest. He took a seat on one of the deck chairs while Macy went back down into the cabin. She quickly returned with a beer in one hand and a Jack and Coke in the other. That was another plus on his list for Macy; she knew how to mix a good Jack and Coke.

Sipping their drinks in silence, they listened to Freddie rant in Spanish while seeming to hit every pot and pan in the galley. When no more noise came from the kitchen, after a few minutes, Freddie appeared with two plates, placing one in front of Macy and the other in front of Spence.

Dinner was grilled swordfish with a side of rice pilaf. Macy asked him to join them, but Freddie insisted on eating at his post, smiling as he made comments in Spanish and rushed away before Macy could reply.

Shortly after they finished their meal, Freddie returned to remove the dishes. Then he brought out a dessert plate of cheesecake for each of them. Spence figured he bought this somewhere too, since he hadn't had enough time to make one himself. Nevertheless, it was very good, and Spence savored every morsel.

Once dessert was finished, Freddie returned once again with a fresh beer for Macy and a newly mixed Jack and Coke for Spence. Quickly clearing away the rest of the dishes, he headed back down to the galley. Once he'd completed cleaning up for the evening, Freddie excused himself.

Macy and Spence remained on deck for a while enjoying their drinks. After a while, Spence stood up and announced he was ready to call it a night. Obviously sleeping on deck the night before hadn't been very restful, he was glad to accept the cabin accommodations. Macy gave him a soft kiss on the cheek before they retired to their separate rooms for the night.

Chapter Twenty-Five

S pence awoke the next morning feeling very refreshed. He glanced at his watch, and then realized he wasn't sure if they were even in the same time zone. Things had happened so quickly over the past several days, he wasn't certain what day it was. He could smell the aroma of freshly brewed coffee, assuming the morning girl had already been up for some time. As he walked into the galley, Macy flashed a big smile and informed him he was just in time for breakfast. She had prepared omelets and bagels, which she placed in front of Spence. Then she poured them both a cup of coffee and sat down to join him.

"What's on our schedule for today?" he asked.

"Shopping!" she quickly answered. "We need to get you some new clothes."

"What's wrong with the ones I have?"

"Well, besides the fact they haven't been washed in a while, you didn't bring very many with you."

She was right. In his hurry to leave the hotel, he tossed most of his clothes into a larger bag he'd left inside the Escalade when he parked at the marina. The small bag he carried with him contained only a pair of jeans and a couple of shirts, and of course, the bug detection devices George gave him. They'd become like an American Express card to him; 'Don't Leave Home Without It.'

After breakfast, Macy cleared the dishes while Spence dressed in the jeans and shirt that was the less dirty of the two. They left the boat together, walking toward a graveled circular drive, lined with parked taxis. Macy opened one of the cab doors, climbed inside, and motioned for Spence to do the same. She barked out directions to the driver and they were on their way. They drove past a section of older buildings in need of repair, continuing until they reached what appeared to be a much more affluent neighborhood. The driver stopped the car in front of a group of shops. Macy handed him some money, for which he thanked her graciously. Then they climbed out of the cab and he drove away.

Every kind of clothing and accessory shop you could imagine lined the street. Spence began wondering where to start when Macy grabbed his hand and led him into the first store on the corner.

"We'll make our way through them all eventually," she said. "So we may as well start here and work our way down the street."

It was not long before Spence felt certain he knew exactly how runway models felt during a show. It seemed he'd tried on more outfits than he'd ever worn before in his entire life. Macy was relentless when it came to finding exactly what she was looking for. She explained to Spence that she wanted him to be dressed in such a way as not to stand out like a tourist, but rather look like he belonged there. It would be easier for him to blend in that way. After a few hours of this torture, he asked if he could just stay on the boat to avoid detection, to which Macy laughed, dragging him to yet another store.

They'd barely been inside the store for half a minute when a rather tall, smartly dressed man with a French accent approached them.

"Bonjour, Mademoiselle et Monsieur," he began. "My name is Phillipe. May I be of some assistance today?"

"We're shopping for my husband today," Macy said.

"I see. You're looking to update his attire to match the current trends?" asked Phillipe, reaching for a pair of trousers. "These colors are all the rage this year," he continued, thrusting several different colored garments in their direction.

"Actually," Macy replied, "we were looking for something more conservative, but not too drab, something that won't stand out in a crowd."

"I see," Phillipe said. "We do not want him to seem, how you say, available, yes?" Macy nodded her approval. "I believe I have just the thing you are looking for." Phillipe beckoned with his hand as he led them to the back of the store. "Tell me what you think of this?" He showed Macy a pair of pleated linen white trousers with a matching jacket and a lime green shirt to complete the ensemble. "Not too flashy, but enough color to say *I'm not dead yet.*"

"This looks splendid," Macy assured Phillipe, while Spence rolled his eyes upward.

"Relax, Spence," Macy whispered. "It's the only outfit we've bought so far that wasn't either a pair of shorts, or khaki, or both." Phillipe also showed them a conservatively styled pleated front pair of navy blue trousers, with a yellow and blue shirt to match. Macy bought those as well. Then it was on to shoes.

Before Macy was finished, Spence ended up with six new outfits, two pair of deck shoes, a pair of semi-dress loafers, a nice pair of running shoes, and of course, the necessary under garments. He was amazed at the cost, but Macy insisted on paying for everything. She actually enjoyed playing the role of loving wife picking out clothes for her husband.

Having finished their quest by two o'clock, they decided to grab lunch. Finding a little corner cafe on the same street, they sat down with their many bags and began looking over the menu. Spence was relieved he could actually order a burger here, but Macy suggested the fish. They would look less like tourists if they ordered what the regulars usually did, and the locals usually came for its catch of the day specials. He was just glad to be able to sit and rest for a few minutes. He didn't understand how women could spend so much time shopping and actually enjoy it. To him it felt worse than a day pouring over legal briefs, which was exceedingly boring work.

After they finished their meal, Macy led Spence back to the corner where they started. It was now five minutes before three, so she stood on the corner until her watch read three. At precisely three o'clock, the same taxi they drove to town in, and the same driver, pulled up to the curb. He got out, said something to Macy, smiling as he spoke, and loaded the packages in the trunk. Then they sped off back to the docks. Obviously, she'd made a very rewarding arrangement with him earlier that morning, as he was determined to follow through with his requested mission. There was no conversation on the way back to the boat, but the driver kept peeking at them through the rearview mirror.

Arriving at the marina, they unloaded their packages, Macy handing the driver what appeared to be more money, then he sped off toward town. Spence carried the packages back to the boat and took them down to his room. As he was putting away his new wardrobe, Macy mixed him his favorite drink. Then she grabbed a beer and they headed up on deck.

Spence collapsed in a deck chair beside Macy and took a long swig of his drink. He was exhausted from the day's events, and wanted nothing more to do than kick back and relax. It was a beautiful sunny day, and they were enjoying basking in the warm rays and the tropical Bermuda air. Freddie was somewhere attending to his duties, being careful to leave them to their privacy.

After a few minutes, Macy turned to Spence. "Now tell the truth. That wasn't so bad, was it?"

"What, being drug over half of Bermuda changing outfits more in one day than a normal man does in a year?"

"Ooh, poor baby!" she teased. "I'll bet if you were playing golf or some other sport all day you wouldn't be complaining."

"You're right," he conceded. "I enjoy doing those things."

"So you don't enjoy spending time with me?" she pouted.

"If that were true, would I be here beside you now? It's the shopping I can live without, especially for that long," he said.

"I'm just teasing," she told him. "And I appreciate you being such a good sport about it, but we just had to get you some clothes and it seemed easier to do it all in one trip."

"Easy for you," he said, rolling his eyes, provoking a laugh from Macy.

He really enjoyed hearing her laugh, so much so that he tried to act the clown more than usual in the hopes she would find something he said or did funny. She was one of a kind, he thought, and felt strangely at ease in her presence. Just when he would start to think he was having feelings for her, the warning light would go off in his head, along with an image of Arlene. He never wanted to feel that much hurt and distrust again as long as he lived. Spence decided to engage Macy in some lighter conversation.

"Tell me more about you, I mean, if you can," he began. "I know you're George's sister. What was it like growing up with him?"

"Actually, George was a very good brother to me," she said. "He and I were a team, and he always stood up for me."

"Well, isn't that what a big brother should do?" asked Spence.

"I believe so," she answered. "But I had several girlfriends whose brothers were complete jerks to them. I felt lucky that George was my brother."

"What sort of things did you guys do together?"

"Well, believe it or not, I was sort of a tomboy, so we played a lot of sports, especially basketball. Our dad put a regulation size goal in our backyard where we would play for hours. When we got older, we would go to the park so we could play on the hard courts. It was easier than trying to dribble a ball on grass. Of course, we had long worn the grass down to the dirt at home, but at the park we could usually find a pick-up game with some other kids." She started to chuckle at the memory. "They had no idea how good I could play, so no one wanted to pick me. George knew, though, and somehow we usually ended up on the same team. They thought they could beat us easily with a girl on our team, but it didn't take them long to figure out they had made an error in judgment."

"Oh, so you're a jock, huh?" he continued.

"Yup," she admitted. "I even played varsity in high school, but I just wasn't quite good enough to make the college team."

"Where did you go to college?"

"My family lived in Kentucky all of their lives, so I decided I wanted to go off to college. I went to the University of Tennessee in Knoxville. Where did you go?"

"Michigan," he answered, taking another sip of his drink.

"You mean you didn't have the urge to venture any farther from home than Ann Arbor?"

"No need to. Michigan is a great school. I knew I could get just as good an education there as anywhere. Besides, I was far enough away from home to have plenty of fun," he said, giving her a devilish grin.

"And I'm sure you did!" she said with a laugh.

"Changing the subject a little," Spence began, "you never told me whether or not you're married. I mean, I haven't heard you mention a husband, so I assume you're not."

"Well, you know what they say about assuming," she said, flashing a smile. "But no, I've never been married. You?"

"Once. A long time ago," Spence admitted. "Actually we met in college. We thought we were in love, so we got married. Then I found out she was more interested in money and status than me. When I told her I was moving to Kentucky and leaving my father's practice, she informed me she wouldn't be going with me. In fact, it seemed she had already replaced me with an old college buddy. By the way, she was also a red head," he added, gesturing a wave in Macy's direction.

"I can assure you," she returned pleasantly, "all red heads are not the same."

"Really?" he said, "Because she was really good in the sack."

"Well, we do share some of the same traits," she said, a soft blush staining her cheeks.

"But you'll just have to take my word on that for the time being."

"What a tease," Spence said, rolling his head back in the chair. "So tell me," he continued, "why didn't you ever marry?"

"The same reason most single people use. I guess I haven't met the right man yet. Of course, I've had several men in my life, but for some reason or other, they never seem to hang around long. I guess a lot of men are intimidated by a strong woman."

"I guess some are," he said, then added. "Wimps!"

"Any children from your marriage?"

"No, we weren't together long enough for that. Besides, I don't think Greta was into kids. Would you like to have children some day?" he asked, almost embarrassed at such a personal question.

"When I was younger I thought it might be nice, but my career really would have made it difficult, even if I had met the right man. Now I'm really too old to think about having kids," she admitted ruefully.

"Nonsense!" he said, "You can't be more than thirty."

"Nice try, slick," she said with a smile. "But I'm thirty-four."

"Well, that's still not too old, especially considering women are having children much later in life than they used to."

"True, but you're forgetting one important thing; no 'Mr. Right'."

"Maybe you've already met him, but just don't realize it. In fact, he could be somewhere close to you as we speak, but the question is, will you know him when you see him?" he asked, trying to disguise the hope he felt.

"How does one truly know when they've met their soul mate, if there even is such a thing?" she asked. "Maybe some people are just meant to live life by themselves."

"You don't believe that any more than I do," he said. "That sounds like someone who's afraid to take a chance on true love for fear of having their heart broken. Believe me, it hurts like hell when the one you trust betrays you, but you can't give up. Call me a sap, but I believe there is a special someone out there for everyone."

Macy laughed. "I applaud your optimism, and hope for both our sakes you're right. How about another drink?" she asked, rising from the deck chair to head back down inside the cabin. After a few minutes, she emerged with another beer for herself and a Jack and Coke for Spence. She handed the glass to Spence, settling back into her chair, letting out a huge sigh as she took a pull from her long neck.

"At the risk of venturing into confidential waters again," Spence began, "you've mentioned a couple of times about your work getting in the way of relationships and children. Can I ask you what it is you do for a living?"

"Sure, you can ask," she answered. "But it's still too early in the game to put all of that on you. You need to learn patience, my friend."

"Game!" Spence snapped, raising his voice. "Is that all this is? Just a game to you? I mean, sure it's not your neck on the line, but it is my life that's at risk. Somehow that doesn't feel much like a game to me."

"Whoa, take it easy," Macy said, holding her hand up. "I'm sorry. I didn't mean that like it sounded. Of course, what you're going through is not a game. Believe me; I'm as committed to your innocence as you are. Sometimes I don't always use the best choice of words. I guess I kind of got lost in our little boy/girl conversation, and for a moment there was nothing else going on except you and me in our own little world."

"I'm sorry I snapped at you. It's just that after the way Arlene acted, I'm still struggling with trust issues," he confessed.

"Hey, I don't blame you. If I were in your shoes, I wouldn't trust me either. But you do trust George, don't you?"

"With my life."

"Then you're safe with me," she said, reaching out to take his hand.

"At the risk of sounding like a total moron," Spence began, "I feel I must confess that I am strangely attracted to you."

"You don't sound like a moron," she chuckled. "Instead, that was a very sweet and romantic thing to say. And since we seem to be in a confessing mood, I too, feel a strong attraction to you. However," she continued, "you know as well as I do that you can't handle any more complications or distractions in your life right now. That is why we need to keep our relationship on a more professional level for the time being. That doesn't mean, though, that we can't talk as friends. I've been enjoying our day together," she said, squeezing his hand.

"I know you're right," he said. "But I just want to know everything about you. Is that so wrong?" he asked.

"Not at all," replied Macy. "But you're not ready to know all about me. Believe me, when the time is right, we'll finish this conversation, but we need to get ready for our dinner guest."

"Dinner guest?" asked Spence. "And who might that be?"

"You'll see soon enough. I just ask that you keep an open mind. Now go take a shower and put on one of your new outfits," she ordered.

"Yes ma'am," he said, smiling and tossing a half-hearted salute in her direction.

Spence retreated to the cabin for a quick shower and change of clothes. When he finished, he returned to where Macy was still sitting, posing for her approval. He was wearing the white linen trousers with the matching jacket, and a bright green shirt.

"Very nice!" she said, smiling approvingly. "Now, you

can relax while I get ready." With that, she rose from her chair and headed down into the cabin.

After what seemed like a longer shower to Spence than the one he took, Macy emerged in a bright sundress with a flowing pattern of yellow and melon-colored flowers. He couldn't help but think how beautiful she was, as the dress accented every perfect curve of her body.

"Wow!" was all he could manage to say, as she smiled back her approval. Freddie came up, whistled at Macy, and then after a few words of appreciation headed down into the cabin.

"What now?" Spence asked.

"Now, we wait for our guest to arrive while Freddie prepares dinner," she answered mysteriously.

Chapter Twenty-Six

Macy left the boat and headed in the direction she and Spence had taken their cab ride earlier that morning. Insisting he remain on the boat while she was gone, he sat waiting patiently for her to return. She told him she had to meet their dinner guest, and felt it best if she went alone. During her absence, Spence mixed another Jack and Coke and relaxed in the deck chair, staring out across the blue water.

Since his back was toward shore, he didn't turn around until he heard footsteps approaching. Assuming it was Macy returning with her guest, he stood up and turned to face them, flashing a pleasant smile. His smile quickly evaporated into a stare of disbelief, as he stood with his mouth half-open, unable to speak as Macy led her guest by the arm.

"Hello, son," the man said, smiling. "I'm sure I'm the last person you expected to see." It was his father, Judge Rawlings. He looked better than the last time Spence had seen him. He had obviously kept very fit, and was now sporting a nice tan.

Spence quickly gulped down his drink, blinked his eyes for a moment as if to make sure he wasn't hallucinating, then stammered, "H...How, w...what, b...but, you're dead!" he managed to say.

"Relax, Spence," Macy cut in. "I told you that you need to keep an open mind. We'll talk over dinner and explain the whole thing to you. Trust me, you'll understand once we've had a chance to talk it through."

Deciding there should be no one watching them here, she thought it best not to take too many chances by dining on deck. Gently taking Spence's arm, she lead him down into the cabin, with the Judge following close behind.

Spence stared at his father without speaking while Freddie served dinner. *'How could he still be alive?'* he thought, as memories of his meeting with James, the funeral, the estate, and everything he was going through all flooded into his mind at once, seemingly choking off his air supply.

Unable to stand it, he leaped to his feet exclaiming, "I need some air!" and headed back up on deck. Macy quickly followed him, as he made his way to the side of the boat. He was leaning over the railing as if he was thinking of jumping off, when she touched his arm.

"I know this must be a huge shock for you," she began.

"That's an understatement!" he sneered.

"Please, Spence, come back downstairs and we'll help you make some sense out of all of this. I promise."

"How could you keep something like this from me?" he asked, turning toward her, his eyes burning a hole through her soul.

"I wanted to tell you, but it was necessary to make you believe your father was dead, for your own safety as well as his," she answered.

"So all of this, everything, has been a lie!" he snarled.

"Not everything, Spence. Please give us a chance to explain—"

Spence cut her off. "Explain what? That my father isn't dead after all? I can see that! I suppose next you're going to tell me that the past few weeks have all been a very bad dream."

"I wish they were," she replied. "But Spence, I've never

really lied to you. Sure, I've kept some secrets, and believe me it was for your own good, but I've never actually lied to you."

"So what?" Spence asked. "Are you looking for a medal?"

"No," she said. "I'm looking for a little trust. Please give us a chance to explain everything. I would never lie to you, I promise. Now it's time you learned the truth about your father. He insisted he be the one to tell you when the time came, so I arranged to have him meet us here. You've been searching for answers to so many questions. Well, here's your chance to learn the truth. I'm here to help and support you while you work through this. And I'll not leave you alone, unless that's what you want."

Spence grabbed her hand and squeezed tightly as he wiped a tear from his eye. "No, I don't ever want to be alone again," he said, taking her arm and leading them back to the cabin. He could feel her strength as she steadied him going down the steps. They returned to their seats, as Macy gave a nod to the Judge. They sat in silence for what seemed to Spence like an eternity before his father suddenly spoke.

"Spence, I'm sorry about having to put you through everything you've had to deal with over the past several weeks," his father began. "But believe me, there was no other way."

"Well, why don't you just start from the beginning and bring me up to speed?" Spence asked, managing a half-hearted smile.

"You were right all along. I guess I had become so used to dealing with the VanWarners that I ignored the truth. You were so right about their activities. I'm sorry I ever let that come between us," he said.

"Then why did you?" Spence demanded.

"At the time," the Judge continued, ignoring his son's outburst. "I felt as if I had no choice. Do you remember anything at all about your mother, Spence?"

"Not really," he lied. "I guess I was too young when she died. Why? What does she have to do with this?"

"Everything," his father said, letting out a heavy sigh.

"You see, I left out a few details regarding her death that even I didn't know until recently. It's true; she died in a traffic accident, but not by a drunk driver. We were at a party that night by special invitation from VanWarner. Your mother wasn't very fond of the man, but I convinced her that he had a lot of influence in the community, and this was my chance to make his acquaintance. I was much younger, and eager to prove myself, looking for any opportunity to reach the 'big time'. Your mother reluctantly agreed to accompany me to the party in hopes it would help my career. I was trying to fit in with the local power mongers, but soon realized I was lacking in both guile and a substantial tolerance for alcohol, quickly becoming severely intoxicated. The rest of the evening was a blur, with only shadows of images I believed to be real. The next morning I woke up at VanWarner's house having no idea of the shock that was to come. VanWarner told me I had proceeded to drive home the night before, but was so drunk I ran off the road. Then he informed me that I had killed your mother in the accident. Immediately enveloped by guilt and grief, I fell apart, crying like a baby. VanWarner remained as calm as ever throughout the entire ordeal. Then, when I started to regain my composure, he quickly pointed out the accident was my fault, but he'd taken the liberty of protecting me. He informed me that he had us followed home, and when his goons saw the accident, they quickly arranged the scene to look like your mother was driving alone and had swerved off the road. They brought me back to the VanWarner house to establish an alibi, should the police suspect any foul play. Of course, given the way his people had arranged the accident scene, the police were well convinced it was an accident, thus there was no further investigation. I, on the other hand, had to live with the fact that I was responsible for the death of the only woman I had ever truly loved. It was almost too much to bear, but VanWarner made sure I was never alone for the next six months. He made me a generous offer to handle some of his legal work. Before I knew it, I'd become one of his pawns. I was afraid that if I didn't work for him, he'd reveal the truth about your mother's death, and I still had you to consider. Besides, I was so empty after the accident I became cold and indifferent to what was going on around me. I tried to put up a good front for you, but now you know why I spent so many nights at the apartment in Detroit."

"So it was you who killed my mother!" Spence interrupted, tears streaming down his face.

"No!" his father denied, raising his voice. "Let me finish telling you the whole story. I believed VanWarner's story while the guilt ate away at me for years. Then, about a year ago, I was working at VanWarner's house, going over some papers he'd asked me to look at. I overheard a conversation between Joey and one of his father's men discussing the death of Joey's wife. Joey made a comment about how they'd taken care of that situation just as they'd taken care of your mother. Then he went on to say how sometimes he felt sorry for me because I thought I was responsible for her death, when in fact they slipped something into my drink that night. Not only was I sober, but also I had never left the house. According to their conversation, they murdered your mother and made me believe I was to blame so they could control me. And it worked for many years."

"Why didn't you go to the police once you heard this?" asked Spence, already knowing the answer.

"Because I had no proof," his father answered. "It would have been my word against theirs. And who do you think the police would have believed?"

"I guess you're right," Spence agreed. "But that still doesn't explain faking your death."

"I'm getting to that," his father said, pushing his hands toward Spence as if to say 'calm down'. "After hearing this revelation, I decided to start collecting any information I could that might incriminate VanWarner. I made copies of all the documents, especially the invoices between the VanWarner companies and the Gregorio companies. Of course, you know about the missing ten million dollars Gregorio was supposed to receive. The fact is that's just a drop in the bucket compared to what Joey has been siphoning off from his dealings with Gregorio. In fact, I was able to gather enough evidence to prove Joey had procured several billion dollars over the course of many years, stealing from Gregorio. I don't think he'd be concerned about ten million if he knew about this."

"Okay, so you found out you didn't kill Mom, and Joey was stealing from Gregorio. I'm still waiting to hear why you faked your own death," he finished, folding his arms.

"I was unable to find enough to go to the police with anything that would prove VanWarner killed your mother, much less illegal activities. He was very careful when it came to putting anything in writing. Once the ten million went missing, however, Joey began putting pressure on me. Since one of my employees took the money, he was convinced I, too, was involved. I kept telling him I didn't know where it was, but he became more and more hostile toward me. Gregorio was pressuring Joey. He was afraid Gregorio would discover his embezzling activities if he began asking too many questions. In the meantime, the FBI had contacted me regarding both the VanWarners and the Gregorios, trying to obtain the necessary evidence they needed against both families. The Feds were convinced I'd be privy to their deepest darkest secrets since I was their counsel. Unfortunately, I had little to offer. In fact, the FBI had been able to piece enough together that they convinced me I'd go down with VanWarner as an accomplice in their illegal operations. They offered me a new identity in their witness protection program if I would testify against VanWarner, but I had seen Joey get to too many people over the years. I knew I'd never survive that way," he said as he took another sip from his glass.

"So, that's when you decided to fake your own death," Spence remarked.

"Not exactly," his father swiftly returned. "Actually, I hadn't even thought of it until I met Macy." He turned toward her, giving her a wide smile.

"Oh, so this is where you come in," Spence said, glaring at Macy.

"Spence," his father interrupted, "Macy has been a very

good friend and ally throughout this entire ordeal. George is actually the one who got Macy involved. He was the one working the FBI case who tried to convince me to testify against Joey. However, he knew as well as I did what Joey was capable of doing. That's when he called Macy."

"But George is with the SBI in Kentucky!" Spence exclaimed.

"Not since 1998," Macy explained, squeezing Spence's hand. "He uses the SBI office in Lexington to conceal the fact that he's actually working for the FBI."

"And who do you work for?" asked Spence, pulling his hand away.

"Anyone in need of my services," she replied, reaching for his hand again.

"Well, you're pretty much up to speed now," his father interrupted. "The evidence I had of Joey's embezzlement from Gregorio is in the apartment adjacent to the one I kept in Detroit. Did you find the key and address in the 'Key Largo' tape?"

"Finally," Spence replied. "Clever clue, Dad."

"I knew you were smart enough to figure it out."

"Actually, I must give Sherrie the credit for that one. She was the intelligent one in the firm."

"I'm truly sorry about your friend. I must go for now, but Macy can fill in the rest of the puzzle for you. Don't worry. I'll see you again soon, that is, if you would like to help me rebuild our relationship," his father told him as he headed for the door.

Spence grabbed his father in a warm embrace, whispering, "I love you, Dad."

"I love you too, son." The Judge walked up on deck and disappeared into the night.

Chapter Twenty-Seven

S pence stood quietly in the darkness, staring at the space his father had just vacated. The air was warm and humid, with a gentle breeze blowing in from the ocean. He could feel Macy's presence next to him, strangely comforting him, as they both stood in silence. Finally, he stirred from his seemingly hypnotic trance, eager to learn the answers to the many questions that remained.

"So, tell me," Spence began, "what's your role in all of this?"

"Like I said before," she answered, "I help people in need."

"You're going to have to do better than that."

"Well, considering what you've been through," she said, "I guess my honesty right now might help your needs. Did George ever tell you about our parents?"

"Not much," Spence admitted, "Just that they were rich."

"That pretty much sums it up," she allowed. "When they died, they left everything to George and me. Of course, you know George's career choice. He's probably more of an idealist than I am. He feels he can make a difference in the lives of people by continuing to work as a field agent, even though he doesn't need the money."

"And what about you?" asked Spence. "Tell me about your career."

"I was your typical rebellious teenager," Macy began, "joining the Navy when I graduated. It wasn't long before Navy Intelligence recognized my unique abilities. With their training and my aptitude, I quickly became one of their best agents. I was in covert operations for five years when I decided to quit the business and pursue my education. After graduate school, I still yearned for the excitement I had when I was in the Navy, but I wanted to do more for the little guy instead of large countries. George was convinced the FBI was a noble calling, and tried hard to recruit me to work with him. However, you know how hard it is for siblings to work together. Besides, I didn't want to be bound by the Constitution should I need to operate outside the law. I have more money than I could ever spend, thanks to my mother and father, and my investments are secure. So, I decided to use some of my fortune to help those less fortunate," she finished, smiling back at Spence.

"I'm still confused," Spence said, shaking his head. "What exactly do you do?"

"Whatever needs doing," she replied simply. "Look, I'm trained in several of the martial arts. In addition, I trained in the use of sophisticated weaponry, all thanks to Uncle Sam, I might add. Often people find themselves in seemingly hopeless situations, with nowhere to turn. Many times George calls me when he has worked a case that has tied his hands and he needs my special touch. Such was the case with your father. Since George thinks the world of you, he immediately thought of me as a solution for your father's plight. I don't mean this to sound like I'm bragging or self-serving, but I guess I'm sort of an avenging angel for the desperate and down-trodden."

"Wow, that's deep," said Spence, starting to laugh. Macy quickly grabbed his wrist, turning it backwards and sending a searing pain up his arm. Then she bent him over a deck table, pushing his face into the surface.

"What I do is not a laughing matter," she hissed near his

ear, as she held him down.

"I'm sorry," Spence gasped through the waves of pain. "I didn't mean to offend you. I'm just having trouble processing all of this information."

Macy released his wrist and tugged him back to his feet, pulling him close to her, locking her mouth over his as she proceeded to give him a long, wet kiss. Then she just as quickly separated their bodies as Spence stared at her, unable to speak.

"I'm very passionate about my work."

"I can see that," Spence replied, still staring somewhat in shock. "Isn't this stuff dangerous?" he finally asked after he composed himself.

"There's a certain amount of danger I must admit," she said. "But I find it much less hazardous than government work."

"So, tell me more about my father's situation." he urged.

"As you heard him say, he felt there was no way he could testify against Joey and live for very long. George learned that Joey found out the FBI had approached your father, and was beginning to feel your father had outlived his usefulness. George was afraid for your father's life, so he called me. I orchestrated your father's death, while he supplied the funeral arrangements and the clues he left behind for you. He even added the bequest to Agnes Morehead so anyone watching the tape would believe he recorded his will many years ago before her death. I decided to rent the apartment in the name of Agnes Morehead just in case anyone came looking for her." Macy paused for a moment. "I've not only been helping your father, but I've also been keeping an eye on you. He was very worried about your safety, especially since he knows what these people are capable of doing. By faking his death, your father was free to travel where he wanted without looking over his shoulder. I reminded him there still wasn't enough evidence to put these guys away, and that he dropped you in the middle of all of this, but he assured me you were smart enough to figure a way out where he was unable. The ten million, plus the insurance money he left you, is enough for you to be able to disappear should the heat get too hot. At least that's what your father believed."

"And what do you believe?"

"I believe no amount of money can make you completely safe from people like these," she answered. "And now that I've had a chance to see you in action, I believe you're not the type of person to run from a good fight. I must admit, the murder charge is a rather large curve I wasn't expecting either, but I believe you'll figure out a way to beat it somehow."

"And what makes you so sure I can?" he asked.

"I don't know," she replied. "Just years of gut instinct say you will."

"Well, I wish your guts would tell my guts how to do it," he put in, "'Cause I'm not sure what I should do next."

"Well, like I said, I'm here to help. So let's go over everything and see where we are. The answer might just be staring us right in the face," she said firmly as she pressed her right index finger against Spence's nose. Then she took his hand and led him back inside the cabin.

Macy led Spence back to the table, gestured for him to take a seat, then quickly removed all the dishes from the table and retreated to her room. After some shuffling noises, she returned carrying some papers and clenching a red marker in her teeth.

"I've been working on an outline of all the events in this case," she began. "I thought we could examine it together and see what we're missing."

"Okay," Spence agreed as she spread the papers out onto the table.

"We know now that VanWarner was behind the death of your mother, and we also know Joey killed his wife."

"Yes, we do. But we don't have any hard evidence to prove either case."

"We know the VanWarners and the Gregorios are involved in illegal activities," she continued as if she didn't hear Spence. "And we know Joey has been siphoning funds away from Gregorio for years."

"Again," Spence interjected, "we have no proof."

"Yes we do," Macy objected. "At least your father has proof of Joey's money scamming."

"But the police don't care about that," Spence insisted. "It's no evidence of illegal activity."

"Not if you're bound by the Constitution," Macy winked. "But I'll just bet there's someone who would be very interested to know the information in the papers your father had in his possession."

"Gregorio!" they both said at the same time as their eyes met.

"Okay," Spence said with excitement lining his voice. "We can get Joey in a lot of hot water with Gregorio, but how will that clear me of Sherrie's death, or did you forget I have a murder rap hanging over me?"

"Didn't you say Arlene offered to make it go away for ten million dollars?" reminded Macy.

"Yeah, but how do I know she'll deliver once she has the money?" Spence asked thoughtfully. "I'm still not sure where she fits in all of this. Hey, wait a minute," he said, his features animated as if a light bulb just came on over his head. "If George is in the FBI, he should know more about Arlene, right?"

"I'm already ahead of you on that," Macy answered. "It appears Arlene does work in OCB, but George couldn't get any more information than that. Supposedly, she's working on a high-level case and deep undercover. Maybe she's legit and can actually help you get out of this murder charge."

"Well, I have a gut, too," said Spence. "And it's telling me that something doesn't smell right. I mean, how can having just the money give Arlene enough evidence for her case? No, something is definitely wrong with this picture. I just don't know what."

"Well, they have some pretty damning evidence against you," Macy said, shaking her head. "Tell me Spence, honestly, did you sleep with Sherrie?"

"I'm only going to say this one more time," he glared, his mouth edging into a thin line. "I did *not* sleep with Sherrie. I don't know how they have forensic evidence that says I did, but we were never intimate."

"Okay, Spence, I believe you," she soothed. "But it seems like this is the thing we've been missing. How could they have manufactured forensic evidence like this, without having every cop on the take? And believe me, George knows the CSI crew who took the samples and he would swear on a stack of Bibles they're not corrupt."

"That's definitely the missing piece of the puzzle," Spence said, nodding his head in agreement. "But I'm still convinced Joey is involved. All we have to do is prove it, and we may get the answer we're looking for."

"Let's take a break," Macy sighed, heading for the bar. She mixed a Jack and Coke for Spence, grabbed a beer for herself, handing Spence his drink as she passed by and crooked her finger in invitation to join her on deck. They walked over to the two chairs they had sat in earlier and collapsed collectively in one large sigh. Millions of twinkling stars filled the sky as they sat silently listening to the water lap against the bottom of the boat. After a few minutes, Spence decided to break the silence.

"So, tell me more about your work, Macy," he urged. "How do people who need your services find you?"

"Well, like I told you, George refers some to me. I also get referrals from attorneys who are familiar with my work, and have clients whom they truly believe are innocent, but there's no way to exonerate them through legal means. Don't get me wrong, I'm not a rogue criminal looking to break every law ever written. But I believe sometimes the law gets in the way of justice."

"A noble statement, but how often does that happen?" asked Spence.

"More than you can imagine," she answered. "Just take your situation, for instance. Did you believe you would be facing this six months ago?"

Spence took another sip of his drink, pondering that question. "No. I can honestly say I never saw this coming in a million years. And what makes it all so frustrating is that I know I'm innocent, but have no way of proving it. But let's get off the subject of me for now and back to you."

"Oh, do you find me that interesting?" she teased, taking a long pull from her beer while flashing that winning smile at Spence.

"I must admit I'm very intrigued by you and your mysterious life. Tell me more about how you came to this point in your career?" he pressed.

"Well, like I said, I was a rebellious teenager who joined the Navy straight out of school. For some strange reason I discovered I had an aptitude for excitement and subterfuge. As soon as I was offered an opportunity to join Naval Intelligence in special ops, I jumped at the chance."

"Why did you decide to leave the Navy and go it alone?"

"The last mission I took involved a covert operation to enter a certain country under the cover of darkness, apprehend a major political figure, and remove him to a safe location for interrogation. Of course you realize I can't give you all the details," she stated.

"Of course," he nodded. "Please continue."

"We made a routine beach landing from a sub off the coast and headed toward the compound where the subject was located. Getting in was a piece of cake for our crack team. It was as if they wanted us to take him. Once we got him to the safe house for interrogation, I realized why it had been such an easy operation. The subject was merely an attorney, like you, caught in the middle of a political struggle between the people who were in power and the ones our country preferred to be in power. This guy held no important position, and worse yet, had no information of any importance to the operation. He was just an innocent by-stander, caught in the crossfire.

"After it was apparent he was of no use to us, I suggested we let him go. Instead, our team leader insisted he was lying and summarily executed the man. This innocent man with a wife and family died a senseless death in order to satisfy the blood lust of a common soldier acting on behalf of his country. At that point, I decided people like this man deserved someone to stand up for them against the bureaucrats, politicians, and bullies who prey upon the weak. Of course, I operate mainly in the U.S. since I lack the connections for overseas operations I had in the Navy. Besides, there are plenty of people in this country who need my help."

"Do any of these people pay you for your services?"

"Some have offered, but I don't accept payment for what I do. I simply ask that in return for my help, they agree to offer whatever assistance they can to anyone they see who is in need. I also give them my card, which has an untraceable number that is routed to an answering service should they need me again, or should they have an acquaintance in need of my services," she said, reaching into her pocket to retrieve a business card, which she handed to Spence. He held it up to the light and read the bold words 'The Avenger' with the number listed just beneath it.

"Very impressive," he mused. "No name, no identity, just 'The Avenger.' I like it."

"Well, at least somebody does. George thought it was ridiculous, at least at first, but I believe he's warmed up to it more after seeing the impact I've had on people."

"You know, I remember an old television show called 'The Equalizer' that sounds a lot like the same thing. Of course he simply ran an ad in the newspaper to attract clients."

"Well, that was television," she replied. "If I ran an ad, there'd never be enough hours in the day to handle all the requests. I try to stay with the more serious cases, like yours, where I know I can devote my full attention to one case at a time, rather than chase a lot of small problems that can best be handled by local authorities."

"Well I certainly appreciate all your assistance," Spence told her. "I don't know what I would have done without your help."

"That's my job," she said matter-of-factly. "Now, back to the issue at hand. What do you think we should do next?"

"I don't know," he replied. "Have you come up with anything?"

"You can always take the ten million and skip the country."

"And go where?" he asked with a deep shrug. "I don't want to live the rest of my life looking over my shoulder, wondering if I'll be arrested and hauled away to prison for a murder I didn't commit."

"Well then, it appears Arlene is your only other option at this point," Macy offered. "Maybe she can help you more than you know."

They sat in silence for another twenty minutes, slowly sipping their drinks as the quiet sounds of night on the water enveloped them. Suddenly Spence sat upright in his chair.

"I've got an idea. Let's head to Miami."

"What do you have in mind?"

"I can't tell you now. Just trust me," he said, as he reached for his cell phone. After a few seconds, Spence spoke into the phone. "George, it's Spence. I've got an idea."

Chapter Twenty-Eight

Macy left to give Freddie the instructions for departure while Spence finished his phone call with George. After a few seconds of animated conversation, Freddie made preparations to get the boat under way while Macy made her way back to the deck to find Spence. He was just finishing his call when she sat down.

"Now can you tell me what your big idea is?" she asked.

"Actually, I was hoping you could help me." Spence carefully outlined his plan to Macy while she listened intently. After a few raised eyebrows and questioning looks, she finally conceded his plan was probably his best and only shot. She quickly went to work punching numbers into her cell phone. When a voice came on the other end, she began barking out orders much like a military commander. It was obvious she was used to getting what she asked for, because the entire conversation took a mere thirty seconds. Then she ended the call and glanced in Spence's direction with a somewhat self-satisfied expression on her face.

"We're all set," she informed Spence primly. "They will be waiting for you."

"Great!" he exclaimed. "Now all we can do is to wait

until we dock."

They decided to retire for the evening in order to get a good night's rest for their big day tomorrow. After a couple of hours, it was apparent Spence was too anxious to sleep. He pulled on his robe and shuffled out of his room into the galley where he fixed himself a Jack and Coke before climbing out of the cabin and up on deck. Apparently, Macy was having the same difficulty sleeping, as Spence found her curled up in a deck chair staring out across the black ocean water.

"Penny for your thoughts," he said, causing her to jump.

"Don't sneak up on me like that again," she demanded. "You could give someone a heart attack. What's the matter, can't you sleep either?"

"No. I guess I'm just too eager to get back. What's your excuse?"

"I guess I'm excited for you. I've been playing out possible scenarios in my mind, trying to convince myself that it will all work out to your benefit."

"And what if it doesn't?" he asked. "Then what?"

"Hush," she soothed, placing a finger in front of her lips. "You must think positive. You're going to be okay."

"I hope you're right," he said, tossing back some of his drink.

"I know I'm right," she said confidently, smiling back at him.

Spence collapsed into the chair beside Macy where they sat for the next few minutes in silence, deep in thought, each staring off into the distance, the night ocean sounds playing a unique symphony as the boat made its way swiftly across the surface of the water.

He woke to the glare of the morning sun shining brightly in his face. As he shielded his eyes, he looked around to get his bearings. Macy was still asleep in the chair beside him. Obviously, they'd both finally succumbed to exhaustion, spending the rest of the night asleep on the deck. He reached over and nudged Macy, who nearly bolted out of her chair.

"What's wrong?" she cried, rising to a half-standing position.

"Relax," Spence answered, stifling a laugh. "Everything's fine. Apparently we both fell asleep out here last night."

She collapsed back into the chair, wiping her brow as she struggled to calm her nerves after waking suddenly from a deep slumber.

Spence made out the formation of land ahead as the boat moved slowly over the water. Freddie appeared from the helm to inform them he intentionally slowed down so they wouldn't arrive in port before Spence and Macy had a chance to conceal themselves in the cabin. Macy applauded Freddie for his astute thinking, especially since Spence was no longer in disguise.

"How about some breakfast?" she asked, heading toward the cabin.

"Sounds great to me. I'm famished," replied Spence as he followed close behind her. When Macy began rustling about in the galley, Spence decided to take a shower.

He could smell the wonderful aroma wafting from the galley as he finished getting dressed and joined Macy at the table. She'd gone all out, preparing eggs, bacon, sausage, toast, and hash browns, and of course, coffee. As he sat down across from her, they both looked at each other simultaneously, exchanging smiles. That was the first time he truly believed everything would somehow work out. There was something about being with Macy, which made him feel warm and secure. It was a feeling he wanted to last forever.

They ate in silence, periodically exchanging glances, as both appeared to have ravenous appetites. Although it seemed like an enormous feast, there was nothing but a few morsels left after they were finished. Macy cleared the dishes quickly, then, rejoined Spence at the table while they sipped their coffee.

"We've got a busy day ahead of us today," she began.

"Yes, but I'm eager to get started," Spence returned.

"Why don't you pack what clothes you'll need to take with you while I grab a quick shower? I'll help you get ready."

"Sounds like a plan to me."

Macy proceeded to the shower while Spence disappeared into his room. It didn't take long for him to throw a few articles of clothing in his overnight bag. After all, he only had the few items he'd purchased with Macy. He zipped the bag shut and carried it outside his door, placing it on the floor near the cabin steps. After a few minutes, Macy appeared in her bathrobe, a towel wrapped around her wet head.

"Do you have all of your papers?"

"Yes, they're in the bag."

"Where is the disguise George sent you?"

Spence retrieved the wig and makeup from his room, handing the items to Macy. "Here they are."

She led him into the bathroom and proceeded to work on his appearance. After a few minutes of placing, smoothing, and cursing, Spence was no longer in the room. Instead, Walter Miller stood examining his image in the mirror.

Spence admired her handiwork. "You did a better job than I ever did."

"Well, I've had a little more practice than you," Macy laughed, giving Spence a slight hug. "Besides, it's always easier to put that garb on someone else."

They could feel the boat turning as it neared the dock. Freddie would secure the craft before giving Spence the all clear to depart.

"Are you sure you don't want me to go with you?"

"No. It's better if I go alone. I don't want to tip my hand."

She placed a hand on his forearm. "Well, whatever you do, be careful"

"I promise." The smile he gave her was warm.

Just then, Freddie came down the steps and advised Spence it was clear for him to leave. Spence walked up the dock to the marina, where he had to pass through customs. Flashing his passport to the customs officer, he patiently waited, trying not to look nervous. The officer merely glanced at the photo, then up at Spence, before waving him through. *'So far so good'*, he thought to himself as he exited through the front doors of the marina. It was exactly eight o'clock, and there was a cab waiting for him. He tossed his bag in the back seat and climbed in, instructing the driver to take him to the airport. The cab sped away from the curb and into traffic.

The Miami airport was a large hub not only for vacationers, but for business travelers as well. Many people traveling to Disney World for vacation caught connecting flights to Orlando from Miami. Miami was also the main port for the Caribbean cruise lines. Boats were leaving port every week for three, four, or seven days at a time.

He liked the idea of a large crowd, feeling he had a better chance of going unnoticed. He waited patiently in the passenger line until a very young and pretty attendant summoned him to the ticket counter.

"Yes sir," she said smiling. "How may I help you?"

"I'm booked on the ten fifteen flight to Detroit," Spence told her.

"Certainly," she replied politely, still smiling. "May I see your I.D.?" He handed her the Walter Miller driver's license.

"Thank you, Mr. Miller," she said, and began punching the keys on the keyboard. "Will you be checking any luggage today?"

"No. I just have my carry on."

She retrieved a ticket from the machine next to her and handed it to Spence. "You are booked on Flight 1110 leaving from gate A23. Have a pleasant flight, Mr. Miller."

Spence winked back and headed off in the direction of the gates.

All passengers had to pass through a security checkpoint and metal detector before they could proceed to the gate areas. Spence had already emptied his pockets of any metal objects and placed them in his bag. He'd found this to be the quickest way to get through security. Once past the checkpoint, he could easily retrieve any items he would need from his bag before boarding the plane. The line moved very slowly while the guards escorted several passengers to the side and scanned them with a portable wand after the metal detector alarm sounded. Finally, it was Spence's turn to walk through the detector. He placed his bag on the conveyor and quickly strode through the screener. He was relieved when no alarm sounded, and quickly retrieved his bag on the other side. Proceeding to gate A23, he waited for the boarding call for his flight.

Spence stopped by a shop to purchase a newspaper before settling into a seat near the corner of the gate area. He adjusted the paper to partially conceal him from the other passengers. There was nothing of particular interest in the pages as he flipped through them. Besides, his mind was a million miles away, concentrating on his mental 'to do' list he had laid out in his head.

A few minutes later, a gentleman in a blue suit approached him, sitting down in the next seat. Spence felt he knew the man from somewhere, especially since the man kept looking at him. The gentleman asked Spence if he was finished with the sports section, flashing a pleasant smile. Spence offered a half smile in return, handing him the section he asked for. Then he silently cursed himself for being so paranoid.

After another twenty minutes, an attendant announced over the intercom Flight 1110 to Detroit was now boarding. Spence waited patiently while the other passengers boarded the first class section. He decided to fly coach to avoid any extra attention. When his row was called, he sauntered slowly to the gate as if he were in no hurry. The attendant tore off the stub, handed it back, and wished him a pleasant flight. Spence walked onto the ramp and into the plane to find his seat.

He'd reserved the window seat and was extremely relieved to find no one in his row when he approached. Placing his bag in the overhead compartment, he settled into his seat, fastening his seatbelt, cautiously observing the other passengers as they continued boarding the plane. Just as he was wondering if the seat next to him was booked, the same gentleman who'd asked for his sports section stood beside his row, placing a bag in the overhead compartment. When he sat down in the aisle seat next to Spence, he nodded in his direction.

Once the plane had completed boarding, it was apparent that Spence and he were the only two seated in this row, so the gentleman took his jacket off and laid it on the middle seat.

As the plane taxied down the runway preparing for take off, Spence sat back in his seat and closed his eyes as if trying to nap. After a couple of minutes, the pilot informed the passengers they were next in line for departure. Within a few seconds, Spence felt the plane move rapidly down the runway, then pull upward as it ascended into the blue Miami sky. The plane climbed for quite a while until it finally reached cruising altitude, leveling off for the remainder of the flight.

He eased his seat back, keeping his eyes closed. He was actually starting to dose off when he felt something against his arm.

"Hey, buddy," whispered the man sitting next to him. Spence opened his eyes to find the man leaning across the middle seat staring at him. "Sorry to disturb you, but do you have the rest of that newspaper you were reading back there?"

Spence pulled the paper from the back seat pocket in front of him, where he'd placed it when he sat down, handed it to the man and leaned back in his seat when the man spoke again.

"Thanks. By the way, my name's Norman Smith," he said, extending his hand toward Spence.

Spence shook his hand. "Walter Miller."

"What line of work are you in?" Norman asked. It was clear the gentleman wanted to engage Spence in conversation that he would be unable to avoid for the rest of the flight.

"I'm a school teacher," Spence lied. "Tenth grade math. You?"

"Oh, I sell life and health insurance," Norman answered.

"Sorry, I've got all I need," said Spence, raising his hands.

"Don't worry," Norman said with a slight grin. "I hear

that all the time. Do you live in Michigan?"

"No. I live in Panama City. Just going to Detroit for some continuing education at a teacher's conference," Spence said.

"I'm from Pontiac," Norman offered. "Know where that is?"

"Afraid not," Spence lied. "Is it close to Detroit?"

"Just a little north of there. That's where the Silverdome is, where the Detroit Lions play football."

"Sorry, I'm not much of a football fan," Spence lied again.

"Married?" asked Norman.

"Divorced," replied Spence. "My ex ran off with our insurance agent," he chuckled as he cut his eyes suspiciously toward Norman. "Just kidding," Spence burst out laughing after seeing the stunned look on Norman's face. "Actually, it was my best friend."

"Wow, sorry to hear about that," Norman said convincingly.

"What about you? Are you married?"

"Yep, twenty years now," Norman beamed, reaching for his wallet.

Oh, no! Picture time, thought Spence, as Norman pulled out photos. He carefully went through each one of his wife and four children. When he finished, Spence felt like a distant relative. He could actually remember some of their names.

They conversed in idle chitchat for the remainder of the flight. Spence didn't mind since it actually made the flight seem shorter. It wasn't long before the pilot came over the speaker to inform the passengers they were ready to begin their descent into Wayne County International Airport. After a few minutes of additional flying and maneuvering, the plane made its final turn, heading down onto the runway. Once on the ground, it was a few more minutes before the plane taxied to a stop at one of the gates. The passengers began the short walk from the plane to the terminal, as the flight attendants smiled, waved, and thanked them for flying.

Norman leaned over and whispered to Spence, "George

said hi," shook Spence's hand and winked as they headed into the terminal. Spence gave him a grateful nod for the escort, heading off in the direction of the rental car counters, while Norman took off in the direction of baggage claims. Three people were in front of Spence, so he watched CNN on one of the many televisions mounted on the walls of the terminal as he waited patiently for his turn. After a few minutes, the counter attendant motioned him forward and asked if she could assist him in renting a vehicle. He asked if they had any panel vans available, to which the attendant replied three, all the same size. He handed her his Walter Miller driver's license and credit card, then pretended to be engrossed in a news story while she went to work typing at her computer. After swiping his credit card, she handed back his identification along with the paperwork and keys to the van, pointing in the direction of the rental car lot and wrote the parking space number on the flyer. Spence headed toward the door as she called the next customer over.

The doors automatically opened on his approach and he walked out into the rental car parking area. He was looking for space number 138, which just happened to be at the far end of the lot. He reasoned that since the cargo vans offered little in the way of sex appeal, the company purposely kept them out of sight in favor of the brighter and flashier cars. The van would do just fine for what Spence had in mind, though. He tossed his bag in the back and climbed into the driver's seat. After a quick adjustment of the mirrors, he drove out of the lot and headed toward the interstate. So far, his plan was going okay, but this was the easy part. Better not get overconfident, he told himself. There was still a long way to go.

Chapter Twenty-Nine

Spence pulled into the parking lot in front of the apartment building where his father used to stay overnight. He remembered coming here once as a child, but it was so long ago he'd forgotten most of the characteristics of the building. It had held up well over the years, and still housed a good clientele, unlike the many other buildings across the city that fell into decay and were used for low rent subsidized housing, if not left vacant and inhabited by addicted street urchins.

He remembered what his father told him about the key he'd discovered. Apparently, the Judge had leased two apartments, the second under a fictitious identity, on which he continued to keep the lease current. He had let his original apartment's lease expire just before his departure, hoping to prevent discovery of his stored papers by Joey or his associates.

Spence looked around carefully to make sure no one was following before exiting the vehicle. There was no one around who seemed to be out of the ordinary. In fact, most of the residents were still at work, so it was very quiet. Spence assumed anyone searching for evidence his father possessed had long since given up on this location after discovering the expired lease. After all, there was already another tenant in his father's old apartment.

He walked to the rear of the van, climbed in the back and proceeded to put on the brown jumpsuit neatly folded and lying on the floor. Grabbing two magnetic labels from inside the van that read 'Allied Moving & Storage,' he placed them on the sides of the van. Once everything was in place, he retrieved a hand truck from inside the van, closed the back door, and began walking toward the building.

Spence made his way to the apartment number scrawled on the paper he'd stuffed into his pants. Once there, he inserted the key and turned the lock. The door opened and Spence entered the room, quickly locking the door behind him. The apartment had very modest furnishings to give the impression someone was living there, just in case the building superintendent ever needed to enter. Spence could tell right away, though, that no one had lived here for a long time. It was also in need of a good cleaning, displaying surfaces of the furniture thick with dust.

Spence left the curtains closed so as not to reveal his presence to anyone outside. There was enough light filtering in through the cracks to enable him to see his way around the apartment. He moved on to the master bedroom, where he found the medium-sized, walk-in closet containing a few items of clothing. They had been hanging there long enough to go in and out of style a couple of times.

Parting the clothes hanging in the closet, he began feeling along the back wall. His father had told him he'd installed a fake back that reduced the overall size of the closet, not enough to notice, but enough to conceal several file boxes carefully preserved behind the secret wall. A small panel opened to access the hidden area. He smoothed his hand over the surface until he was able to locate the loose panel. After a few seconds of working the panel, he removed it, revealing an opening to the remainder of the closet.

Spence entered the small space and looked around to survey the contents of the secret area. At least a dozen file boxes were stacked along the left wall in three columns. He grabbed the top box and carried it out of the closet, placing it in the middle of the bedroom floor. He carefully opened the box and examined the contents. Although he was not a party to the business dealings between Joey and Gregorio, Spence was able to follow the paper trail.

His father was right. There was definitely some misappropriation of funds on Joey's part. The Judge had obviously been collecting data for quite a while. Spence couldn't help but smile as he placed the papers carefully back inside the box.

He carried the rest of the file boxes from the closet to the bedroom, loading four of them onto the hand truck and rolled them down to the van. Three trips were all it took to empty the apartment of all the file boxes. Once he tucked them away in the back of the van, he climbed back into the driver's seat and sped off in the direction of the interstate.

"So far so good," he muttered to himself again, glancing in the rear view mirror to make sure no one was following.

He drove the two hundred miles from Detroit to Muskegon in approximately three hours. It was now late afternoon, as the shadows were beginning to grow longer in the fields along the highway. Spence decided to spend the night in Muskegon, rather than risk anyone spotting him in Traverse City. Feeling certain the authorities were staking out the estate, he wanted to wait until the last possible moment to make his arrival there. Besides, he still had one more journey to make.

He noticed an old motel just off the highway that looked like it had been around for a hundred years. Only a couple of cars sat in the parking lot, most travelers opting for the nicer accommodations, he supposed. However, since he wanted to maintain a low profile, and the rooms were somewhat secluded from the main view of traffic, he decided this place would suit his needs.

The office was located at the north end of a long row of rooms. Spence walked into the office and rang the little bell sitting on the counter. After a couple of minutes, he heard someone shuffling toward him from somewhere in the back. Soon, a lady emerged from the room behind the counter, wearing a faded, pale blue dress that looked much worn, and knee-high stockings that had fallen down to the tops of her equally worn bedroom slippers. Her short disheveled hair was mostly gray, and came to rest just below her ears. She had a pair of horn-rimmed glasses dangling from a chain around her neck, and a cigarette hanging from the left corner of her mouth, the ash at least three inches long.

"What do you want?" she snarled, squinting at Spence.

"I'd like a room for the night," he answered somewhat timidly.

"Fill this out," she ordered, shoving a register in front of him. He scrawled the necessary information on the sheet and handed it back to her. "Fifty bucks!" she demanded, the long ash still clinging to her cigarette.

He reached into his front pocket and pulled the money out. The old woman grabbed the cash from his hand and tossed a key in his direction, which landed just in front of him on top of the counter.

"Room eight!" she barked, "And no wild parties!" Then she turned and disappeared into the back room.

Spence walked out of the office and back to the van. He parked directly in front of room eight and grabbed his bag from the back. Cautiously entering the motel room, he locked the door behind him. One full-sized bed took up the middle of the room, and a small table with two chairs sat in the corner. At least the television had a remote and cable, he chuckled, but was the only sign of modern civilization in the room. The furnishings looked as if they'd come over on the Mayflower, and smelled like it too.

The small table nearly collapsed when Spence placed his bag on it, so he quickly moved it to the bed. He was afraid to sit in either chair, fearing they were in just as bad a shape as the table.

Spence sat on the edge of the bed and pushed the button on the remote control. It took a few seconds for the picture tube to warm up before the television sprang to life. Obviously, the old woman got out as cheap as she could by only ordering the basic cable package, which consisted of the local channels and HBO. There was also Spectra-vision, a selection of adult movies he could order with the remote at a cost of six bucks each, but you needed to provide a credit card to pay for them. He reasoned this place was most popular among people looking for a place to have a quick rendezvous while cheating on their significant other. He just hoped the old lady had recently washed the bed linens.

Spence crashed on the bed while watching an episode of the Sopranos on HBO. He woke up at around one o'clock in the morning, used the bathroom, and pulled back the sheets to return to his slumber, switching the television off. He slept soundly until seven, awakening to the sound of a couple in the room next to his. It seemed they were continuing their love ritual from the night before. Probably regulars, he thought to himself, getting up and dressing to begin his day.

After tossing his bag back into the van, he dropped the room key at the office and drove off in the direction of Grand Rapids, stopping long enough to grab a biscuit and coffee, which he ate while driving down the highway. It took approximately forty-five minutes before he arrived at the airport in Grand Rapids. He parked the van in the long-term parking lot and grabbed the two duffle bags he brought with him, walking to the terminal where he waited patiently for his turn at the ticket counter.

The wait was much shorter than Detroit, as Spence was motioned to the counter within a few minutes. He requested a one-way ticket to Lexington, Kentucky. The attendant began punching her keyboard and informed him there was a flight leaving in about an hour. It had one stop in Cincinnati before continuing on to Lexington. He handed her his Walter Miller license and credit card, while she continued to punch the keyboard. She asked if he had any luggage he would like to check, but he declined, tapping one of the duffle bags which contained the other one rolled up inside. The attendant handed him a ticket and pointed in the direction of the security checkpoint while telling him the gate number for his flight.

Spence walked over to one side and removed all of the metal objects he had in his possession. He carefully placed them inside the duffle bag and proceeded to the security checkpoint. Surprised no one was waiting in line; he placed his bag on the conveyor belt and stepped through the metal detector. After hearing no alarm and receiving a, "have a nice day" from the guard, he grabbed his bag and headed to the gate. Very few people were waiting, most appeared to be business travelers. He was relieved to be able to sit alone and collect his thoughts while he waited for his flight to begin boarding.

Since he had no one to talk to, the wait seemed longer than the flight from Detroit, but after about forty-five minutes the airline attendant announced the boarding of his flight to Cincinnati with continuing service to Lexington. The jet was small and seated about fifty passengers, so there was no first-class section. The flight was about half-full, and no one sat next to Spence. He could actually sit back and try to take a nap without anyone bothering him the entire flight.

He'd barely fallen asleep when the pilot informed the passengers they were beginning their descent into Cincinnati. Spence sat up and gazed out the window. The overcast sky was typical for Cincinnati, he thought to himself. The plane landed smoothly and taxied to the gate. He remained on board while the remaining passengers exited the plane. A few passengers boarded for the flight to Lexington, but the plane was now about one-third full when they pushed back from the gate. Again, Spence had the row to himself, so he lay back as far as the seat would recline and closed his eyes. The flight to Lexington was even shorter than the previous flight, so he never fell asleep. It was cloudy in Lexington as well, as a few raindrops fell on the window of the plane. Once the plane came to a complete stop, the passengers began to exit the craft and enter the terminal.

Spence made his way to the rental car counter, where he rented a mid-sized sedan. Again, he used the Walter Miller license and credit card, but rented from a different company than the one he rented the van from, just in case it would raise a red flag to have two vehicles rented from the same company at the same time.

Handing Spence his papers, the clerk pointed in the direction of the rental car lot. Locating the car, he climbed in and headed out of the lot on his way to Frankfort.

His first stop was at the first bank he'd rented the safe deposit box. He let himself in the vault and placed his key in the lock, opening the door to the vault that held his box. He removed the box and carefully placed its contents inside one of the duffle bags. Then he reinserted the box, closed the door, and locked it securely. He walked out of the vault and noticed Amy was sitting at her desk talking on the phone. As he approached, she quickly ended her call and placed the telephone receiver in its cradle. Obviously a personal call, Spence thought.

He made up some story about being transferred out of town and needing to close the box. Amy flashed a pout face at him, then smiled and assisted him with the necessary forms to complete his transaction. He returned the key to her and thanked her for her assistance. She stood and shook his hand before he turned and walked out of the bank and back to the rental car. Next stop … State Street Bank.

He entered the bank much the same way as the other one, moving steadily to the vault to remove the contents of the safe deposit box, placing the cash in the other duffle bag, closing the door and relocking the box. Making sure the door to the vault was secure, he moved on to Carol's desk to close out his account. He used the same story on her as he had on Amy. Of course, she acted disappointed to see him leave also, but wished him well and thanked him for his business. He returned to the rental car and tossed the duffle bag in the trunk next to the other one. Concluding his business for the day, he drove off toward Interstate 64.

Since the airline would only allow one carry on, Spence booked the rental car where he could return it in Grand Rapids. He didn't want to risk discovery of his cash by checking the bags, or even scanning them through the X-ray machine, deciding it would be safer if he drove back to Michigan with the money. Spence felt a little more at ease now that this part of his plan was complete. Besides, the long drive would give him time to replay his plan in his mind, boosting his confidence in its positive outcome.

The traffic was moderate heading west on the interstate. The trip would take him through Louisville, then north on Interstate 65 to Indianapolis, continuing north to Michigan. It was about a seven and a half hour drive, but Spence was in no particular hurry this time. He maintained the speed limit for fear of being stopped by the police, feeling they would have a lot of questions should they discover the contents of the duffle bags in the trunk of his car.

He stopped in Indianapolis to grab a bite to eat, parking the car where he could see it from the restaurant, making sure it was securely locked before walking away. Since it was between lunch and dinner, very few people were inside. Spence requested a booth near the window. It took only a few minutes for a waitress to get his drink order.

He noticed her nametag read Gladys. She was probably in her mid-forties with blonde hair and blue eyes. No doubt she'd been a real looker in her younger days, but the hard life of a waitress had taken its toll. She still had a very pleasant smile, though, as she asked Spence what he would like to eat. He ordered a club sandwich and a soda. She gave him another nice smile, took the menu, and retreated to the kitchen to place his order. A short time later, she returned with his order.

He would've liked to take more time eating, but he still had a long way to go. He finished the sandwich, left a couple of bucks on the table for Gladys, and went to the counter to pay for his meal. Gladys was playing dual roles as both waitress and checkout clerk, taking his money at the cash register. He thanked her for the great service and whispered he'd left her a tip on the table. She gave him a grateful smile and thanked him for his business, asking him to stop in again. He turned and walked out of the restaurant and back to his car, driving back to the interstate to resume his journey.

Carefully making his way to the airport in Grand Rapids,

he removed the bags from the trunk and turned the rental car in. Walking to the long-term parking lot, he located the van, tossed the bags in the back with the file boxes and drove out of the lot. He had decided to spend the night at his father's estate since it would be dark when he arrived. He had cleaned out the empty bay of the garage when he was there before, so he felt he could park the van beside his dad's car and no one would be able to see it.

It took a while, but he finally arrived at the estate. He turned off the headlights just before turning into the drive, just in case someone was watching the house. He knew the driveway like the back of his hand, so navigating in the dark was a cinch. Once at the garage, he quickly opened the door, removed the light bulb from the opener, and pulled the van inside, closing the garage door as quickly and quietly as he could. Jumping out of the van, he grabbed the bags from the back and entered the house from the side door, careful not to turn on any lights.

Spence tossed the bags on the floor behind the desk in his father's office, and felt his way up the stairs to the bedroom, where he closed the shades completely before turning on the bathroom light. It would give him just enough light without being seen from outside. After his normal pre-bedtime routine, he turned off the light and climbed into bed, certain it was going to be a long night.

Chapter Thirty

Spence woke early, having slept restlessly the night before. He kept thinking about what tomorrow would bring and what lie in store. He wondered if he was doing the right thing, but convinced himself it was the best plan of action available. After lying in bed for a few minutes, he groggily pushed himself to his feet and headed to the shower. He spent an extra amount of time just letting the warm water cascade over his body, struggling to wake up. He was still somewhat sleepy when he turned the water off and climbed out of the shower.

He dressed casually, and headed downstairs for some coffee, hoping that hit of caffeine would jolt him awake. As the coffee began to brew, he grabbed a doughnut from the box he'd purchased the day before, taking a big bite while placing his cup on the counter. By the time he ate half of the doughnut, the coffee was ready. He poured the hot liquid into his cup, savoring the wonderful aroma. Spence had always loved the smell of freshly brewed coffee.

He grabbed another doughnut and headed into the den. Turning on the television, he hoped to catch up on the latest news. He continued to sip his coffee and munch on the doughnut as he listened to the latest news stories. He must be old news since there was no mention of him, he mused. Stories died quickly when no new information captured ratings.

Spence finished the second doughnut, licking the glazed icing from his fingers. He made his way to the kitchen to top off his cup, switching off the pot and unplugging the cord. It had become a habit of his to always unplug the coffee pot when it was not in use after he'd heard about house fires being caused by appliances left unattended. He chuckled to himself as he thought about his current financial situation. It would be easy to replace the house if he decided he wanted to. However, old habits were hard to break, and he needed the property—at least for today.

Walking through the side door to the garage, he retrieved one of the boxes from the van. He carried the box back into the house and placed it carefully on the floor of his father's office beside the desk. He straightened the desktop, placing every document inside the top drawer. There, he thought, it looks much better now. By now it was only ten, still four hours to kill before two. To kill time, he moved back to the den to surf the channels hoping to find something worthwhile to watch while he waited. He was just starting to nod off when his cell phone rang.

"Is everything okay?" Macy asked.

"Fine," Spence answered, "Just waiting for the fireworks."

"Don't worry. Everything's all set."

"Thank you, Macy," he replied, pressing the button to end the call.

Turning off the television, he pushed to his feet, stretched and went back to the office. He sat down at the desk and began writing on a legal pad, deciding to make a few notes, just in case things didn't turn out as he planned.

Spence smiled a few times as he continued to write down his thoughts. He spent an hour comprising several pages of text before laying the pen down and pushing the chair back from the desk. He walked into the kitchen to grab a soda from the fridge, careful to stay away from alcohol, even though he could really use a Jack and Coke right now. However, he needed to keep his senses alert. Returning to the den, he switched the TV back on. He quickly surfed through the channels, settling on the noon news update.

He watched an hour of news, then another forty-five minutes of an old Clint Eastwood movie before glancing at his watch. It was one forty-five in the afternoon. Time to prepare for his guests, he thought, as he punched the off button on the remote and walked back to the office to wait. Everything was in place. Now all he could do was to wait.

At exactly two o'clock, the doorbell rang. Spence made his way through the foyer to the front door. Looking through the glass, he could see it was Arlene. Taking a deep breath, he slowly let it out, then opened the door, flashing a smile.

"Thank you for coming Arlene."

"Well, I didn't feel like I had a choice." She smiled as she sailed past Spence into the house.

Spence closed the door and led her to his father's office, motioning to one of the wing chairs in front of the desk. She took a seat in the left chair, seductively crossing her legs. She was wearing a bright red dress that barely came to mid-thigh, exposing her long sexy legs. She was definitely dressed to make him regret not keeping their relationship intact. He sighed with remorse but offered her a drink, to which she gladly accepted. He left the office and went to the kitchen, returning with the bourbon on the rocks she'd requested. He handed her the drink and moved around behind the desk. Just as he was about to sit down, the doorbell rang again. He excused himself and walked to the front door. A glance through the glass told him Joey was on the other side, a big smile on his face.

"Thank you for coming, Joey," Spence said.

"My pleasure," he replied. "I see we're not alone," he continued as he thumbed toward Arlene's car.

"No," Spence said. "I took the liberty of inviting someone else. I hope you don't mind."

"Of course not," Joey assured him, "As long as they're okay."

"Don't worry," Spence said with a slight smile. "I think you'll be pleased."

Spence invited Joey into the house, led him through the foyer, and into the office. He introduced Arlene as a close friend and confidante. Joey and Arlene shook hands politely, Spence taking note that Joey was beginning to drool over Arlene's legs. He slid into the chair next to her, still staring. Spence hid a grin, moved behind the desk and sat down in his father's chair.

"Joey," Spence began, "I understand you've been missing something of interest that you would like to recover, and that you believe it was in my father's possession. Am I correct?"

"Damn straight!" Joey said without hesitation.

"I'm sure you are aware of my predicament with the law."

Joey nodded. "Yeah, I heard something about that."

"Well, as it turns out, Arlene here has offered to clear my name if I give her the property you're after."

"Is that so?" Joey asked, looking at Arlene.

Arlene stood up and walked toward Joey, suddenly sitting down on his lap and proceeded to give him a long passionate kiss. As their lips parted, Arlene purred, "Joey, baby. You know I was only trying to get your money back for you."

"I know, babe. I'm the one who suggested it, remember?" he chuckled, winking at Spence.

Spence feigned a shocked look, waiting for a minute before speaking. "You mean you two were in on this together?"

"Of course we were," Arlene scoffed, giving Joey another kiss.

"But I thought you worked for the OCB?"

"Well, I did for a while," she confessed, then let out a giggle. "But let's just say Joey made me an offer I couldn't refuse."

"So everything you told me was a lie," Spence remarked, feigning hurt.

"Maybe not everything, but most of it."

Spence decided to switch gears. "I know you killed my

mother, Joey. Tell me, did you kill my assistant too?"

"Killing your mother was just good business. We needed to be able to control your old man," snarled Joey. "I didn't have anything to do with your girl's death."

"I find that hard to believe," Spence said, a frown dragging his brows together.

"Believe it," Arlene interrupted. "Killing Sherrie was all my doing."

"Why? What had she done to you?" demanded Spence.

"Nothing," answered Arlene, lifting one shoulder nonchalantly, as if taking Sherrie's life was of no consequence. "I just needed some leverage to make you turn over the money. Framing you for her murder seemed like the best way to get you to cooperate."

"But how...?" Spence barely got the words out before Arlene continued.

"That night we slept together," she confided, "I slipped something into your drink so you'd sleep soundly for several hours. I was able to retrieve some of your sperm, and put it in the freezer until I could slip it out the next day. I was also able to place the gun in your hand to obtain your fingerprints. At the time, I wasn't sure if I'd even be able to use them, but collected them just in case. Then when I overheard your assistant flirting with you on the phone, I decided it wouldn't be too difficult for people to believe you'd kill her over an affair gone awry. I entered the front door of your office and locked it behind me. I pretended to be in need of legal assistance until I could maneuver close enough to her. Then I killed her and planted your sperm inside her. After that, I searched the office for any indication of where the money might be, but found nothing. After you turned down my proposal, I planted the gun in the dumpster and phoned in an anonymous tip. And the rest, as they say, is history."

"But how did you plan to make the evidence just disappear?" he asked.

"Well now, you see, that's the funny part," Arlene joked. "I had no intention of making it disappear. With you in prison, there'd be no one to interfere with me and Joey," she said, leaning over to give Joey another long wet kiss.

"This has been a very interesting conversation," Joey said, breathing heavily. "But since you brought the money, I think it's time we take the money and run, so to speak." He laughed at his own joke, pulling a gun from under his jacket.

"Now Joey," Spence warned. "You don't think I came here with nothing but the money, do you?"

He looked around him. "What do you mean?"

"Well, it seems my father had gathered more than some of your money. He also had a collection of papers showing where you've been siphoning money from your business dealings with Mr. Gregorio. This box—" Spence pointed to the box beside the desk— "is one of many that contain these documents. I was hoping we could work out some sort of deal."

He waved the gun at Spence. "Gregorio's a chump. He has no clue, and I plan to keep it that way. I tell you what, instead of a deal, why don't you just hand over the papers before you end up like your mother?"

Just then, the sound of footsteps scuffed across the carpet. Gregorio, along with two of his thugs, suddenly appeared in the office doorway.

"Joey, Joey, there's no need for that. Now why don't you put that gun down like a good boy?" Gregorio said as one of his goons pointed a semi-automatic weapon directly at Joey.

Joey let the gun slip slowly from his grasp, it hit the floor with a loud thud. "M...Mr. Gregorio," he stammered. "How long have you been here?"

"Long enough, Joey," Gregorio replied. "And I must say I'm very disappointed in you. I trusted you, Joey, and you betrayed me."

"W...Wait a minute, Mr. Gregorio. It's not what it looks like," insisted Joey as beads of sweat immediately appeared across his brow. "I was just yankin' this guy's chain, you know. Please, Mr. Gregorio, I didn't mean any disrespect." He clasped his hands in front of him in a pleading gesture.

"How did you say it?" Gregorio asked, one bushy eyebrow raised. "Oh yes, I'm a chump who has no clue. I believe that's what I remember you saying."

"Mr. Gregorio, I'm so sorry," apologized Joey. "I was only trying to impress Spence. I'll return all of the money, I swear."

Gregorio walked up behind Joey's chair. "You know, Joey, I learned a valuable lesson a long time ago I'd like to share with you now. No matter how good or bad a person lives their life, everyone must eventually face their day of reckoning," he said, and with that, he pulled a wire from his jacket pocket, slipped it over Joey's head, and began choking him from behind.

"Now is the time of your reckoning, Joey," Gregorio said as he continued applying pressure until Joey's lifeless body slumped in the chair. Arlene wanted to scream, but was in too much shock to move. She simply sat there, tears streaming down her cheeks. Spence hardly flinched at what he saw. In his mind, justice was served and a reckoning now imposed for the death of his mother, and a final reckoning for the murder of Lorraine. Spence hoped this would be the end of his recurring nightmare.

Chapter Thirty-One

M r. Rawlings," Gregorio spoke, "I assume that box has the papers you called me about."

Spence nodded. "Yes, along with eleven others in the van parked in the garage. You're welcome to take them all. Just have one of your guys drop the van back at the rental agency when you're finished with it." He gestured in the direction of the garage.

Gregorio's two men began removing Joey's body from the chair, moving the chairs from in front of the desk to lay Joey's body on the large Oriental rug. Carefully, they rolled the rug up concealing Joey inside.

"Mr. Rawlings," Gregorio continued, "I would like to purchase this rug from you. I believe ten million dollars would be a sufficient price for it. Do you agree?" he asked, nodding at the bags.

"Certainly," Spence replied as they exchanged smiles.

The thugs gathered up the rug with Joey stuffed inside and carried it out to the van. One returned to retrieve the box of papers beside the desk, while the other one started the van. After he placed the box inside the back of the van, he slapped on the side and the driver pulled away, heading down the drive. The other one opened the door of a black limousine for Gregorio. Once Gregorio was securely inside, he climbed into the driver's seat and sped away, following the van. When they reached the end of the drive, each one turned in opposite directions.

Arlene started coming to her senses as the shock began to wear off. She looked up at Spence. "I'm sorry for all of this. Joey made me do it. I swear, I love you. I can make the evidence against you disappear. We can split the money if you don't want to be with me after all that has happened. I'll understand. I still have friends in high places. I can make it go away, I promise. What do you say?" After she finished her plea, George stepped into the office from the adjoining room.

"That won't be necessary," he affirmed. "We have your confession to Mrs. Barbour's murder on videotape. Smile for the camera," he said, pointing to the wall clock positioned behind the desk above Spence.

"Did you get it all?" Spence asked.

"Every detail," George answered.

"Great." Spence turned to Arlene. "Sorry, no deal."

She hung her head as two uniformed officers approached, one placing handcuffs on her wrists while the other read her rights. Then they led her outside to an awaiting squad car.

George held up the tape, saying, "I'll make sure your attorney gets a copy of this."

"What about Gregorio?"

"Don't worry, we've got a car following the limo and one following the van. We'll wait until the one starts to bury the body before we move in. Besides, we have Joey's murder on tape. No way he'll get out of this one."

"Thanks, buddy," Spence said, shaking George's hand.

"Thank you," George replied. "This will be a good bust for me. I may even get a promotion out of it." He laughed, slapping Spence on the back.

Once Arlene and the other agents were gone and all of the surveillance equipment removed, Spence turned to George. "Okay. Now can you tell me who was bugging the place?"

"Actually," George confessed, smiling at Spence. "It was us. That's how I knew you needed my sister's help. I was hoping to be able to get the evidence on my own, but it was obvious you had no clue upon what you had stumbled. I just hate there wasn't enough sound from the bugs in your office to determine who killed Sherrie so you wouldn't have to go through today's charade. I'm just glad your hunch was right. Oh, by the way, say hello to Macy for me next time you see her."

He turned quickly, headed out the door, and sped away in his car. Spence was alone again, but relieved it was all over. He walked to the kitchen and mixed a Jack and Coke, needing a drink badly. After all the excitement hell, he deserved one. He took a long swig, walked back to the den, and collapsed on the sofa. As he flipped on the remote, he suddenly realized how emotionally and physically drained he was. It was just too quiet without some kind of noise.

Spence woke to the realization he'd fallen asleep on the sofa. He looked at his watch and discovered it was seven o'clock, but the sun was rising, so he must have slept there all night. He had a terrible crick in his neck from the awkward position he'd been in. He could hardly believe he'd slept so long. Catching up for all of the restless nights he'd endured when it seemed the weight of the world was on his shoulders, he supposed.

He rose and walked upstairs for a shower, afterward dressed and came back down stairs and headed out to the garage. Since George had promised to have the rental van returned after they finished with Gregorio, the only vehicle he had at his disposal was his father's car. Considering he was the only heir to the estate, it was his now, he decided he might as well make good use of it.

Spence drove out of the garage and headed toward town, grabbing some breakfast, before going to finish settling his father's estate. Once that task was over, he vowed never to return to Michigan. As he was driving along, his cell phone rang. It was Josh Treadway.

"Spence, Josh here. I just wanted to let you know the

D.A. dropped all charges against you. You're officially a free man."

"Great! Thanks, Josh. By the way, do you happen to know a good attorney who would be interested in a small practice like mine?" Spence asked.

"Try Bill Fisher just down the street from you. He hasn't been there long, but he has great potential and is hungry for business. I think he'll service your clients well."

"Thanks for the tip," said Spence gratefully.

"You're welcome. And don't be a stranger, pal," Josh said as he ended the call.

Spence smiled, as he thought 'don't count on it.'

He stopped at a convenience store and grabbed a biscuit and coffee, sat in his car as he ate while waiting for the bank to open. At nine o'clock, he parked in front of the bank and walked in, made his way to the teller window, and informed the teller he was there to close the account he'd recently opened. He also closed the estate account, advising the teller he'd be opening another estate account once he settled. He thanked her for her help and walked out with two cashiers' checks, one for the balance of his account and one for the estate account.

Next on his list was a realtor. Spence had already selected one from the phone book before leaving the estate. He pulled up in front of Greenway Realty at nine-thirty, walked into the office and told the receptionist he needed to speak to someone about listing a property for sale. She motioned to one of the chairs in their waiting area, then, called one of the agents. Shortly, a middle-aged lady approached Spence. She was wearing one of the blue company blazers with matching slacks. Her hair was short, peppered with gray, and was very petite in stature. Her nametag read 'Joan Eastman.'

"Hello, my name is Joan," she greeted, extending her hand.

"Spencer Rawlings," he replied, taking her hand.

She led him down the hallway to one of the offices on the right. Once seated, she asked Spence what she could do for him. He explained about his father's passing and that he wanted to sell the estate along with the boat and personal property in the house. She told him she was familiar with the property as she wrote down all of the necessary information. She also told him she'd need to physically inspect the property and measure the dimensions for the real estate listing. Prepared for that request, he handed her the keys and asked if there was any way he could sign a power of attorney so he wouldn't have to be there for the sale. She said it was possible and proceeded to gather the necessary paperwork.

After he signed all the documents, he gave her his cell number as a way to contact him. He told her she could keep the keys since he wouldn't need them anymore. Finally, he told her that once the property sold, he would give her the necessary account information so she could wire the funds to the estate account. Once they finished their business, she thanked Spence and shook his hand, flashing a pleasant smile. Walking out of the office to his car, he felt confident things were going smoothly at last.

Now that he had concluded his business in Michigan, Spence headed for the interstate. It was several hours back to Kentucky, but the long slumber from the night before had recharged him. He decided to ride with the top down since it was such a beautiful day. He caught himself smiling in the rearview mirror, having weathered the storm of the last several weeks only to finally come out on top. It felt good knowing he was no longer a fugitive.

Finding the banks were closed by the time he arrived in Kentucky, he just drove on home. He parked his father's car in the garage beside his own, taking one last look around to make sure no police were watching, mainly out of habit, before entering his house for the first time in what seemed like ages. He placed his bags carefully in the bedroom closet and headed down to the kitchen to fix a drink, settling in his chair to watch the news.

Gregorio and Arlene were still making headlines as they aired very unflattering pictures of both. Spence was glad not to hear his name in the reports, whispering a 'thank you' to George under his breath.

After he'd watched all the news he wanted, Spence mixed another drink and settled in to watch a movie. He fell asleep two-thirds of the way through it and missed the ending. Of course, he'd seen it before, so he really didn't miss anything. By ten-thirty, he decided to call it a day. Knowing tomorrow would be another busy day for him, he wanted to get plenty of rest. With a clear conscience, it took no time before he was sound asleep.

Chapter Thirty-Two

S pence woke in the comfort of his own bed. It felt good to be home and yet he felt so alone. He found himself thinking about Sherrie and the horrible fate that befell her. He had surely lost a very dear friend. His thoughts turned to Macy and he wondered if he would see her again. She'd told him before he left she'd be waiting in Miami for a recap of this last excursion, but would she be there or had she already left for some other person in need?

He pushed to his feet, heading into the bathroom to take a long relaxing shower. Afterward he threw on a pair of jeans and a polo shirt. The first stop on his agenda for the day was his local bank. He arrived shortly after nine o'clock. Both his personal and business accounts were there, making it very convenient both for banking and for leaving. He walked into the lobby and looked around for his personal banker.

Spotting Julie talking with another employee, he took a seat outside her office. When she glanced his way, she quickly finished her conversation and walked over to where he sat. She was in her mid-thirties with short brown hair, deep brown eyes and cute dimples. She was only five feet three inches tall and very petite.

"Spence," she greeted politely, extending her hand. "How have you been?"

"Okay, I guess," he acknowledged. "I need to close my accounts."

"Is something wrong?" she asked, alarmed at his statement.

"No. Nothing like that," he assured her, then went on to explain about his father and Sherrie.

He told her he was moving out of the area, at least for a little while, and needed to have ready access to his funds wherever he ended up. He promised Julie that if he returned to Kentucky he'd bring his business back to her. She gave him a smile and expressed her sympathy over his recent setbacks. Her fingers flew over her keyboard, typing in the necessary information and the printer spit out several documents. After it finished, she gathered the papers and left the office, returning a few minutes later with two cashiers' checks.

"I made out two separate checks even though both accounts were solely in your name," Julie explained, "just in case you wanted to keep the business funds separate from the personal."

"Thanks, Julie, I appreciate that," Spence said as he took the checks.

He thanked her for her prompt attention and the way she had handled his accounts since he'd first become a customer. Walking out of her office, across the lobby, he returned to his car, driving off in the direction of Lexington, and in just a few minutes, he was sitting in the parking lot behind his office. He hadn't been there since he and Josh came just after Sherrie's death.

The police tape was still up since no one had been there to clean the office. Spence entered the back door and looked around, hoping to find Sherrie hard at work. He flashed back to the harsh reality of her death as he surveyed his surroundings. His eyes focused on the pool of blood still remaining, reminding him of what Arlene had done to one of his closest friends.

Since the files seemed to be intact, even though many

lay scattered about, he decided the office was in good enough shape not to worry about cleaning it. That, he thought, would be for whoever came after him.

He walked down the street to Bill Fisher's office. According to Josh, Bill had only been in town six months, and was fresh out of law school, having graduated with honors and passing the bar with excellence.

He walked up to the receptionist and asked to see Bill. The office was much smaller than Spence's. It appeared it was just Bill and his assistant, much like Spence and Sherrie's arrangement had been.

Bill came out of his office to greet Spence, shaking his hand. Spence gave him a brief summary of the events that led up to this moment, which Bill admitted he'd heard a little about some of it. Spence went on to explain he was leaving town and wanted to turn his clients over to someone who was capable of providing the same quality service that he and Sherrie had.

Bill seemed flattered at first, but then informed Spence that since he hadn't been practicing long, he lacked the necessary funds to purchase a practice the size of Spence's. Spence smiled warmly and informed Bill there was no asking price, and he was welcome to move to his office if he wanted, especially since he'd paid the lease in advance for one year. Of course, he probably would want to have it cleaned first, he told him.

Spence handed him the necessary paperwork he'd prepared in order to turn over the business to Bill. Bill was at a loss for words at first. Then he asked Spence why he'd chosen him. Spence declared that he felt Bill was a trustworthy individual, one who'd come highly recommended. Bill beamed with pride after Spence's last comments and thanked him again for his confidence in his abilities.

Spence left Bill's office and headed back home, feeling good that he'd successfully taken care of everything on his to do list. Now all he needed was to get all of his papers in order and pack a few clothes. He could use his own passport now since there was no need to resurrect Walter Miller. He decided to hang on to the disguise and fake identification, just in case. You never know when something like that might come in handy again, especially considering the events of the past several weeks, he reasoned.

He pulled his car into the garage and climbed out of the driver's seat, walking into his house and on to the bedroom. Grabbing a few clothes, he packed them neatly into his travel bag. Then he made sure all of his papers were in order and arranged them with care, along with the cashiers' checks, in his briefcase. He made sure he had the two duffle bags, and was now all set to go.

Spence was in the same predicament as before, not being able to fly for fear of someone discovering the money and raising too many questions. He decided to drive to Miami, which would take approximately sixteen hours. Well, might as well get started, he thought as he placed all of his bags in the trunk. He pulled out of the garage and headed toward the interstate, thinking about calling Macy, but decided to surprise her and hoped she'd still be there.

He drove the first eight hours straight, stopping only once for gas. He pulled off the highway at a rest area to take a short nap before continuing. Several other cars were parked in the area, so he felt like it was safe to stop. He leaned the seat back and closed his eyes, falling asleep after a few minutes, and remained that way for four hours. When he awoke, the rest area was almost deserted. He climbed out of his car, stretched and headed for the restroom. After relieving himself, he washed his face in cold water to wake up. Grabbing a soda from the vending machine, he hurried back to his car, anxious to be one his way, started the engine and continued on his journey.

After another couple of hours, he was hungry again, so he exited the highway near a small town and searched for a place to eat. Finding a truck stop, he parked in an empty space and went inside. Several truckers were already eating and telling tales from the road. Spence sat down at the counter between two couples who appeared to be married team drivers. The waitress scurried over and asked if he would like some coffee while tossing a menu down in front of him. He nodded his approval and began to study the menu.

Just then, the man to his right leaned over and said, "Just stick with the ham and eggs. It's the only thing fit to eat in this joint," he said, letting out a big laugh, then he introduce himself.

"The name's Max." He jerked a thumb toward his companion. "And this is my wife Patty." She nodded at Spence and smiled. "We're from North Carolina, but drive together all over the country. This is one of our favorite joints."

"I'm Spence," he said, returning the nod. "I'm from Kentucky."

"You don't look like a trucker, Spence. What do you do back in Kentucky?"

"I'm a lawyer, or at least I was. I'm in the process of moving out of state."

"Where to?"

"I'm not sure yet. Any suggestions?"

"Hell, there's a lotta good places," Max said. "Me and Patty, though, we like the open road."

"Have you guys been driving together long?" asked Spence.

"Goin' on eight years now."

"Ever get tired of each other's company?"

"I don't," answered Max. "How about you Patty?" He looked at her and winked.

"Never," she said, smiling back at him. "Every day is a new adventure."

The waitress returned with Spence's coffee and asked for his order. He decided to follow Max's advice and ordered the ham and eggs. She scribbled on her pad, picked up the menu, and returned to the kitchen.

"So, are you headed any place in particular, Spence?" asked Max.

"Well, I'm on my way to Miami for now," Spence said.

"Am I right in assuming there is something or someone waiting for you there?" he asked and Patty interrupted saying, "Now Max, don't be so nosy. It's not polite."

"That's okay," Spence chuckled. "That's the part I'm not so sure about, Max. Hopefully there will be someone there."

"Well, for your sake, I hope so too. You seem to be a fine upstanding young man," Max said, patting him on the back.

"Why thank you, Max," Spence said. "That's the nicest thing anyone has said to me in quite a while."

The food came and Spence began devouring his meal. Max and Patty had already finished eating, said goodbye and headed out to their rig. As they pulled out, they blew two short blasts on the horn as a farewell to Spence. What nice people, Spence thought. He hoped they would have safe travels.

After finishing his meal, Spence headed to the restroom before hitting the open road again. Walking back to his car, he stretched his limbs before climbing in, his muscles growing stiff from sitting so much. Wanting to get to Miami in the shortest time possible, he pulled out of the parking lot and drove to the on ramp and back on the interstate. He drove with the window down for a while to help him stay awake.

Spence arrived in Miami around three o'clock the next day, making the trip in good time, and was glad it was over. Butterflies fluttered in his stomach as he thought about going to the marina and what he would find when he got there. Deciding he no longer needed his car, he stopped at a dealership and asked them how much they'd pay for it. The owner of the lot paid Spence the wholesale value for his car, considering he had no real need for cash, seemed fair to him.

Even if Macy had already left the area, Spence decided he'd take a taxi to the airport and fly away somewhere exotic. Calling a cab, he directed the driver to take him to the marina. He climbed out of the cab, paid the driver, and walked in the direction of the docks, looking around anxiously for the 'Hole in the Water,' but didn't see it anywhere. Suddenly, he felt very alone and sad at the thought that Macy was gone and he had no idea where she was.

As he turned and started walking back to the curb to catch a taxi to the airport, someone touched his shoulder from behind. He spun around quickly, instinctively cocking his arm to throw the first punch when he realized it was Freddie.

"Freddie!" Spence exclaimed. "I thought you guys were gone."

"No sir," he replied with a grin. "We have to change the name of the boat every so often so no one can determine who we are. It's now 'Spence's Quest.' Macy picked that out herself in honor of you. You didn't hear it from me," he whispered conspiratorially, "but I believe she likes you a lot."

"I certainly hope so, because I'm crazy about her."

Freddie grabbed some of Spence's bags and led him to the boat. Macy was lying in a deck chair facing the ocean. Freddie held his finger to his lips, and took the rest of Spence's baggage to the cabin below.

Spence walked stealthily up behind Macy, reached over the chair to cover her eyes and started to say, "Guess who." Before he had the chance, Macy reached up quickly and flipped him over the chair, where he landed flat on his back in front of her.

"What the...?" Spence began, reaching behind him as he sat up to rub his aching back.

"Oh, I'm so sorry Spence," Macy said, rushing to help him up.

"You could have killed me!" he shouted.

"Sorry, but that was the way I was trained," she explained. "Just remember not to sneak up on me again unless I know it is you."

"Well then it wouldn't exactly be sneaking, now would it?" he snarled.

"We could pretend," Macy said coyly, touching his back.

Spence decided to milk it for all he could, even though his back was hurt much less than his pride. He stumbled and fell into her arms. She helped him into the deck chair and pulled one up for her. Freddie suddenly appeared with a Jack and Coke for Spence and a beer for Macy. Obviously, Macy had been instructing Freddie in the nuances of their guest.

They sat in silence for a few minutes, Spence still winc-

ing as if in pain. The silence was comfortable, as each felt
secure with the other one present. After a few minutes,
Spence broke the silence.

"So, where are we off to now?"

"Wherever you want to go."

"You mean you don't need to go rescue another soul in
distress?"

"That's the beauty of my job," she said. "I can work
when I want. Besides, I feel like we both could use a little
vacation."

"How about the Bahamas?" Spence asked.

"Sounds good to me," Macy replied as she called
Freddie over to inform him they were ready to leave.

She rose and entered the galley, returning soon with another drink for Spence and a beer for herself. As he watched
her, it seemed she'd become even more beautiful since the
last time he saw her, if that was possible.

"Have you thought about your next move?" asked Macy.

"Well, it was going to be on you before you nearly broke
my back," Spence said jokingly.

"Well, maybe we can get the kinks worked out together," she said, a naughty smile flashing across her face.

"I'm seriously considering retiring," Spence said. "How
about you?"

"I have a job," Macy replied. "Have you ever thought
about using your skills and money to help others in need?"

"You mean we could be like an injustice fighting duo,"
he said.

"Kinda," she answered with a cute giggle.

"I don't know. Why don't we both think on it while we
take our little vacation together before we decide?"

"Okay," she said, leaning over and giving him a long
sensual kiss. Spence felt as if he could just melt at that moment. Then she took his hand and led him toward the cabin.
"Now let's go work on those kinks."